T0164003

The Last Rock Star Book
Or: Liz Phair, a Rant

by Camden Joy

❧ VERSE CHORUS PRESS ❧

First published in 1998 by Verse Chorus Press
PO Box 14806, Portland OR 97293
www.versechorus.com

A portion of this text was previously published in *Puncture* #38

Cover photograph ©1969 Gordon Beck / *The Montreal Gazette*

This novel is a work of fiction. With the exception of those
persons appearing as well-known personalities under their own
names, albeit in fictitious circumstances, all other characters bear
no relation to living characters and any resemblance to actual
persons, either living or dead, is entirely coincidental.

The publishers wish to thank Dennis Stovall, Linny Stovall,
Ruth Gundle, Tom Booth, Bill Donahue, and Kathy Molloy
for their generous advice and assistance

Country of manufacture as stated on the last page of this book

ISBN 978-1-891241-07-9 (paper)
ISBN 978-1-891241-85-7 (e-book)

Library of Congress Catalog Card Number: 98-60029

This book belongs to my sister

Okay, I'm back. Now I've rewound and this works.

So.

How should I begin? I consult the Pocket Secretary 21 User Guide and it tells me, *slide the one-button control fully upward and talk directly into the microphone. Ambient noise will be reduced proportionally to the distance at which the microphone is held.*

Let's see.

This morning I received a phone call from an older guy named Gabriel Snell. He was calling from Florida, on a cell phone. He asked me to call him Gabe. Highway sounds came across the phone, rushing wind (the winds of Florida), brakes, swerves, decelerations. He explained that he puts out music-celebrity profiles, his particular expertise being picture books about ill-fated pop celebrities who have vanished or met with bad ends. Gabe was quite frank about his motives. He said he has cared nothing for popular music since Elvis got inducted into the army. His only interest in modern music is how often its silly dramas provide, and here I quote, "a ripe market." For reasons too numerous for Gabe to list, there is presently such a delightfully swift turnover of rock celebrities as to guarantee at least six individuals per year on whom he can commission profitable quickie where-are-they-now?–style biographies. He explained his formula for determining which newly departed faces deserve a farewell rock bio, but I have to say that like most marketing lingo his formula escaped me. I stopped listening, as I am apt to do, and spaced for a time, and when I tuned back in mention was being made of logarithmically deducting demographics from an "optimal franchise base" to calculate a "percentile of controversy" (honest to god) and all the polls you'd expect as well as the stuff about sales having once approached three hundred thousand units and the hint of a hit single. Gabe admitted he had never even noticed this Liz Phair when she was around but felt, from the surveys he had consulted, that some people must have, and they might be missing her, wondering where she had gone. Thus, Liz Phair was "ripe" (that word again!) for the Gabe Snell treatment. At the same time, he was nervous the memory of Liz Phair's career could disappear any minute. He told me he had once published a very well written book about a similar young female singer/ songwriter named Laura Nyro who at one time was expected to accomplish great things, but never did. But Gabe had been too cocky and had waited too long, waited until she'd completely fallen out of sight before he commissioned the bio, and nearly lost his shirt in the lack of interest the book stirred. When I told him I'd once owned a copy of that book and had quite liked it, he seemed genuinely surprised. He said his failure to profit from the Nyro book taught him two things: run lots of photos and hurry it into print. "Don't wait till the body's cold," was how he put it. "I missed the forest 'cause I was too busy farting around in the trees." If he had worried less about what

4

was written and had included more snapshots and gotten out the Nyro book when the market indicators were "lit," then he might have made some money. Instead, since Laura Nyro had sunk from memory, all his book could do (in a marketing sense) was go down after her. I said I could see his point.

Having spotted my name in a pile of press clippings on budding rock writers, Gabe hastily decided to commission me to dictate a book about Liz Phair and where she is now. I protested that I was no rock critic, that whole rap was a mistake. I had been a little sick in the head and had taken to writing things on the walls of big cities, and publishers had turned around and published what I'd written without me knowing. I didn't know enough rock criticism to fill a pair of shoes, much less a whole book. I knew a little, but I was mostly a musician.

"But you're familiar," he dramatically revealed, "with Liz Phair."

"I am?"

"Not familiar, maybe that's not the right word, none of these kids are even around long enough to be familiar, but she's your age, I just bet you could tell her story with your eyes shut. I know you've seen her picture."

"Oh, is she that one who suckles pigs with her shirt all like unbuttoned?"

"That's another one. That's someone from TV."

"So how do you know I've seen her?"

"Babe, was she high-profile a few years back! Giving out Grammies, on the cover of *Rolling Stone*—"

"Nope."

"No matter, no matter."

He wants twenty hours worth of microcassettes mailed to him in five days. He indicated he was sending me half the money now, the other half when he gets the microcassettes. (When he pronounced that word—*money*—I admit I suddenly became very intrigued by Liz Phair, and *Yeah!* I practically shouted into the receiver, where has she gone to, why don't we hear of her anymore? whoever she is). He feels I'll accomplish the task more quickly if I dictate it, because he knows how careful and precious writers start to be with their manuscripts, and has indicated that he cares very little what I say. Oh, was he smooth. He went back to assuring me I don't have to know where she is now to write a where-is-she-now?–style book. I don't even have to care or find out. He told me it's not about words but about pictures. He has hundreds of photos already picked out, on his car seat right beside him as we speak, pictures from Liz Phair's childhood of her dressed up at Halloween, that sort of stuff, as well as shots of her big moments in the media spotlight. He simply requires a bunch of verbiage he can wrap around the pictures to make them look a little more highbrow. He has a woman on staff who does nothing but transcribe microcassettes sent in by various writers around the country.

He said he would Fed Ex me everything I need—press clippings, her CDs, a ton of bio material—but he'd prefer I didn't wait for them to arrive before starting to dictate. "Remember Laura Nyro," Gabe kept saying. "We thought we had all the goddamn time in the world." When I repeated I didn't know what I had to say about Liz Phair because I couldn't even recall precisely who she was, he said that didn't matter. His experience has been that people buy his books for the pictures. "No one reads these things," he told me. "And no one remembers them."

So today I went out and cashed my disability check and snapped up this little Pocket Secretary 21 and here we are now, just the two of us. She takes AAA batteries. An accompanying booklet assures me *the Pocket Secretary 21 epitomizes the continuing quality of portable recorders offered by Lorenz. The sleek styling, coupled with an unprecedented use of microelectronics, provides you with an extremely reliable and easy-to-use Thought Processor.* I'm sitting in the park near the room I rent in Sioux City. I'm staring out at the trees along Thermaducian Court, remembering what that Joyce Kilmer chick said about trees, how one is fine but two divine, or something like that. I'm attempting to Process My Thoughts. I'm back in Iowa, home sweet home. I don't really know what to include and what not to include. I just ate a red-white-and-blue popsicle I bought from an ice cream truck. I bought it because I liked the popsicle's name. It's called a Bomb Pop. I think I'll rewind and see how this sounds so far.

I should say something about Liz Phair now, since I guess we've gotten this far, and like me you might well wonder who or what she is.

So, okay. Liz Phair. I went to the library and looked her up in the periodical guide. I put in a request for a 1993 article about her first CD *Exile in Guyville*. The article was called: "Liz Phair: The Reluctant Star's Frank Tales of Male Betrayal." That issue was no longer available. The librarian felt sure that it had been stolen. "Someone steals all our magazines," she informed me pleasantly.

So: Liz Phair. *Exile in Guyville*. The Reluctant Star.

By now, these words either resonate for you or they don't.

LIZ PHAIR AT A VERY YOUNG AGE

7

Perhaps you never knew her or perhaps you have forgotten her. Soon she might be the question to an obscure *Jeopardy* answer ("Uh, yes, Alex. Who is 'Liz Phair'?"), under some challenging category like "Feminists of the Past" or "Artists Who Choked under Pressure" or "Indie Disappointments."

Or perhaps you are thinking, Oh my god, that's right, *Liz Phair*—where *is* she now?—in these dire times it is most surely her strong presence that can provide the balance and reason so lacking of late. (Of course you're not reading these words anyway, you're looking at the pictures.) I really don't know what else to say about Liz Phair here. She stood a thousand feet tall and made the natives tremble. She drove the jeeps that made the children well. Liz Phair: cook at 350 degrees, basting all the while; serves eight. Liz Phair, consistently rich and delicious, cup after cup. Liz Phair—crush ¾ tsp. for use in eggplant, zucchini, and green beans. Liz Phair, brewer, patriot, and revolutionary. Sodium Free Liz Phair, refrigerate after opening. This is really hard. Now I've gone and made myself thirsty. I think I'll stop for a while and drink a glass of water.

This is easier for me if I think of it as writing a journal. A journal like my last girlfriend used to keep. Although the thing about her was, she was super private about the journals and when she finally did share one with me I didn't get what was happening and I blew it by saying a few real stupid things. Still, in the long run, I think the journals helped her straighten some things out. My girlfriend's name was Shaleese (her name was really Elisabeth but apparently when she was real little she pronounced it "Shaleese" and it stuck). God, she was so damn talented. I always thought that, you know, but I never really knew for sure.

Talking about it, that's supposed to make it all go away or something. So that's what I'm doing. Talking.

I know the first thing you want to know is all that Holden Caulfield kind of crap, but that's not where my story starts. It starts with this idea that everything in my youth was suffused with futility. As a youngster, I'd hear that these were the best years of my life and I'd know, just know, that this was a complete lie. I'd hear about how I had my whole life in front of me though I knew clear as could be there was nothing the hell in front of me. What were they talking about? How dumb did I look? And please note I did not begin here by saying, "Everything in my youth was suffused with futility *except rock and roll*." No, I'm sorry. Rock and roll seemed just as futile and stupid as anything. To say merely that we felt a little let down by rock and roll would be about like saying the Japanese felt a little let down when they lost World War Two. By the time we inherited it, what could anyone say was really so great about rock and roll? Either you're some naive longhair or you're some humorless skinhead, either you're nothing but beautiful or you're everything and pompous. When there are still Gabriel Snells publishing pretty picture books to argue that the Doors were actually good or Jim Morrison was actually smart, leaving people to close the book swearing that Morrison was our culture's phallus and his band the American orgasm, when this crap is what they call rock and roll, how can you say rock and roll is still significant? Well, I'm sorry, it isn't. At best, there might be a few good seconds in a couple of rock-and-roll songs—some choice snippets, an occasional subtlety, an incorruptible fragment, but that's really about it.

When I was young, we approached rock and roll like that, that it had been broken open and sucked dry by greedy adults and nothing remained of it but a few shards. The Rolling Stones, for example, could be reduced to the mumbles and guitar jabs at the start of "Stray Cat Blues," the submerged clatter of "I Just Wanna See His Face," and the line in "Respectable" about smoking heroin with the president. Three fragments. And I'd have to say that even that was pretty generous of us. The Clash and the Who were each reduced to just two fragments. My friends and I called these "moments," and we constantly bickered over the merits of this or that "moment." I'm the one who said the moments occur when a performer strays from the script, when you sense they haven't practiced this part but aren't worried what to play. It was Roy who said these moments were "steered entirely by the majesty of impulse." I always loved that, "the majesty of impulse." Made passion sound like some kinda key to royalty.

I even played rock and roll, for a long time tried to get a band happening with Acey. We knew this thing about "moments," and we struggled ourselves to attain the majesty of impulse, but it never worked right. It was a great idea when you applied it to other people's songs, but you couldn't consciously start out aiming for it or you'd never get there. Probably there's some Chinese proverb that beautifully captures the frustration of this phenomenon, but I've never found it. The high school I went to was not particularly big on teaching us Chinese proverbs.

To go back to Liz Phair for a second. I honestly want to say I recollect her, but it's like looking over a familiar scrapbook—you can't tell if you really remember the original events or if it's just that the pictures make you think you do (when we count one to ten, this fellow patient once explained to me, we do not actually count but just repeat words we learned long ago). I do have more than a little trouble distinguishing memories of this Liz Phair from (say) Lisa Germano or Lisa Loeb or Lisa Bonet, not to mention others I've overheard people talking about, like Joan Osborne and Alanis Morissette and Tori Amos. I repeat the name over and over (Liz Phair, Liz Phair, Liz Phair, Liz Phair) to see what it kicks loose. I'm not a total ignoramus, I have flipped through more than a few popular magazines in the places I've wound up. Was she the twiggy one with accusatory lyrics and the weak voice, was she the shirtless, top-heavy punk chick who wore electrical tape on her nipples? Was her chosen topic for interviews the Princess Syndrome, or the methods employed by post-capitalist revanchist society to keep women barefoot and pregnant, or lost-little-girl dreams of Barbie betrothals and flying horses with horns? Did her albums show her furious at men who revealed an overt incomprehension of her polygamous desires by terming her a "slut," or did she basically just perform nonsense poetry backed by two loud bass guitars and a fiddle? Which Liz Phair was she, the one with some sort of Christ affliction who complimented soul singers of the sixties, or the willing one wearing nothing but a teeny pink tube top and black pants, placed on the page of an important music magazine as their near-nudie encouragement to resubscribe? Long-legged, crooning her synth-dance hits, always in sunglasses, so tall she made the natives tremble, always lovely in vinyl wrap-around skirts even long after new wave was passé—was that Liz Phair, with the breasts too big to truly believe?

And what's with this "reluctant star" bit? Given the situation, one would think her early interviews would reflect a measure of delight at having been in the eye of so many beholders, the eye in a tornado of bids.

Did she not want to get famous?

Did she not realize that thousands of musicians are killing themselves to get the kind of recognition she got (I was one!)? Seeking notoriety, they snap their souls like chicken bones and feign total casualness as the marrow is laid open. They send out demos and flyers and practice day in, day out, they bore their friends by speaking of nothing else, they consciously write songs to appeal to the broadest audience (if they are gay or Jewish or intelligent they do not mention it), they waste no moment, they map out song arrangements on their laps while taking a crap (that was me!), lunch breaks are spent on the telephone to local rock writers, recording studios, managers, record companies, music-store owners, clubs, they carry portable Pocket Secretarys exactly like the one I'm holding now, on which they dictate every melody that occurs to them (lacking this, they will call home and sing it to their answering machine), they concoct crazy schemes to get tapes to celebrities, they plead with booking agents to put every A & R rep on their guest list, they enshrine each set list in wax paper to document the Salad Days. They work to develop an attitude. They deride bands who use songs to curse and complain as acting "fed up," they scoff at bands who are iconoclastic and independent as "collegey," they dismiss singer-songwriters as "topical." When just for the heck of it their drummer suggests they play a show completely naked, they grow so frustrated at his weirdness they almost kick him out of the band, until they read that some other cool band got famous playing naked and then they consider it. When someone claiming to be a record producer agrees to find them shows if they pay him $500 for each gig, they consider themselves lucky; when this supposed record producer suggests they revamp their material and play mostly nonoriginal tunes, they earnestly implement his advice; when he buys them silly outfits, they proudly wear them (after all, the Beatles did it for Brian Epstein); and when they find they are booked into a birthday party at a supper club where they are obliged to buy a meal and pay for their own drinks and the audience leaves after they finish a completely ordinary version of "Happy Birthday" and the "record producer" takes the proceeds and says he'll call them... they still don't get it (this actually happened). The next day they are at it again, laying themselves open for the taking, hinting there is nothing they wouldn't do for a chance at the Big Time...

"The Reluctant Star"—the phrase yearns for independence, as though no one ever informed Liz Phair of the impossibility of maintaining such a thing in the supermarket that is the United States of America. The article's title makes me think she quaintly did not realize that when you call for change in America they do not hate you but love you for it, they love you until you can't see straight, their hearts brim over with love until they love the change right out of you. But I doubt people told her that; compromise would've dampened what I imagine to be the spirits of this Liz Phair.

You can almost hear the reluctant star wishing this fate on someone else: why me? why me? You can almost imagine her praying that if this is what it is to be a rock star—interviews every hour with nervous admirers and phone calls every day from eager stockbrokers—well then, so be it, she will be this rock star they seem to want so badly, but let her be the last rock star, and let this toll never be inflicted on another. Let none come after. Even if I do not last, she prays—for I will not last so long—at least let me burn so brightly before I fade that like a pure candle lit and put to the tabloid page this world emerges from flames a better place—though tattered—though lost   in

LIZ PHAIR WITH HER FIRST GUITAR

victory—we're free.

The reluctant star. I mean, really, how quaint.

I know people my age who claim to remember Kent State first-hand, or things that happened in the year they were born, things like Chicago's Days of Rage, or even before that, the riots follow-ing Martin Luther King's assassination or the civil disturbances in Detroit, or even longer ago than that, Watts or Newark or Harlem. Not me. I can remember when I was ten, nothing before that. My earliest memory is watching the neighbor buds chase my sister away. But even that's pretty choppy. I remember the bong and the Visine on the picnic table in back, next to a baggie of pot, my parents gone for the evening, Marlboros and mints out to disguise the breath, munchies ready to scarf, Styx playing on the stereo louder than Styx should ever be allowed to play, the screen door open between the picnic table and the stereo, my brothers going in and out trailed this way and that by their friends, the neighbor buds and freaks, Brock and Wayne and Rogers and George. I remember later on we played kick-the-can in the cul-de-sac in front. I was the youngest and the only one into it, all the others used it as an excuse to find my sister (who was twelve at the time) or corner my sister or hide with my sister; some, like George and Brock, used it as an excuse for rougher stuff: to trip my sister in the street, get on top of her, pin her arms down, thump her chest, put their hands in her shirt. I remember Brock announcing to everyone how cute my sister was. I didn't think she was cute—she was just my sister—but I didn't vocalize my disagreement. She had her ponytail woven in one of those long, complicated knots. She wore shorts and sandals and a yellow blouse. Brock grabbed the can we were using as the can in kick-the-can and placed it on his crotch and thrust himself against it. "Boy, am I horny!" he yelled. I didn't know what that meant, but I hooted and giggled anyway. "I'm

14

so horny I could make it with this here can!" And then the game changed and Brock and George led everyone in chasing my sister, who didn't laugh or cry or anything, she just ran and ran and ran. I watched her do one loop around the neighborhood, like a farewell lap, taking her followers up past the identical one-story, white-with-yellow-trim tract homes on the left side of the street then down past all the identical one-story, pink-with-berry-trim tract homes on the right side of the street and then around the corner and then I never saw my sister again after that, she was just gone. Every guy in the neighborhood followed, a big yelling mob that flowed up the left side of the street and then down the right side and then disappeared around the corner in hot pursuit and I was left in the cul-de-sac alone, hopping around on one foot and calling for everyone to come back, my thumb snapping the top of the can we used as the can in kick-the-can. I remember it took hours for everyone to trail back home, they stumbled back in groups of two and three, but my sister wasn't among them and like I said, I haven't seen her since.

So yes, Shaleese was my girlfriend. Although, truth to tell, the only reason I ever even asked Shaleese out was because I needed an alibi. We had this thing we called the Big Bang, it was coming up this one Friday, and we had all our tracks covered. The potassium nitrate was fertilizer that Jimmy had inconspicuously amassed; the lengths of pipe were salvaged from Spencer's sub-basement, the powdered sugar was shoplifted from a drug store, the fuses were... well, I don't remember and it's not important. There was no way to trace the bombs, really. Just to be safe, though, we needed alibis.

I went to McDonald's, looking for Shaleese. She was in her booth. Naturally. It was like she lived in that booth.

"Um, hey," I said.

She continued writing in her journal.

"Hey," I repeated.

"Just a sec," she said, then finished writing her whatever and closed the journal. "How you, Camden?"

"How come you never look at me?"

"How come *you* never look at *me?*" I assumed she was joking, though I couldn't be sure. She was staring at the table-top.

"Yeah. Whatever." I coughed. "So..."

"So?"

"So," I motioned at her journal, "So, what are you writing now?"

"Oh. Same as always. This story."

"What about?"

"Family. Crud my mom told me. I dunno."

"Can I read it?"

She frowned at the table, lightly rapped on the journal, shook her head. "Sorry."

"How about you read it to me, then?"

"We'll see."

"Someday, huh? If I'm good."

"If you're real, real, real good," she snickered. "Right."

"So..." I began again.

"So?"

I was watching from the window as they wheeled the grease barrels around the kiddie park and out to the thatched garbage area. My friend Acey and I had worked here for two months when we were sixteen, which is when I first noticed Shaleese. After school, she was permanently attached to this one booth, always scribbling in her journal, drinking iced tea by herself, looking out the same window I was now. Our jobs then had been to do exactly what these clowns were doing now, to wash dishes in scalding jets of water and mop the floors with industrial-strength ammonia and unload the bun truck and empty out the boiling oil from the french-fry vats. We'd drain them and, more often than not, would find disgusting things gathered at the bottom, things which looked soggy and embarrassed, things dropped in sometime during the day by other employees, things barely recognizable as what they had once been, a plastic model of the White House that had melted or a pet guinea pig that had been boiled alive during a slow shift. And after we'd drain the oil into a barrel, we'd unbox a new white five-pound cube of congealed frying oil and plop it into the vat, then we'd steer the grease barrel out into the disguised trash area in the middle of the parking lot and let the whole mess solidify over night.

"I did that," I said, nodding at the clowns outside. "Remember?"

"Yup."

Acey and I left after the first salary review. They had this award they'd give their favorite back-room employee, this thing called the Silver Spatula. What a joke. They took it so seriously. Neither of us got the award but that's not why I left. I just couldn't stand the stink anymore, the smell of frying oil in my hair, my closet, my pillow at night. It was a smell I couldn't lose. The clowns offered me a pretty good raise, twenty-five cents over minimum wage, but I left anyway.

"Hey, Shaleese, you want to go out Friday night?"

"Fine. What you wanna do?"

"I dunno. What you wanna do?"

"I dunno."

We sat there, wrestling with the silence like it was a math problem we were working on.

"Hey," I said after a while. "You here that time those guys snuck up and firebombed those grease barrels out there?"

Her hair slanted low over her face and her head was turned, but I could see enough of her cheek to tell that she was smiling. "Yeah. You know I was here, Camden."

"Yeah," I said, smiling. "Yeah, well I thought I saw you, you know. I looked back and it was all kinda lovely, like lit all sweet, this absolute mammoth geyser of flame and you painted up all orange."

She chuckled. "Yeah."

"But that won't compare with the Big Bang we're gonna have Friday."

"Us?"

"Um, yeah. I mean, sure."

"So what you wanna do?"

"I dunno, I dunno. Got anything you wanna do?"

She and I still hadn't decided what to do when I picked her up Friday at McDonald's in my daddy's car. I knew I had to get away for an hour between 8:30 and 9:30 to light a couple of fuses, distract Fire and Rescue with some false alarms, and read a manifesto over the phone to whoever answered the phone at the mayor's office. But what to do till then? There just wasn't a lot to do in my hometown. There were plenty of parks, but once dusk fell the parks were officially closed and the cops would swing by and belittle you with shrewd riddles until you'd be so embarrassed you'd give up on your woodsy evening and just go home.

But if the cops stopped us that night and ordered us to head on home, I could see a certain problem developing. I had absolutely no sense of where or what home was for Shaleese, and together we had no real sense of direction.

"We could hit the County Drive-In," I said as we drove, though my mind wasn't really on what I was saying.

"Except I don't have any money, really, do you?"

"Not really." I was thinking of... well, this sounds dumb. And it has no relation, really. I was actually thinking of the Black Hawk Indian rituals involved in the killing of buffalo, thinking of the elders and the children who ran a herd in tight circles for hours and gradually guided the whole, dusty, prancing mass up Iowa's famously high limestone bluffs. I was thinking of the one buffalo who at last lost its footing and was trampled, signaling that the herd was approaching exhaustion, and I was thinking of the line of elite Sac warriors who quickly advanced on horseback, howling, shaking branches of fire high above their heads, and I was thinking of the whole herd as it went mad, spooked and galloping with all they had left, and stampeded off the bluff to their death. "Not on me, no."

"Great date."

"Yeah, well. Sorry." I was too embarrassed to admit that usually me and my friends just hung out on the high limestone bluff above the drive-in, watching the four screens pour movie light all over the valley and the cars and the buffalo ghosts. Each night we liked to imagine the cars had been stampeded to their deaths down there, but really it looked more like a giant tidal wave full of new-model automobiles had just crashed against the drive-in screens and then withdrawn back to nowhere, leaving in its wake this deposit of sea-polished vehicles. I was too embarrassed to speak to Shaleese about any of this because usually when me and my friends went like that, to watch the cars reflect movies, Acey would imitate the movie stars and make up some dialogue or we'd sit and re-tell the rituals of buffalo stampedes or we'd just watch anything that transfixed us, but since we never paid admission we never really got to follow the film, it just happened before us, silent and metallic, like something quietly oozing from a wound in the earth's skin, from the spot where it had been lacerated by the stabbing fall of so many buffalo horns.

"How 'bout the video arcade?"

"Fine," I answered. "Only. What time is it?"

"Seven-oh-five."

"Then nah, let's not. I don't have the money for it anyway."

"So what? We'll just look."

"Well."

"C'mon."

"No, I mean we can't. I mean right about now I got this

feeling the video arcade is full of shrewd cops trying to disentangle this dangerous-looking kinda contraption."

"Sounds exciting."

"Well yeah, and it'll work 'cause there's nothing much there but wire and empty pipes and a clock."

"Ah. Dull."

"Except instead there'll be this explosion in the drugstore next door that takes down oh about half the roof and hopefully hurts nobody too badly."

"Exciting."

I kept driving us around and around, down Cadillac to Bedmore, right on Bedmore to Guthrie, right on Guthrie to Cadillac, down Cadillac to Bedmore, right on Bedmore to Guthrie, and so on. Towns in Iowa have only so many roads.

"We're losing the light," she said.

What I think she meant was that things were winking out of sight, the hills and creeks and trees—the things of nature—disappearing with nightfall, as if swiped by some invisible jerk with huge hands who would return them to us at dawn. The only things we could still make out were artificial and lit by porch lamps and streetlights and parking-lot fluorescence and supermarket neon and car headlights. Pilots peering down would be able to put together the squiggle patterns of our neighborhoods by tracing the town's toylike lights.

"But the drive-in, you think, is safe?" she asked calmly.

"Oh, until about eleven, eleven-thirty."

"And then?"

"I'd rather not say."

Minutes passed.

"Didn't we just pass something that looked a little like this?" she asked as we went by the same row of houses yet again.

"Yeah. But that's because I'm driving us in circles."

"And it doesn't make you dizzy, going in circles?"

"Yeah. In fact, I'm a little dizzy right now, since you mention it. Dizzy and a little sick to my stomach, even."

"In a way this is a kinda fun date. I mean, I guess I wasn't expecting a corsage or anything."

I sighed. "There is a motel, it's got a swimming pool and it's really easy to crash it."

"A motel."

"We could go swimming, I mean. I could see that settling my stomach. Though you probably didn't bring a suit. But it's always dark. There's like no light there. I wouldn't see anything... of yours, I mean, whatever."

"Motel over there? Ragdin and Brown?"

"You know it? It's kinda creepy, I know. Like I've never seen a real guest stay there. And there's this weird German bitch of a lady who runs it, I guess—she lives there, and if you splash in the pool too much she screams for the cops."

Shaleese laughed. "Yeah. I do know her."

"But the cops won't even come 'cause it's such a fleabag kinda joint, you know?"

"And is this place, um, gonna meet with some catastrophe soon? Like is it safe, you think, this motel? Delta force or something gonna land on it tonight, you think?"

"It's safe. We thought, well, I mean, whoever's behind these attacks figured, it was owed something, for all the free swims it's given us."

"Well. Then."

"Wanna try it?"

"Fine."

We parked a few minutes later in the alleyway behind the motel. I pushed the locked fence taut for Shaleese, directing her to squeeze beneath the chain. I followed after. There were no lights on, there never were, except from the front office where the German woman sat tending her TV while it softly muttered to itself.

The sound of sirens zipped past, Fire and Rescue headed

this way and that. I could see next to nothing in the dark. I heard the sound of Shaleese unzipping her jacket and pants and then she slipped into the water. I took off my Pendleton, wadded up my Levi's. Standing naked on the diving board, I glanced to the south, craning to see over the dilapidated roof of the motel's second story, where the night sky chuffed with a rich amber smoke.

"What's going on?" whispered Shaleese from the black pool. I could hear her treading water.

"Who knows?" I answered, trying not to sound too ecstatic or proud or anything. I took two steps, slapped the board with my right foot, bounced high into the air, hugged my knees to my chest and, hearing Shaleese giggle deliriously below me, I yelled, "Geronimo!"

We were not revolutionaries, really. Even at eighteen, we understood the impossibility of maintaining a revolution in the United States of America, though we knew it was deserved, though we knew that any democracy in which less than half the people bother voting is one lousy democracy, though we recognized that ten minutes into any TV show or two pages into any article the same alluring temptress would drop out of the digitalized sky, the true leader of our people selling us images of ourselves as a disfigured people in need of beauty-care products, detouring us into a loop of unquenchable desire, glamorizing youth's golden opportunities and maligning the tragedy of maturity, though the things sold to us as the Joys of Life were mere momentary distractions, and we realized what must be changed, broken, destroyed. It had become difficult to do so in these United States of America because whatever else was said there remained so very much love here, it leaked from the sympathetic eyes of shrewd policemen and politicians, all that gooey heartsickness and unsureness and wondrous naiveté.

How could we hurt people because of their own gullibility? How could we wrestle ourselves free from their brave but wrong choices, their misguided intentions, their warm compassionate embraces, turn our backs on these kind ones and order them shot?

You will call for a revolution in America and they will love you for it, they will love you until you can't see straight, they will hand-deliver you baked goods and put you in advertisements and forgive you everything, their hearts will brim over with love until they love the revolution right out of you. And it is real, all of it, their love, and this abiding need to smash a few of their gullible, stupid eggs.

The problem is, how do you distinguish the participants you trust from the life you trust so little? What was it Bremer said in his diary, as he decided against shooting Wallace at the airport for fear of injuring those two innocent girls? The problem is, there are people there every time you turn around to start your little revolution. People who must be sparked to revolt from the melancholy of the structures binding them so severely. And yet you will find, hiding within each suspicious structure, still more people who want to love you and want you to love them, who will hand deliver you baked goods and forgive you anything.

Where are the ones who must be shot? How do we do this? What is wrong in this free land of ours that so many healthy folks truly perceive themselves as sullied and disfigured and in need of beauty-care products, even—especially—the very ones who invented this sales strategy?

For us at eighteen, it was all very simple. To revolt in America, you isolated an evil and made it yours, to embrace or erase. Now, hitting the water of the motel pool, sinking into its lagoonlike dimness, I held my breath for twenty seconds and flailed joyously; my friends and I had isolated "compromise" as an evil. Easy to isolate, difficult to attack. Compromise was in the unfulfilled looks of most everyone, in their inability to stop asking themselves *What if...*, in their regrets that some treasure they sought was too easily surrendered, that they did not suggest drinks with the gentleman of their dreams because they sensed his rejection, they did not make that move to Seattle because they distinctly sensed failure, they did not pursue performing or writing or mountain-climbing or frigate-hopping or professional sports, because someone hinted they'd appear foolish in doing so; in that crucial instant, they laughed along at themselves, and they compromised.

How can you tell such a frail and gullible people that they must not compromise? You can't. All you can do is to alter their given reality for a night, place them upright and fully mobile in a scary, liberating situation, and induce them to puzzle it out for themselves. They may awaken with a rekindled faith in themselves, they may see—as if from a stranger's perspective—just how bold and loving they can be in a perilous environment; they may emerge somehow more independent.

My head broke the water. I could hear Shaleese laughing. The motel lady was squealing in a high-pitched voice, but she was squealing in German. "Blah blah blah blah blah blah," she was squealing. "Blah blah blah blah. Chalice." She said the last word quite clearly.

"She knows your name?" I whispered but Shaleese was too busy answering the woman.

"It's okay," she laughed. "Really. It's okay, Mom."

The German woman mumbled at her slippers and scuffed back inside, valiantly pulling at the screen door to make it slam but finding the hydraulic door fastener only permitted the door to close with a gentle sigh.

"Mom?" I repeated. "Oh, I get it."

"You're fast," she replied. "A regular Bernstein."

"Einstein, you mean."

"What."

"A regular Einstein. That's the phrase."

"Bernstein, Einstein... Whoever."

"It's not like it matters," I agreed.

We splashed around a bit more and then, well, a not un-expected thing occurred. Though I hadn't planned on it at all. All these vacant motel rooms, all these empty beds. Shaleese and me, naked and dripping wet. We tried a few doors until we found an open one, just going in for the towels, taking our clothes into the room without bothering with the light, and soon enough found ourselves passionate on the bed.

It was awful.

I don't know if she'd been with anyone before, but I had only been with Monica, and she was much different. Monica was amenable to anything and didn't mind those occasional breaks when you just need to call a time-out and get up and stretch, checking to make sure which arms and legs are yours.

Shaleese seemed desirous of something less purposeful, some act of supreme subtlety. "Wait," she kept saying. "Wait. Hold on."

I guess I wanted to believe that maybe it was her first time.

She lit a dim candle at the bedside but I couldn't slow down. I hugged her sturdily about the shoulders, locking her into place with her head turned to one side, my head to the other. Sirens throbbed all around, Fire and Rescue striping the ceiling with peppermint-candy lights. They were all I could see. She lay limp beneath me. I didn't want to interrupt to crudely ask about protection and I had no rubbers so I just shut my eyes tight then pulled out and came all over her belly. I thought this ended it, but then she broke my heart with a longing kiss.

"You have to give me some more time, sweetheart," she murmured, clearly unfulfilled.

I groaned, eyes closed. "What time is it?"

"Eight-thirty."

"Shit." I jumped up, shoved my legs into my pants, buttoned only the top of my fly, threw my shirt up around my shoulders.

"Wait," she whispered.

"Shit," I said again. "Shit, I gotta, I gotta do some things. I'll be back in like, an hour." I had my hand on the doorknob.

"Camden," she said and I felt it in my stomach. That yearning in her voice. That yearning which seemed to bathe her like honeyed perfume. I weakened against the door frame. I was this close to compromise. I had just wanted a date, something simple, something we could shrug off, whatever, an alibi, nothing more, for that night, the one night me and my friends had determined to force the issue, the one night she lay vulnerable behind me on a scratchy polyester bedspread, pleading. "Camden. Look at me."

"I can't," I answered at last. "Not right now. I got some things I gotta do first." I sighed, wondering what I was compromising now. "I promise I'll look at you later."

Brock, of course, turned up dead not much later, his skull busted when he misestimated a Soft Shoulder sign. Since he was the one I held responsible for the disappearance of my sister, I can't say I cried. I did go to the funeral, but it was closed-casket.

What sort of girlfriend was this Shaleese? We moved to Sioux City together only a few weeks after our first date. And we found a tiny clapboard place on quiet little Kimballton Avenue. And after that, well, Shaleese was the sort you saw flitting about the campus of Morningside College, one day giddy, the next day not, the sort who blended right in with the other artsy chicks at the Nighthawk Coffeehouse, always weighed

IN HER JUNIOR HIGH YEARBOOK, LIZ WROTE THAT HER GOAL WAS TO
BECOME THE AMBASSADOR TO THE UNITED NATIONS

down on one side by a thick, cracked-leather shoulder bag full
of books and pads and pens. She was not the sort who ever
wore heels but the sort who always wore flats, and most often
a jeans jacket or an oversize black V-neck pullover covering
a dropped-waist floral-print dress, and underneath the dress
most often she wore black tights.

But that tells you zilch. That says nothing about her mood
swings, how she'd be doing nothing for weeks and then all
of a sudden some part of her would open right up and huge
amounts of drawings and paintings and stories would pour
from her, streaming out from some mysterious source. Then
she'd meekly close up again, refuse to show me any of what
she'd just made; as far as I could tell, she'd do nothing again
for a few more weeks. Oh, but that's not it either. That says
nothing about how when it rained, for example, she'd admit
she only wanted to run and catch it in her mouth. She couldn't
keep her eyes on the traffic. And the highways filled with water and the water moved the vehicles along. The sky billowed
with splendor and the sun set in five colors. The road was

27

hard to watch, so cars crashed with a sickening noise of heat, and people swerving were also surprised, and often caused the more dangerous secondary pileups. Cutting through the thunder would come the peal of ambulances. Rain had once meant things were being cleaned, but Shaleese began to fear it, afraid for the ones who had to die on the highway because of it.

"In the future," some mayor of New York once said, "Everybody will be famous for fifteen meals." Which, by my calculations, is about five days, the length of time Gabe Snell has given me to dictate this book. These are my fifteen meals (now I have only thirteen left).

I can't believe today's only my second day with my little Pocket Secretary. What was it Gabe said—"None of these people are even around long enough to be familiar." We are really quite familiar, despite our difference in weight and age, despite the fact that I am white and male and she is black and plastic. These are truly unimportant differences in the big scheme of things. Last night we slept together. It was our first time and when I cradled her in my palm, she emitted only a small purr of electronic delight, a joyful whirring. I'm getting downright casual spilling my guts to her. I feel like I've been talking forever, but I've only filled up one little microcassette. Jesus, this is hard.

I dictate this while I walk the street. Wide walks, grassy fenced-in lots, Sioux City. I'm hungry but I hesitate to spend too hastily on one of my fifteen meals. At the nearest bus stop a poster for the expensive vodka Krazkow features a little drama: *She was following him. Everywhere he went she'd show up alongside him, going his way. She knew his every path. She'd surprise him at the kiosk, in the waiting room, on the train. Who among us has not been the sole source of some lonely someone's delight? Turning* the corner of the supermarket aisle, with the universally admired Krazkow in his cart, Gregory Haldz would discover her before him. "Hullo," he'd say evasively, working with the dangle of his hands, his suddenly nonchalant posture and underwhelmed tone of voice to convince her it was futile to wish for something special between them, there was no point. Why—when such a celebrity was so instantly recognizable she apparently could have anyone—why was she determined only to get Haldz? She'd not talk—how could she, from the billboard or the magazine cover, Haldz was not so crazy as to expect THAT—but always her accusing eye, the significant glance his way would not stop. Krazkow? Why was this famous woman pursuing him and his world-renowned vodka, he wanted to know. And more importantly—what would it take to make her stop?... Krazkow... You can't escape the attraction.

LIZ LIKES ALL KINDS OF MUSIC !!

There is a plaque on the house I just passed identifying it as the site where a certain famous Iowan actress grew up. To us in Iowa, she was a stage actress, but to the rest of the world she became something bigger. Back in the early seventies, age twenty-three, she was the rage of the state. People would drive from other parts of the country to watch her perform, she was this thing the Chamber of Commerce wrote brochures about. You all know her name by heart, if I spoke it you'd go "Ohhh-hhhh! Her! Yes, yes!" I'm just saying she was something else to us here before you city folks got hold of her and plopped the weight of the world on her shoulders. She resisted the pull of Chicago's theaters, impressing the locals with what they perceived as her loyalty. Probably she was bargaining. For when she finally left—as was inevitable, what talented individual sticks around these parts for very long anyway?—she went the other way, west, to Hollywood, and commanded an uncommonly high price for some commercials and films before settling into a comfortable role as a certain character we all knew intimately in a certain popular soap opera. By now you know who I mean, and, too, you know what happened. And we all knew her before we had to share her, when she only had eyes for us. She was definitely famous for more than fifteen meals (shows what big-city mayors know!) but you know what happened next, and the way, after a time, after you'd gotten what you wanted, you delivered her back to us literally in pieces, after the headlines informed us of her dismemberment by a creep who broke into her Mulholland Hills home with a knife one night to exact some vengeance for a thoughtless line her character had spoken on the soap opera a few weeks prior. You called her murderer "a fan," which shocked our neighborhood terribly. The house where she was a little girl during the late fifties and sixties was back there a way, that's really the only reason I bring this up.

I mean, have you never lost something or does everything with which you were born still surround you, crammed into close-by cabinets, laid out luxuriously in spacious rooms, engendering only pure and uncompromised feelings of fulfillment? You ask what is my point, but what remains for me from people, places, and things I've seen? I'll tell you, when I stand before the mirror, what I see of me is this: disappointment. You have probably observed me passing through your town like a puke cloud, and glancing out through the window of a donut store or a copy shop you have pleaded to avoid my fate. Oh, forget I said anything. I'll sign off until there's something definite to report.

When I was young I remember learning about how Napoleon defeated Russia in a battle which cost so many men that it was the equivalent of a jumbo jet crashing every three minutes from breakfast to sundown. I don't remember much else I learned when I was young. Frankly, the only reason the comparison stuck with me was that when I was young, a jumbo jet did descend every three minutes from breakfast to sundown, going what seemed to be straight down into our neighborhood.

That's what comes of living in the flight path.

Not only that, but the sky was crowded with flashing, colored lights—orange and green taillights, red and turquoise wing-lights, white nose-cone beacons. Before any of them could descend, each jumbo jet had to perform circles in the sky, and they'd get backed up and it would look almost like someone was slowly spinning a lasso made out of blinking Christmas lights. The lights swirled overhead constantly, seeking authorization to land, tracing perfect ovals in the heavens. Then one lucky jet would get an okay and it would dip its wings and fall away from its pals like a curious vulture and become a splendidly huge roaring thing of metal coming right at us, making the sound of a fire-breathing monster, blinking hungrily as it approached. This was a novelty for a while, then a mere inconvenience.

Of course, all these jumbo jets weren't coming to feed on us and they weren't crashing; they were just arriving for repairs, tune-ups, to have their wings and engines re-bolted and their black boxes checked. They didn't carry passengers, only an occasional navigator or pilot and a few cabin attendants. These planes landed here because a few years earlier, back before I can remember, a major airline had purchased thousands of roll-ing acres outside our town of Crazy Horse Junction, off Plains Highway 12, where it crossed an insignificant prairie path called N-238, and the airline had leveled all these acres and sprayed them with a special sealant to form the world's largest runway. Everyone joked about it at first because, after all, this was Iowa, and though our tornadoes and dust storms didn't come as often or as bad as they did in, say, Kansas, still we hardly possessed what could be called ideal flying conditions. But the airline knew what they were doing: they explained that our unique position-ing in terms of climate and geography would allow them to experiment with fancy new forecasting gadgets. They also guar-anteed we would never see an airplane crash, from bad weather or whatever, because their revolutionary new instruments were far too delicate. This did a lot to reassure everyone, except for those of us who were kinda counting on an occasional crash to liven up our days. So anyway, this became an unofficial hub city for the airline, a sort of resort where they could test their little machines and fix their little planes and instruct their little pilots and cultivate their little stewardesses. They called this place Site 3. There was gambling in Site 3, and drinking at age eighteen, and lax enforcement of local ordinances prohibiting prostitu-tion. After a time, the mayor and city council of our town of Crazy Horse Junction decided we should be incorporated into the booming airline town, and we surrendered the name of Crazy Horse Junction to become one with Site 3.

Suddenly every school kid was required to know everything about airplanes. We had classes in recognizing different models by their bellies and wing-spans, and weekly visits from airline workers who spoke enthusiastically about their exciting careers. On some lucky days, the stewardesses would even speak to us. They'd arrive at our school in limos, their first names pinned to their chests, escorted everywhere by big security guards as if they were porn starlets or big-time beauty queens or politi-cally significant aerobics instructors. They'd toss their ponytails and never stop smiling. We'd collect their autographs, get our pictures snapped with them. They were our cheerleaders of the heavens.

We became familiar with the gust of exhaust that follows a plane's takeoff, how when you stare through it everything distorts into a watery mirage. We would lie still on the ground, looking at planes so high up they appeared to be pausing in mid-air, and there would be nothing at all between us and the belly of an airplane but five or six miles of air.

Anything that had ever carried a radio signal in our town now emitted cockpit conversations. They traveled on every frequency. You'd be on the telephone talking privately with a friend and there'd be this feeling like the phone going dead and suddenly a deeply distorted, throaty male voice would pipe up, "Roger, gauges and levels responding as normal, over." We never knew who was talking or who was listening. It was hard to feel any of your secrets would be kept when the skies were filled with observers and everything was incessantly under radar surveillance. You'd pull up to the drive-through window of a fast-food place and be about to spout an order into a statue's electronic mouth when suddenly the statue would begin to talk pilot gibberish for a few minutes. People who had outfitted rooms in their houses with intercoms found their intercoms carrying the talking-airplane show. Kids with metal fillings or braces heard in their mouths the intimate details of every landing. It was all a hassle, but as with the lights in the sky, we got used to it.

We had an incentive. Our incentive was that when we joined up with Site 3 we were linked with fast-food outlets and drugstore chains and supermarkets and four identical strip malls with fabric centers and film-processing booths and yogurt places and souvenir shops and smelly stores full of bath salts and candles and soaps, all of which meant that suddenly people had steady jobs, this being when Daddy got into the union, unprepared for the way its compromises would wreck his life soon after.

I want to say she came every time we made love. But never once in all the times Shaleese and I got naked did she come, even the time in the evening seclusion of my uncle's log cabin, on our big vacation back into the mountains of New Mexico, when wild horses stood outside the window scratching themselves against the porch's support beams and deer pranced towards the ripening dusk and she dipped her long nails between her legs and identified her labia and clitoris for me before coaching me through cunnilingus. Even there, in that cabin without electricity, some necessary sexual spark failed: after a period of lapping noises, she slapped at the sheets and asked me to stop. Then, frustrated, she slid from my grasp and twisted her body completely away from mine. Her mouth made a sound, a chuckle maybe or a sob, I don't know. I felt it in my stomach. Suddenly I needed to see her face really bad, to register her expression. For some dumb reason, it was important to make sure she wasn't laughing at me. I grappled for her on the bed, wrestling with her slippery, naked shape in the failing light. "Dammit, Shaleese," I said. "Damn you, dammit. Show me your face, girl. Show it to me." I was surprised by her strength, that she was so fluid and impossible to hold. When at last I pinned her, I don't know how much time had passed but night was completely upon us and it was too dark to see anything. "I gotta see your face, baby." My arm shot out, plucking up the unlit oil lamp from the bedside table. I held it firmly aloft in one hand. My knees scooted up to pin her elbows, freeing up my other hand to reach for the box of matches.

Her arm snaked loose. Flailing desperately, she knocked the oil lamp from my grasp. It was a little like pitching a Molotov cocktail, an extremely formal one with an unlit wick. It was, I'd like to think, an accident.

The lamp hit the floor with a crash.

We lay panting for some time, motionless heaps on the bed, surrounded by broken glass.

The drama of it all settled on me like amnesia. I no longer wanted to see her face. In fact, the reason we were fighting had now completely slipped my mind. Have I mentioned the dark? The cabin, built facing south, caught no moonlight. The stink of kerosene sank into the floorboards beneath the bed. We could see nothing. Lighting a match would have incinerated us. Getting up would have sliced open our feet.

We lay there all night, unclothed, not speaking.

The next day I drove us twenty-some hours straight back to Sioux City. I recall it still as the worst travel time of my life. The landscape, steeped in romance when we'd driven through a few days earlier, was now bleak, like black-and-white photos. We passed bleary cowboys, abandoned motels, abandoned bars, abandoned gas stations, abandoned drive-ins, ghostly things. We passed these things in dead silence, and I drove in dead silence, though to be truthful I could coax a syllable or two from her if I really worked at it. At night we were wax gargoyles lit by the dashboard light, stroking the radio dials like prayer beads in a worthless show of faith. The radio insisted on playing only those unhappy, old-timey hits that would've bored even our parents. And all that time, all that silence. Throughout Colorado, they were playing songs by the band Chicago, and I tried to get into it, I remember humming along to "Color My World" as we got ready to enter some real deep, dark thing outside Boulder called the Eisenhower Tunnel. I couldn't begin to guess what was going on in her head. I could only imagine she was building her case against me, indicting me through some mixed-media masterpiece of literature and art she was quietly conceiving that whole time.

Fed Ex just drove up (our Fed Ex guy's named Franklin), had nice Mrs. Dannerby sign for a flat package sent from Snell Publications. So what was in this package? Well, Gabe sent me my check, one-half the total payment, but he forgot to sign it and there's just one press clipping, no CDs, and no biographical shit about this Ms. Phair. My check, nothing else (who's complaining? Well, I mean, it is unusable, it's not signed, how very true). Oh, and attached to my worthless check was a post-it note which read "Hope this helps! Hurry, Joy! Remember Laura Nyro! Twenty hours of tape due this Fri!" and then he signed off "Joy to the World! Gabe."

The place where the Fed Ex package arrived, the environment I inhabit, the room in which I live: a metal desk with framed pictures of cats, a long, creaky bed with blankets of orange and green, the happy shag-rug face of a large latch-hook clown smiling down from the wall. A mirror and a closetful of suitcases. My window shows the stained and spotted back of an old apartment building which appears unoccupied. If I

LIZ PHAIR WITH OSCAR TOYLE, THE FIRST BOY SHE EVER FRENCH-KISSED

stick my head out the window and look straight down, I see an alleyway through the trees. Couples sometimes walk this alleyway, furiously fighting to the sound of car alarms, the woman choking back tears, the man pleading, basic public disagreements, one treating the other like dirt for not recycling bottles and newspapers while the other retorts that the trash men take everything to the same dump no matter the color of garbage bag or civic policy, the inevitable breakdown in communication, one ridiculing the other for reading too many magazines and not living more in the real world while the other responds that watching television is not the real world, listening to popular radio is not the real world, don't speak to me about the real world, asshole. One furious at the other for dropping an important letter into the mail chute from high in the building without suspecting that it might get stuck and go nowhere, going on and on about how much better their situation would be if only the other one thought once in a while, where does your brain go, all I'm saying is show a little sense.

There is faith and there are those who despise you for it. But, there is faith. One small example: it is astonishing, when you think about it, how there is no guard before the women's rest room, no mechanism of any kind to insure that only females enter. It is merely an unlocked door, if that; in stadiums and airport terminals there is simply a cavelike gap in the wall (more like a missing tooth than anything else)—yes, faith and trust! for what could be more easily broached, what secrets are more tempting to penetrate than those held in the ladies' room?

Mrs. Dannerby has generously rented me the room with the CD player in it, but I have nothing to play on it until Gabe comes through.

Just now I realized these microcassettes also fit in Mrs. Dannerby's answering machine downstairs, which means I can tape any conversation I have. I put the tape in the machine and dialed Gabe, thinking I could record our conversation as I complained to him about not getting more of the stuff he promised. But all I got was a young woman who answered, "Snell House." I left my name and number and said it was crucial that Gabe call me in the next few hours.

That was twenty minutes ago. The phone has not rung.

When I was twelve, we chased lizards but we never caught them, me and Spencer, in between playing soldiers with our plastic army men and jumping from tall willows into Abingdon Creek, and we learned nothing in school that year except where to hide cigarettes for lunch recess, and the sunsets were so vivid and intense that we used magnifying glasses to focus the sun's rays onto our arms and legs to increase our super powers because we'd heard how the light at dusk is magic, and I was accused of shoplifting at one of the drugstore chains even though I had no idea up to then such a thing was even possible and after I protested my innocence and they let me go home I resolved to shoplift something from a drugstore every day for the rest of my life, and I hit .167 for our baseball team with no RBI's and a freak twister carried off every single stalk of corn that was growing in our county and one of my brothers graduated from high school and I got up the nerve to ask my daddy if he knew where my sister had gone and he met my eyes, smiling hopefully, and answered that as soon as he got more work he'd square himself with the private-investigation firm he'd hired and then he'd get the nuts and bolts himself and be able to fill me in and I salted slugs and spat on ants and squashed beetles and swatted lightning bugs with my badminton racket to make my badminton racket glow and my mom insisted on resisting all those entertaining two-step-gourmet dishes they advertised on TV because they made cooking look like such easy fun and, un-like my daddy, my mother appeared to have real trouble with any notion of easy fun so instead she boiled spaghetti for forty-five minutes until the noodles were expanded to the thickness of insulated extension cords and stuck in your teeth for days and that's all that happened when I was twelve.

What sort of girlfriend was she? I'd come home late from band practice and our house would be full of candles, all of them lit. The windows would be open, a breeze bringing in traffic noises. As I'd come in, I couldn't help thinking, "She knows how to create an atmosphere." She'd be lying lifelessly in bed. I'd get two cans of beer from the fridge and advance towards her. It would not be the first or last time I'd glance around for a suicide note. The cans would be cold in my hand and I would want to wake her to join me for a drink—I'd kiss her forehead and massage the bottoms of her feet, but she would not move. Still, I knew that if I just breathed on one of the candles among us Shaleese would stir as the flame stirred, and she would stretch and speak. Instead, I always let her lie. I'd sit on the carpet, watching the walls swoop in and out with the flicker of the candles, trying to remember the color of her eyes as her pupils swam beneath her clenched eyelids.

I found that with my hand in the small of her back, I could put Shaleese to sleep and this made me rethink my hands. I had only known my hands to heal small hurt things or hurt small things even more, to masturbate or play guitar or raise beer bottles. I always knew the important verbs were invented for my hands, but now that they could lay Shaleese down to sleep I grew wary of them. What magic was this? I felt I had to watch my hands very closely.

I would say she slept like an angel except that angels do not sleep. And even if angels did sleep, I cannot say that they would sleep this way. For Shaleese was the sort whose nightmares always had her thrashing in her sleep, nightmares so vivid and overwhelming that they would virtually leak out of her while she slept and overwhelm me as well, so that ly-

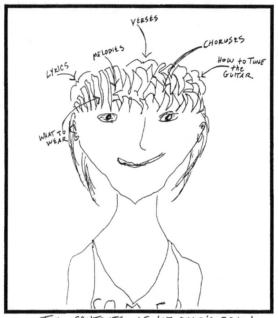

THE CONTENTS OF LIZ PHAIR'S BRAIN

ing next to her I would be forced to share them with her. Her body temperature would plummet. She'd shiver in her sleep. I would move to clasp and comfort her, glancing about the room to realize that once again (this happened every time) I had forgotten to extinguish the candles. Anything visible about Shaleese was indistinct, cast into shadow. She never awoke. And the nightmares grew. With lips slightly parted, her mouth would utter names, not the names of personal acquaintances but names from magazines, names from television. "Ted... Turner... Kath... leen... Turner... Mary Tyler... Moore... Demi... Moore..." They came out as sounds, frightened sounds, panicked syllables in broken meter, too scared to carry any real meaning. "Foz... zie... Pig... gy... Ker... mie... Snoopy, Lucy, Schroeder..." And I'd rub her unyielding arms and legs as if to say plainly, "I'm here, I'm here," my newly powerful hands fumbling to call forth some magic which might replace these recurrent nightmares with good dreams. Then I would make a wish and blow the candles out. In the morning, she'd say, "I missed you last night. I'm sorry I slept. I missed it all."

I have now read the article Gabe Fed-Exed me. A very good piece of writing. In it the journalist confesses digging each act on Matador Records, as he was sent them—first Superchunk ("beneath the churn of 400 guitars an unmiked voice screams to be heard"), Pavement ("bored but coolly in control: songs like terrorist acts, words like ransom notes"), then Bettie Serveert ("imagine a lisping version of Crazy Horse from Holland, their feelings hurt, their sound resembling the canals of Amsterdam, by turns reflective, murky, deep, inspiring"), then Christmas ("troubling lyrics set to perfect pop melodies sung by a woman whose voice, wrapped in wax paper, could be sold as candied confection"). Eventually, the writer admits, Matador acts became all he wrote about. His editors complained. He promised to be better, but just then Matador slated another release, and sent him a CD called *Exile in Guyville* by a singer/songwriter from Chicago named Liz Phair.

The writer claims he could listen to nothing else for a month (are we to believe this?). His editors label her a media hype. What is it with Liz Phair? his editors ask. Did men just discover that women can play rock and roll too, is that such a revelation? You would think there was nothing else to write about. The only reason you want to write about Liz Phair is because you get so turned on by her filthy mouth.

The writer defends himself by saying he'd been waiting for just this CD since Madonna first appeared. He speaks of some dramatic surge of feminist music that I only vaguely recall—people like Throwing Muses, Sinead O'Connor, PJ Harvey—I wonder why Gabe didn't just hire this writer to dictate my book? He's very well informed. Too expensive? He wouldn't accept unsigned checks? I'm gonna read the rest of the article aloud, read it into the record here:

"The trend continued for other bold women artists like L-7, Kim Deal, and Tanya Donelly, jumping with such quick readiness from obscurity into popularity that their record companies were left scampering to keep up with the demand. The sudden presence of so many strong women at the microphone—singing neither as folkie angels nor hard-rock whores but simply as women—abruptly made a shambles of marketing strategies. It can be blamed on the tasty melodies and arrangements of the Breeders and Belly. Suddenly, in 1993, there arrived a glorious flood of female talent—during one week I received advance copies of albums by Bratmobile, Juliana Hatfield, Brenda Kahn, Penelope Houston, Barbara Manning. I heard a cassette of cool, screeched fusion lullabies from a West Coast band called Lava Diva and a tribute album to Victoria Williams as well as a flexi-disc spotlighting the hilarious, intelligent, tremulously sung material of New York singer Julia Douglass. I was blown away by an unsigned Los Angeles trio named Wheel (led by the indecipherable growls of bassist Sabrina Judge, a sound like Joan Armatrading fronting Galaxie 500). I read in *People* magazine acclaim for the simplistic grit and guts of Olympia-based Tiger Trap, for Bikini Kill and Huggy Bear. Yet there was still more I needed to hear, a release I anxiously awaited which would synthesize the allure of Sinead O'Connor with the melodies of the Breeders with the directness of Bratmobile with the musicianship of Belly. This was when, to my eternal misfortune, Matador mailed me *Exile in Guyville*."

When I was thirteen, I missed three ground balls in a row at tryouts and for the first time missed making the baseball team, I threw rocks at birds and boulders off overpasses, I rode my brother's motocross bike everywhere, my oldest brother married a stewardess named Lauren who was really sweet to me and really a fox and she gave me books on art and the Navajo and I wrote her a letter asking her to sleep with me because I was ashamed of being a virgin and everyone laughed and passed the letter around, then my other brother kicked my ass while my daddy made clucking noises with his tongue and Lauren and my oldest brother moved to Oregon and made me promise to visit, and I broke Spencer's arm and felt really awful about it until I realized it meant he could hang out with me because he was injured and the team couldn't use him, and I met Roy (this was the first time he came to live with his father) and we taught each other words like "lezzie" and "nympho" and "b-j" and "cum" and the three of us—Roy, Spencer, and I—all went to some drugstore every day and every day I stole something, and I began to spray-paint things because I had all these cans I had shoplifted and once some former coach recognized Spencer when he was keeping a lookout with his arm in a sling while Roy and I did graffiti and Spencer lost his nerve and told us that if the police arrested him he was gonna have to rat on us or his father would be devastated and his athletic career would end and we called him "Rat" and he said "Yes, yes" and we said "Rat" and "Narc" and "Jock" and "Wuss" like they were interchangeable and Roy said how he should go hang out with muscle-headed jerks who were more like himself and he said "Sure, sure" and rode off, and someone dared me to ask my mom if my sister was dead and Mom yelled at me, "Your sister's great, but I've just about had it, will I never hear the end of this, she doesn't belong to us anymore okay, all right, she's no longer our daughter, plain and simple," and I made it to third in the school spelling bee before I got out on the word "fuselage," and we listened a lot to Bob Dylan and this Cree Indian named Buffy Sainte-Marie who we liked because she sang tunes about people dying on codeine, and my mom kept making bad spaghetti, and I met an exchange student named Flore in the record section of the library, she was three years older than me but she seemed to like me, and we went to the video arcade a lot though getting there was a drag because Flore didn't have a bike so I always had to wait for her to catch up with me and we would smoke cigarettes and she would shake her head at me and say "Nobody does Dylan like Dylan" and we exchanged addresses when she left and we kept up a fierce correspondence that slowly dwindled and dwindled and died and I forgot her face utterly and that's all that happened when I was thirteen.

What sort of girlfriend was she? I would come home to find globbed-up paint brushes stuck to our placemats, Shaleese using the nice napkins to swab the walls with turpentine, a dim red bulb screwed into the bathroom socket, the tub clogged and reeking of photo fixer and developing fluids. I would never find art. Just the raw tools, bruised and filthy. She'd already put everything else out of sight. She always said she was ashamed of her stuff and that I would be embarrassed for her if I saw it. She said this with complete conviction, though I know she was simultaneously sending slides of her artwork to galleries and winning distant contests with her photographs. When I asked how it was she could share her artwork with the world but not with me, she told me she guessed it was because the world's opinion just didn't matter. She was weird about a lot of that stuff but I never thought I would lose her to it so that was okay. And besides, I was happy with her in a way I had never been before, felt contained and sure. It was a happiness peculiarly shaded by her gestures and nuances, my affection for her centered in a few specific unconscious movements she made, the way she pointed and laughed, the way she so unabashedly involved herself in the world around her.

What I mean is, despite these things I've said about her potential suicide notes, her moods and privacy and nightmares and fears for the weather, despite all that Shaleese still had these qualities that begged for a name like "Pumpkin" or "Silly." Like "roller coaster" to her was "rolley coaster," "soda pop" was "sodey pop," "balloon" lasted about thirteen syllables and came out as something like "ballooeeyen." Like every dog passing by she'd have to name, not by breed but by some human name—"Oh hello you must be... Fred. And your cute little friend there, is that Babette? Well boom-boom-boom, hello Babette!" Or she'd have these classic American idioms that she would always misquote. Probably she was just quoting her German mother, but who knows. I'd always be a little embarrassed for her mistakes and I'd feel like it was nice of me to offer corrections. But she usually went right back to the wrong phrase, giving me these wild justifications and arguing my corrections. Like, for example, she'd say that someone was "off his rocket" instead of "off his rocker," and then tell me she liked the first one better because she could envision someone jetting around to get so much done that he'd simply fall right off his rocket. She also thought the expression was, "He lied like a mug," and explained that it referred to the way a criminal might hold his face when he gets his mug shot taken. "Trial and error" and "trial by fire" became, in Shaleese's mind, "trial by error." "That's what makes horse racing" and "Close only counts in horseshoes and hand grenades" became "Close is what makes hand grenades." "I don't give a hoot" and "It doesn't add up to a hill of beans" became "I don't give a hoot of beans." To make the point that she was comparing things of like value she'd say, "Oh well, it's six and half a dozen of the other." I'd cautiously inform her that by my calculations that totaled twelve for "the other" and none for this, but she'd always ignore me. All these expressions, all these garbled clichés. "Pumpkin," you'd want to call her. "For all intensive purposes," she'd say, "It's a doggy dog world." You'd want to pat her head and say, "Oh, go on, silly."

At dinner tonight, I tried to tell Mrs. Dannerby about my easy new job that just dropped out of the clear blue, but she was skeptical. What do you mean they don't care what you say? She put her spoon down and looked at me gravely. She said it was her ex-husband's policy to disbelieve all things until they were completely proven. That way you were never wrong. Mrs. Dannerby loves to talk about her ex-husband. He died some-how, I can't remember, though I've heard about it many times over dinner.

I told her I could stand to learn a thing or two from him because it seemed I had always been wrong. She patted my hand and gently asked if that was why I still wore the bracelet.

"Is that something your ex left you with?"

I was stunned that suddenly Mrs. Dannerby should speak to me this way (has she been listening at the door? Almost certainly!). I have never mentioned Shaleese to her.

LIZ ATOP CHICAGO'S WORLD-FAMOUS SEARS TOWER

More, I was concerned that she should have noticed the bracelet. Though I have been careful to cover it with my sleeve whenever I'm with her, apparently I've underestimated the keenness of Mrs. Dannerby's sight.

"Yes," I told her. "It's a reminder, is all."

She collected our dishes, sighed, and brought out dessert with a sympathetic shake of her head.

There has been no reason to hide this. I knew you would drive me to it eventually; that's what makes this particular talking technique so successful... I knew that eventually you would wrestle everything out of me: on my left wrist I wear a plastic bracelet.

It's not what Mrs. Dannerby thinks. The bracelet bears my name and patient number and I apparently require some special institutional gadget to remove it, something like that valuable instrument the assholes hide behind the counter and bring out only to snip off tags at the clothing store so that the shoplifting alarms won't be activated by your new purchases, the plastic on the bracelet is that thick, too thick to cut, I have tried and succeeded only in bending and ruining a pair of scissors lent to me by Mrs. Dannerby without her knowledge. I struggle to tell you all I know about it, but the bracelet bears no other information, like an institutional name or city district, so I can't be positive if it stems from that hospital visit I made in New York, which happily was a willing one (New York? was this Passaic maybe? Outside the window, stick-bare windswept trees of winter spoke of witch trials), or that one other time, a grassy facility with ping-pong tables in North Carolina, which was against my own wishes but now and again I think maybe for the best. I will hopefully get better at putting down an exact chronology. Somewhere in here too I was transferred to another place, further outside of town, which was where I collected the first names of a few people, as one does with people one calls friends. Perhaps that was my third stay in an institution, I don't know. It doesn't matter.

I hear the television blaring downstairs as Mrs. Dannerby sits and waits for her crime show. A voice comes on to summarize last week's plot: *Haldz has done everything and anything to get the attention of the girl he loves: flowers, candies, valentines. Wealthy, becoming more and more well known, she will no longer acknowledge this poverty-stricken man's existence. After years of this treatment, Haldz is horrified to realize that the love letters he had addressed to her from prison gave her the idea for her newest film. Will she only take from him, first his heart, next his words and gifts, then his very thoughts, in the form of movies? Do you honestly understand what it is to be frustrated? In this week's episode, Haldz determines to ask her exact intentions. But can he handle her answer?*

When I was fourteen my daddy's union went on strike out of sympathy with the metal workers and my mother had to start working and Roy went back to live with his Mom and I met Doug Prendergast who was this beautiful, slick-haired dude and he taught me how to wring money from a Konelco change machine using Xeroxes of dollar bills and I had nothing to do with all the money so I bought records and porno magazines and I studied them intensely and I taught Prendergast how to fingerpick that codeine song of Buffy Sainte-Marie's and we laughed at anyone using drugs because the song made them out to be so pathetic and I was propositioned by Monica, who I thought a little stuck-up and didn't really like very much at first, though upon her asking I did like she wanted and met her down at Abingdon Creek and we made it but then she wanted to make it again as soon as it was over and I felt dumb though later this skinny runt named Adam Charles who went by his initials but wrote A.C. out as "Acey" told me that Monica was always that way and she and I started making it quite frequently except she continued to make it with at least Acey that I knew of and some others and because my mom was always working my daddy started cooking dinner but my mom complained he never boiled the spaghetti long enough so she quit her job to stay home and cook and the governor asked for authority to fire the striking workers and then the union met and decided they had best go back to work even though none of the metal workers' demands had been met and my daddy was so upset by this so-called compromise that he argued and argued until they kicked him out of the union and then even though he was a local boy and everybody's favorite pal he was blackballed everywhere and no one would hire him and I also met dumb Jimmy that year and that's all that happened when I was fourteen.

I remember one Saturday, one beautiful spring day when we awoke and suddenly realized I didn't have to work and she didn't have class and we had the whole day to play. We went out to breakfast at the Nighthawk coffeehouse (she loved their butter-smothered giant cinnamon rolls), which despite its name was open quite early. Then we wandered down to the sloppy Missouri, its banks lined with little tramp villages and burnt-up hulks of cars, and we took turns hurling pennies at Nebraska and South Dakota, both of which lay just across the river, looking silver in the late-morning sun. Then we wound up where we almost always wound up, at the one hip place in Sioux City, a bookstore called Adventure Books. The big, jolly guy at the register beamed at us like always, with this misplaced air of jubilance, like we were his pet project, like he had taught us to walk, taught us to read, like it was the victory of a lifetime getting us to laze around in his store.

Adventure Books not only had a good selection of books on weird subjects but beanbag chairs and sofas and hidden nooks and free coffee. Shaleese and I would start looking for something interesting. The first one to spot something got to read it aloud while the other slouched on the sofa and spaced out.

The only thing that had started to bug me about Adventure Books was their growing collection of rock-star books. When we first started going there, a few limp, dusty books had been shelved in a tiny section in back underneath a hand-drawn, scotch-taped sign: Celebrities. Gradually, that section moved forward in the store, up and up the unswept aisles, expanding all the while with books from Snell Publications, until now the section had been renamed Rock Biographies/Artist Histories and had become one of the most prominent displays in the place.

This morning, as we strode in, the early light made it seem even bigger than usual.

"Rock stars," I grumbled. "We all want to know every scrap of detail about the lifestyles of the rich, we just must know what rock stars are doing."

"Oh, Camden, don't."

"Did I read you that thing about rock stars being like royalty in the Middle Ages, roaming the countryside, pillaging as they go?"

"Such a nice place and you immediately have to pick up on the one thing you don't appreciate."

"One thing I gotta say about punkers is they at least despised rock stars, until they died and became rock stars themselves. Did I read you that interview with Johnny Rotten where he goes like, it's just been announced that Elvis Presley has died, this is like 1977, and they ask Johnny Rotten whether he has any comments on the death of Elvis and he goes, 'Too bad it took so long.' Isn't that great?"

"I guess."

"And then he says 'I hope Mick Jagger's next.' Isn't that great? That's the kind of thing you never see in these rock-star books: one of them dancing on another one's grave."

"Maybe it's in that book," she said, pointing out *The Collected Insults of Johnny Rotten.*

"Oh no," I moaned. "Oh, man, it is just so gross living in

this time. I mean, think about it. How come every rock star—you see this in like interviews with Pete Townshend and, even, god, even with Billy Joel—they all mock themselves, say all they did was live recklessly and write little ditties, they don't deserve to be rich and famous, and this sorta makes them disappointed in how shallow we've become, because they deserve to be dead and unknown and instead they're not, instead they've each got a little biography written about them."

"Are you asking me?"

"I mean, god. It's like every rock star living or dead gets some lousy book written about them. Aren't they ever gonna run out of rock stars? I mean, here's one about Cracker already, here's one about the Go-Betweens. Jesus! Like I care how they live."

"You *are* flipping through the books."

"Just to make sure. Nothing wrong in knowing the enemy. Hate to just preach to the converted, you know."

"Hey." From the corner of my eye I saw her reach into her bag, pull out a fragile clothbound book. "I got something I want to read you."

"That your journal?"

"This? Uh, no."

"Can I see it a second?"

"No. Sit down. I want to read it to you."

"It looks like your journal."

"It's a library book, okay?"

"All right, all right. I guess it wouldn't be your precious journal."

"It's a book, a book I found, and it seems important to me, real important, and I... it's about Brian Jones—"

"Great! More dead rock stars! What'd he ever do but drown? They've done every member of the Rolling Stones now three times, individually and in various groupings. You want to know what I predict?"

"Listen," she said, the Brian Jones book open before her.

"'Having had his fill of couscous, goat's meat...'"

"Oh. And I want to know about their every meal, too. Yeah, right. This is what I predict. I predict there's gonna start being books about one-hit wonders like the 1910 Fruit Gum Company or whoever, and it'll spark some bizarre nostalgia and probably be a real successful trend and whatever. But then there'll come a book—listen to me now, I'm serious—"

She shut the book politely.

"A book whose subject we forget as soon as it comes out and you know what that'll be? It'll be the last rock-star book."

"That's great. Okay now, sit down, I'm gonna read this to you."

"After what I just said, you're gonna turn around and poison my mind with this dead-rock-star crap?"

"Yes."

"Okay."

"Now sit in that beanbag—"

"I'm sitting, I'm sitting—"

"—and please hush up. Here goes. 'Having had his fill of couscous, goat's meat, and dimly conveyed translations, the British superstar excused himself from the table and stumblingly surveyed the rest of the restaurant—'"

"Oh Jesus. The fictionalized ones are the worst, where they constantly try to figure out what a certain celebrity would be thinking at every moment."

"Now, please. I listened to you. Now you listen. This is important to me."

"Important to you? Right."

Having had his fill of couscous, goat's meat, and dimly conveyed translations, the British superstar excused himself from the table and stumblingly surveyed the rest of the restaurant. The master musicians of JouJouka, the Pipers of the Rif Mountains, the ones he had traveled all this way to record, the people of Pan, nodded politely as he left.

The room stank sweetly of hashish. Through the kif haze and the faint green lights, the superstar could be spotted in his exotic furs and flowered cravat and maroon brocade jacket and broad-brimmed, yellow-and-pink-polka-dotted hat, struggling just to hold himself erect, lurching to and fro like an animal seeking warmth at sundown, then landing with a startled grunt at some other table across the restaurant. He looked up groggily, as if astonished to find himself once again sitting, two bloody soft-boiled eggs for eyes and lemon sunshine hair and a wax visage, the jazz alto saxophonist from Cheltenham who had traveled down to London to become blues guitarist Elmo Lewis, the father of countless illegitimate children, and founder of the world's most notorious rock-and-roll band—

"I hate this kind of writing."

—the one who insisted they call themselves after a Muddy Waters tune, the one who brought sitar to "Paint It Black," the one with the longest rap sheet, the short one, the bully the girls adored, the one who couldn't keep his mouth shut, the scapegoat for Scotland Yard's most celebrated drug busts, the pedantic hustler, the frail Stone.

"Far out," he muttered at the young tourist across the table. "Really, far out."

"Ich kenne Sie, mein Herr?" she asked. Do I know you? *Her spine stiffened as she said this, for she had been rather content sitting by herself.*

He squinted at her, blinked a few times. "German. The enemy. Far out. Me Grandad pro'ly shot at your Grandad, know that? What a wonderful world. I was a lad growing up, I used to tell me Dad, one day I'd bring him home a Nobel prize. What in, he'd say. He never laughed, not once. Always supporting me. Other parents, they'd

53

laugh, they'd joke, right you are, sonny, sure, sure, et cetera—but not me Dad. There's this way he always was—

"Like they know exactly what he said to this woman."

—I was failing at school, still he'd be, "What area you going to win your Nobel prize in, son?"

She studied the tears running down his face. Large, wet teardrops like summer rain.

"Here, luv. You don't get English at all, do you?"

"Some," she said, working to keep her accent down. She cautiously shifted her silverware, straightening the fork, clinking the knife against the spoon. Underneath the table, she ran a sandal into her knapsack, securing her passport between her toes.

"Who are you?"

"Elsa."

"How old are you, Elsa, sechzehn, siebzehn?"

"Siebzehn, ja."

"All alone then?"

She shook her head vehemently.

"Parents, chums, what? Boyfriend?"

She nodded.

"Oh well, that." He suddenly lost interest. "Groovy," he said listlessly. Then he invited her to a party, mumbling some directions, and lunged past her and out the exit.

After he had gone, Elsa opened her travel log and wrote a complete summary of the events that had occurred. The earlier pages of her log were filled with descriptions of fire-eaters and jugglers and snake charmers and acrobats and silver-hung belly dancers and Berber drummers, detailing the thirteen days since her boyfriend abandoned her here in Morocco. The mounds of brightly colored spices sold in the souks of Tetouan. The oppressive web of alleyways in the labyrinthine medina. The babbling storytellers of Tangier's Grand Socco bazaar. The pomegranate gardens and low, pink houses of Marrakesh. Now the encounter with the British superstar in a French colonial inn in the foothills of the Rif mountains. She wrote of his sad gaze, his drooping hat, his pointed Edwardian button boots. Then Elsa wrote down his directions to the party.

"Can I go on?"

"Go on."

"It's sorta hard for me to read with all your comments."

"Tell it to the author."

"You aren't about to stamp off in a puff or anything, are you? The part that's really important to me, it's coming up."

"In a huff."

"Hmmm?"

"The expression is *to stomp out in a huff.* Not puff. Huff."

"Oh, I like puff better, don't you? Like a puff of dust, like what happens in cartoons when one of them leaves in a hurry. There's no reason to be so literal. So I can keep reading?"

"Fine. Got my coffee. I'm nice and cozy here."

Elsa followed the desert howl and the bleating of farm animals beyond the village and through the Little Hills to a lone shanty. Coming upon the musicians perched outside on the porch on footstools, Elsa was pleased to realize it was not the desert she heard howling but these wrinkled pipers, dressed in caftans and djellabahs, fingers and ears studded with glass and silver, playing tunes as old as the world.

She found the superstar inside with some other Englishmen, within the shanty's astonishingly lavish inner chamber, beaten metal lamps flickering in every corner, gold fringe winking at her from curtain trims and tablecloths and hanging tapestries.

"Anita!" he cried, kissing her cheek, a near-empty

bottle in his hand.

*"Anita!" Elsa cried gamely in return. She assumed
it translated as "welcome" in the native tongue.*

"She sounds a little like you there."

*The superstar giggled, spun on the others. "Doesn't she
look just like Anita to you lads?"*

*The bubbling of the hookah was the only response.
"Well?!"*

*"I'm bleedin' sick to death uh all this Anita crap,"
one of them croaked. He exhaled lungsful of smoke, then
continued in a gentle tone. "And I would not like to discover what your intentions are in regards to this chick.
Somehow it's always me who has to tend the broken ones,
you know, and I'm fucking sick uh it. You remember now,
that was me in Tangier that time, putting in the call to the
home office to tell them you broke your sweet little hand
in some climbing accident after you clobbered Anita. And
now… What's that new chick's name?"*

"Suki," someone offered.

*"Suki, right. More fisticuffs. Who was it called the
bloody ambulance to the Hotel Minzah—why just last
night I do believe it was—after you pummeled your be-
loved Suki unconscious? Why, that was me too, come to
think uh it." The man stood. "So fuck off, all this Anita
crap." Pushing past to join the musicians on the porch,
he quietly concluded, "You're a goddamn bloody menace
is all you are."*

*Only one of the English entourage, a large balding
man with tattooed arms, would even look at the seven-
teen-year-old German girl. "Okay, right," he answered
Brian, after peering into her face. "Maybe a wee bit like
Anita. More like Suki though, you ask me, Brian."*

Elsa was shown to the hookah by the tattooed man.

56

"E's a bit touched, y'know?" The tattooed man pointed a fat finger at his smooth head. "Ha-lucy-gens. Falls into a dream state, then—" The man delicately whistled the sound of an approaching bomb. His whistle faded into the howls of the musicians outside.

She lay down to inhale from the pipe, breathed out slowly. In no time, the superstar was upon her. "I told Mick he could keep the fucking group!" he screamed, his face pressed to hers, his lips an inch from her eyes. Elsa recoiled, struggled to push him off, grunting.

"Ich kann nicht atmen." I can't breathe.

"I told him in his position they could really do some good in the world, and not just bum everyone's trip, man. I said that, dig? I said groovy, you got some problems, I got some problems, we all got some problems here that like need working out, and Mick, man, you got to be kinder to the women of this world. Can you fucking dig it, Anita?"

"I am... Elsa!"

The tattooed man appeared, looming above the superstar, shaking his head. He would not interfere.

With one hand the superstar unzipped himself, with the other he held Elsa by the hair. "I told Mick he was cruel to chicks, dig! I told him—here—like this'll show you—"

"Stop!" Elsa screamed in his ear, and he leapt enough for her to wriggle free. She scampered to her feet, flushed and panting.

"Oh it's going to be like that, is it?" murmured the superstar, lifting a knotted velvet cord to strike her.

The tattooed man appeared again. "No," he told the superstar, grabbing away the cord. "It's not gonna be that way at all." He shoved him deep into the cushions of the sofa. "Come now, lad. Make our new friend here a little welcome."

The superstar swept the strands of yellow from his

eyes. His mouth worked but no words came out. He trembled the way a marionette might as its wires are pulled out. His head fell into his hands, his back convulsing with sobs. His teeth were chattering. "I'm so, god, I'm so... what is this?"

Elsa stepped outside. The lights of the village were dimly visible below through the oaks and cedars and olive trees. Goats nibbled shrubbery in the moonlight. Elsa believed she could hear the waves of the Mediterranean in the far distance.

"They have a way of breathing in while they exhale." It was the Englishman who had fled to the porch earlier. He was motioning at the master musicians of Jou-Jouka. "Allows them to play uninterruptedly. They never have to stop for a breath."

Elsa nodded. "I... am hearing you," she said. "Yes." She sat down with her legs crossed, took a sip from a bottle with an American label, made a face, took another sip.

They sat in silence. A small herd of newly shorn sheep jangled into view, small bells knotted about their ankles, emerging along the same worn mule-path which guided Elsa here. The tinny bells joined the sounds of far-off waves and hypnotic pipes and contented bleating.

Brian Jones appeared at her side. He looked ruddy and smelled freshly bathed. "Please come inside. Please. I'm telling you, I'm really quite sorry."

Elsa looked curiously at the other Englishman. "Yes?" she asked the Englishman.

"Go ahead," the man assured her. "Humbled, the giant can no more roar. You'll be fine."

Once inside, they found Elsa a clean glass and filled it with the brewed mead they were sharing. Each man politely asked for a chance to dance with her, to hug her while turning in slow circles. She assented. It began with the tattooed man and at last she found herself back with the superstar, except that now the roles were reversed and she held him up, for he felt fragile and slight in her grasp. Elsa clung to him as he moved like a woman against her. For hours, it seemed.

"May I tell you why it is I like you so?" he murmured, showing no trace of his earlier sinister self.

"Yes."

"I like your feet. They're so... big, you know? Anita had, or I should say 'has,' I suppose, has these delicate little china-doll feet, Suki too. But you... you're the real thing. All these other chicks, with their teeny-tiny perfect feet, I seem to get what I want. But you fight back and I, well, while I can't honestly say I enjoy it, I do respect you more for that. You know? I mean, you're around me long enough, you hear me speak a lot of lines to a lot of chicks but what I'm saying here, this is no line. I respect you. And I respect your feet. They're big, god. They're big as mine, you know that?

"Here, try these on. You see? You can fill my shoes. And while I can't say I know what your trip is or anything, I can see you changing me all around, you and those big feet, getting me back to normal. I could anchor myself to you and you'd just haul me out of all this... this shit. I see a chance with you. Tell me. Say you'll help. I mean I respect you and all. If you don't want a sexual sort of occurrence tonight, that's cool, I understand, you're welcome to stay, hang out, et cetera. But I'm not simply speaking of making love. I want... I want you to promise you'll join me in Sussex. Of all bloody things, I'm moving to the House at Pooh Corner. Come stay with me. We'll be ever so happy. Six bedrooms, three baths. Three reception rooms. A staff apartment. Bentleys and Rolls Royces. Eleven acres. Pooh. Piglet. Christopher Robin. Oh, and a heated Grecian swimming pool. We'll go swimming."

"We wait... and see," Elsa said, in careful English.

*Compared to the torment she had put up with from her
former boyfriend, the superstar was easily managed. She
laid him down in the makeshift bedroom and kissed him
to sleep.*

"I've read about the Rolling Stones. But I've never heard of
this Elsa woman."

"No?"

"No."

"Well."

"Is any of what you're reading, any of this stuff you're
reading me, Shaleese... Is any of it true, I mean, or is it all
some novelized fictional thing?"

"She's my mom."

"I'm sorry?"

"Elsa."

"Huh?"

"Seriously."

"No. Your mom who runs the motel back home, you're
saying that's this girl, Elsa? No. Sorry, but no."

"I admit... it's kinda weird... telling you."

"Right."

She said nothing.

"No. It can't be. Come on, really. It has to be someone
famous, like Pierre Trudeau's wife or Grace Kelly's daughter
or something. That's how these books work."

"Oh."

*Elsa could not stop sniffling nor could she seem to find
the right temperature. With her sweater she roasted, without it she shivered. It was the afternoon of July 2, 1969,
and the German girl—now eighteen—was on her first trip
through the British countryside, on the way to Cotchford
Farm, former estate of A.A. Milne. She had traveled up by
train from London, had telephoned Brian from Haywards*

Heath station. He sounded overjoyed that after all these letters and phone calls and excuses and delays she was actually coming to him. His last package to her had contained, of all things, shoes: he had sent her a pair of shoes, one size which would fit both him and her, the soles handcrafted pieces of cherrywood painted with crescent moons and smelling heavily of Moroccan paprika, the leather glistening with gold sparkles. An apt gift, shoes, a wish for forward movement, for he was now—officially, as of last month—an ex–Rolling Stone, and he needed her now not so much as an anchor but to help get him moving again, to start him rolling. Elsa sneezed into her hands again and the taxi driver blessed her.

As they entered the wide-swung black gates and stopped before the tall stone facade of Cotchford Farm, Brian and his dogs were there to help her from the cab.

"Ah! You're wearing the shoes! So you received them all right. Aren't they wonderful? Makes one want to walk forever!"

He looked paunchy and tired.

"T'ey are... t'e best!" Elsa exclaimed enthusiastically. She sneezed.

"Ah, what's this? Touch of cold?"

"How vould you say... Heufieber."

"Oh. Hay fever."

"Hayfeber," she repeated diligently.

"Today's bad." He held up an asthmatic inhaler. "Must keep my squirter with me at all times on days such as these."

He presented her to his two dogs and showed her about the grounds: the Eeyore sundial and Christopher Robin statue, the bridge over the stream where the game of Pooh-sticks was invented, the brick walks and overgrown fruit trees.

Several times Elsa tried to tell Brian about a man

she had observed on the way in, a beekeeper at a local Sussex honey farm with his body suit covered head to toe in honeybees. She didn't know the English words. It struck her so vividly: the ill-fitting body suit, allowing the beekeeper to move only in fitful, jerky motions; the honeybees, a shifting organic swarm, stinging the body suit, constantly changing place, moving and vibrating. It had occurred to Elsa as she watched that this thing was a robot: Nature angrily attacking a robot. All she could say was, "It vas vonderful, vat I saw." Brian agreed it sounded quite wonderful.

The decor inside the house seemed to mix the musician and the Morocco tourist: a tomato-red guitar propped on a lime-green velvet sofa, a grand piano laden with flamboyant silver candelabras, a mellotron upon a Marrakesh carpet, under intricate hanging fabrics from Tangier; a record player among silk cushions, weathered trunks, glass curios. Woven burgundy curtains hung limply in the heat. When Brian drew the curtains back, Elsa was momentarily blinded by the gleam from the ornate pool.

"Ah," she said, shielding her eyes. "It is beautiful... but my head." She motioned towards her temples, her stuffed-up nose.

"Yes. Indeed. You've been traveling and you are fatigued. Weary. Listless. May I show you to your room now, Fräulein?"

Elsa nodded. He took her hand in his to guide her to a banister. He led her up a broad set of dark wood steps, turning left at the top.

"And here we are, so soon." Her room was composed of still more dark wood, and was many degrees chillier than the main hall. Her eye scanned the room—the bed piled with yet more Arabian patterns, the built-in writing desk, full-length mirror, mahogany bedside tables, more Moroccan carpets—and a window. She moved to the window, looked down on the pool ringed with dense bushes, the fruit trees covered in bird netting, a band of construction workers busy around the other wing of the mansion. In the distance Elsa could make out a number of cottages.

"All t'is belongs to you?"

He was sitting on the side of the bed, pale and sweating, wheezing on his inhaler. "Up to a far line of cypress trees you can see there. That's the windbreak. It demarks the property."

She was trying not to sneeze, her finger beneath her nose, her eyes shut tightly.

"Oh, go ahead and sneeze."

Elsa let it out, then found she could not stop sneezing. They exchanged rueful looks, that they should meet at last on such a pollen-heavy day.

"You want something for hay fever, we got that." He pulled a series of pills from his pocket, examined each closely, then selected one and held it out to her, a white tablet pinched between two yellow fingers.

She squinted at it and shook her head.

"Make you a tad drowsy is all." She watched him, still wary. He shrugged, but as he started to put the pill away, she thought better of the offer, snatched the pill from him, threw her head back, swallowed. Then she sneezed again.

"You see. Better already, pretty missy."

She sat on the bed beside him, mussing his hair, rubbing his sideburns, kissing his neck, his ears, his mouth. He tasted of wine and of medicine.

She fell back on the bed and reached up to help him untie her blouse. "Everyt'ing... off!" she cried with enthusiasm, pulling at his shirt.

"Yes, everything," he said. "Everything off."

"Everyt'ing but t'e shoes... I never must remove t'e shoes."

They made love as best they could, given his asthma, given her hay fever. Later it did not seem particularly memorable. She'd remember him popping out every time she sneezed and, coughing heavily all the while, repositioning himself strenuously each time with his hand before reentering her. She'd remember him climaxing with such a groan that she feared his life was leaving him, and holding him as he lay upon her afterwards. He said, "I can't believe you're truly here. You don't know how happy this makes me." She was aware of him climbing from her as she felt the cool of the room harden her nipples. She was too weary to cover herself.

"It's okay," Elsa heard him say. "You rest. We'll have lots of time to talk, lots and lots of talk." He covered her with a blanket, bent and kissed her shod feet. "God, I love these feet," he snickered. He patted her shoes—his shoes—their shoes—and drifted away, gently closing the door behind him.

She awoke hours later. Her head was turned to the side and she could see nothing. Gradually, as her eyes grew accustomed to the dark, a strange object came into focus, a robot's eye staring at her from only inches away. She caught her breath. She could hear the voice of Ernestine the Operator wafting from a television set in another room where they were watching Laugh-In. *Elsa stared back at the robot's eye, waiting for it to blink. It did not blink. She heard convulsive fits of laughter drowning out the television set, friendly shouts drifting in from the swimming pool. And still the robot did not blink. At last she took a trembling hand and slapped at it. It struck the wall with a loose, cracking sound, bounced to the floor, rolled beneath the bed. It was Brian's inhaler, which he'd left upright on the bedside table. She blew her breath out, unsteadily got to her feet, naked but for her shoes. Taking up the bedspread to wrap herself, Elsa crossed the room.*

From the window, she could make out a group of men, the tough-looking workers she had seen earlier around the mansion's other wing, roughhousing in the pool, swigging from bottles. Brian was swimming towards them, his bloated white torso resembling a languid piece of gristle bobbing in a clear broth. She wondered if he would be all right without his inhaler. She thought for a moment of walking it down to him, but instead she returned to bed. She watched the ceiling ripple as the underwater pool lights refracted up through her window. She dozed off again peacefully.

She had a dream. Her mother was alive and pleading with Elsa to come back to Heidelberg. She could hear her mother calling from far across a green pasture, and a moist wind carried Elsa's name off into the welcoming woods, until she doubted whether her mother was calling her at all.

She awoke at Cotchford Farm to a great crashing of glass. She leaped up. The door to her room was wide open. Downstairs, men were shouting. She ran to the window. The Cotchford floodlights were on. The grounds were swarming with people, not people in swimsuits, not people with gay expressions, but older people in faded clothes, barking out orders, uprooting shrubs, working to pry up the Eeyore sundial and Christopher Robin statue, directing one another with waving pitchforks and flashlights. Bonfires, not just one but several, glowed throughout the property. And what were they burning? Elsa squinted at the bonfires, picking out things she recognized: gold fringe winking at her from cloths and tapestries, exotic furs, a tomato-red guitar, flowered cravats, the maroon brocade jacket, and broad-brimmed, yellow-and-pink-polka-dotted hat. On the decking of the pool there lay an indistinct shape, lifeless and gray as a robot's corpse. She threw on some clothes, tucked the trailing ends of her unknotted blouse into her pants, grabbed her bags. She did not feel the broad, wooden steps beneath her feet as she bounded downstairs in a panic. "Brian!" she shouted. Villagers were busy in here too, perhaps twenty of them, with their caps pulled low and their expressions tight, pulling down textiles with both hands, scooping up armfuls of glass curios and beaten-metal lamps, smashing record albums, arguing about how best to hoist the lime-green velvet sofa.

"Brian!"

"You're too late, luv," someone turned to inform her, and when he lowered his stack of satin pillows she recognized him as her taxi driver from earlier in the afternoon. "Brian Jones is dead."

A thwacking sound erupted from the front doorway. She bolted towards it, found men swinging axes at the door jambs so as to carve out a path for the grand piano.

Elsa ran to the driveway and kept running until she was outside the open gates. Then she turned to look back on Cotchford Farm through the fire-flecked night. Feeling her feet cold against the asphalt she wept, not only because the chill told her she was not dreaming, but because her feet were bare. The shoes must have been taken from her while she slept. From here she could see a row of vehicles pulled up along the drive, their owners scampering about, arms piled high with Brian's belongings. Elsa thought of the bee swarm, the lifeless robot at the side of the pool—should she brave returning to locate her shoes? Would she pull the shoes from the flames if she found them in a bonfire? A gleeful singing erupted from Cotchford Farm just then, the voices of the villagers united in a savage-sounding hymn. She turned her back and fled, wandering the roads lost for most of the night, eventually circling in on the train station in time for the 8:30 a.m. to London.

Elsa read only one British newspaper in her life after that, the one which carried the coroner's explanation that Brian's death was "by misadventure." His life was discussed without sympathy, his death recounted without pity. They treated him as a mighty monster who had at long last been slain. They reproduced unflattering photos and wrote of how after enduring busts for cocaine, cannabis, and methedrine, how after beating Anita Pallenberg too many times and losing her to Keith Richards, how after giving up hashish and sinking so deep into paranoia his fingers could no longer hold an instrument and he did nothing but phone his worries and dream his worries, how after suffering some (if not nineteen) nervous breakdowns, Brian Jones continued to experiment with the varieties of LSD (and STP, mandrax, desbutal, amphetamine, and barbiturates) available to Londoners in 1968. The newspaper implied that Brian was so untrustworthy and manipulative that when he spoke to everyone of his intent to return to Morocco to record some pre-Islamic musicians there, it was only because he liked how it sounded—it sounded upbeat and promising, like a rebirth. In truth, according to the paper, everyone was very dubious about the prospect of Brian Jones ever returning to roots music.

His court-appointed psychiatrists were stunned by the death and had no comment. Pete Townshend was quoted as saying, "Oh, it's a normal day for Brian. He died every day, you know." Keith Richards was quoted as saying that a satisfactory resolution of what killed Brian Jones was as likely as resolving who killed JFK. All he would add was that "some very weird things happened that night."

Police were said to be seeking a teenage girl, blond, perhaps German, for questioning in connection with the incident. The girl was observed fleeing the scene on foot soon after the drowning was reported.

But what baffled newspaper writers most was how suddenly and entirely the mansion's contents vanished. They quoted sources who said that millions of pounds

67

worth of antiques, art work, and other possessions had disappeared in a matter of hours.

"So if I am to believe that Elsa's your mom," I said, "Then you're saying your dad is…?"

Sucking in her lips, eyes on the floor, Shaleese did not answer. She jumped to her feet and gestured absurdly, throwing out an arm, as if to convey frustration at what I'd said. But something in the movement alerted me. What had happened to the library book? It was no longer in her hand.

"Oh, pumpkin," I said. "Oh, Shaleese."

She was crying.

I pulled her onto my beanbag chair and cradled her in my arms, glancing around all the while to see if maybe the book had disappeared into her bag, had fallen to the carpet or slipped behind my chair. Had she tossed it onto a shelf somewhere? I caught a glimpse of it then, lightly wobbling atop the celebrity cabinet. As I watched, it stopped wobbling and the weight of it slid from view, disappearing with a klunk behind the cabinet. Dammit! Was it my fault she'd toss away something important to her? (And who would owe the library fines for the missing book? it would be me! of course!) I just wanted to get to know her was all. How like her it was to hide or give something away to strangers rather than share it with me, to acknowledge it. I knew I had to get her out of the store—Mr. Jolly Register Guy was heading over to make sure everything was okay—but I made a promise to myself to come back here some time, alone if necessary, and shove the cabinet out from the wall so I could reach a long brave arm in there and retrieve the rest of the story.

Finally found one short intact interview with Liz Phair (it was contained within an article I'd seriously assumed was an archeology piece about fossilized remains called "Women in Rock"). The interviewer asks if *Exile in Guyville* is meant to be a song-by-song refutation of the Rolling Stones' *Exile on Main Street* (an album that came out when Liz Phair was about two) and Liz Phair says no. The interviewer then asks why the albums' song counts are exactly the same and the layout of cuts (4-5-5-4) perfectly matched; Liz Phair calls it a lucky accident. And the interviewer asks for her reaction to the inevitable "Liz Phair Backlash"—those women artists who'd argue that Liz Phair is *not* a revolutionary voice despite what the male rock critics are writing, female indie heroes saying that Liz Phair is popular only because a lot of guys want to sleep with her, calling Liz Phair a "media darling" and "good but not that good" and "just way overrated"; and Liz Phair responds with something very calm about how she'd probably say the same thing if she were in their position.

When I was fifteen my mother told us she didn't love my father but some other man and my parents split up and my remaining brother also got married to a stewardess, this one named Bunny, who reminded me a lot of this girl we saw at school who we code-named "Stench" 'cause her eyes always sparkled and she always twirled around all the time like she was in some perfume ad, and I re-met Roy when he came to live with his father again, and I introduced him to Prendergast and Acey and Monica, and Roy tutored me special so we could both join the Big Brains field trip to Chicago and we went and snuck away from the chaperons to go visit the sites of the Chicago riots and we reverently touched the buildings on Madison and LaSalle streets that had been hurt by the Weathermen during the Days of Rage, and back home I found this book in my daddy's closet called *1969—The Year in Review*. I was flipping through it for photos of Dylan at the Isle of Wight when I came across a black-and-white

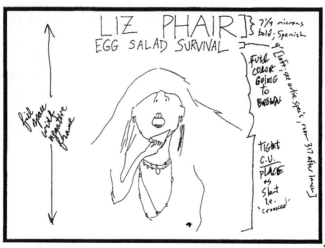

EARLY SPEC ART FOR DEBUT. NOTE ATTEMPTED SANDWICH TIE-IN (LATER REJECTED)

photo from the *Montreal Star* taken the day before my birthday, the day before Chicago's Days of Rage in October 1969, when police and firemen struck in Quebec and the separatists took to the streets and riots ensued. This photo shows the broken front window of a shoe store and a girl reaching in with one hand for a pair of shoes while to her left are two calm boys, one with his thumbs hooked in his pocket looking the other way, the other walking away, a little bored, and the glistening light from the window display illumines the night; the girl (straight dark hair, vinyl jacket, micro-miniskirt, the bare length of her lithe legs) occupies half the photo: one leg is bent so she can reach in, the other leg straight to support her. The huge platform shoes stand atop several inches of glass shards. Her jacket falls open, a hint of large breasts, her other hand calmly in her jacket pocket, she turns her face away so you can't tell what she's thinking. I wondered what had become of this girl, most nights in bed, before I fell asleep, where previously I'd thought about baseball players or Bob Dylan. I insisted Monica wear micro-minis and platform shoes when she came over and I had her turn away from time to time and make me guess what her expression was and I got better at guitar but worse at algebra but Roy kept me afloat, and a woman started phoning all the time asking for money and claiming to be my sister, but Daddy kept screaming "Tell me who this is and why have you done this to my family" and "I have nothing left to give" and staring at me wet-eyed as he rushed to put down the receiver, all the while daring me to react or say something and that was all that happened when I was fifteen.

❧

"What."

"Hello, Gabe?"

"Who's this?"

"Camden."

Pause.

"Camden in Sioux City. I'm dictating this book for you—"

"Joy. Camden Joy. Yeah sure, I remember you."

"Yeah, well I—"

"You got the check?"

"Yeah, I got the check."

"You already cash it?"

"Not yet, no, I just—"

"You can cash it, if that's what you're calling about. The check is good."

"Oh okay. But you didn't sign it."

"So how's the book on Liz, uh... Liz Smith?"

"Liz Phair."

"Liz Phair. How many hours we up to?"

"Um. I don't know. Listen, Gabe."

"Yep."

"You need to send me her CDs and some bio stuff. I'm really winging it, you know—"

"Great."

"Yeah. I don't know, though. I don't have a lot to go on,

just articles that are listed in the periodical guide that have been stolen. It's sort of ridiculous. Maybe I could interview her, you know. I could find out where-is-she-now, that kind of scoop."

"Where is she now, what inspiration! Of course, of course. Wait a minute! Wait one nose-pickin' goddamn shit-fuckin' minute. You saying you got the check but not the clippings file?! And no CDs. Damn that girl! Shit. Office help these days is for shit, you know? Don't blame her, though, they call that a weak management strategy. My own fault, my own fault. I accept full responsibility, is that what you want to hear, Joy?"

"Um. Okay."

"I'll get it off to you today, this minute."

"And mark it for next-day morning delivery."

"Right, right. Got it. Anything else?"

"Well. You could send me a signed check. Other than that... I mean, I don't know what I'm doing."

"Who really does? And who cares?"

"No, I mean... Like, here's something I'm thinking of including—"

"What are you talking about? You haven't got it written down, have you?"

"Well, just for now, yeah—"

"Joy, Joy, listen to me, babe. Cash the check. Are you listening? Cash the check, talk to the tape recorder. That's all. Don't write anything down for god's sakes, got that? Legally, it's just a lot more... It's a whole lot faster if you don't fart around with the written word. Trust me on this one, I know this business. No one reads these things, no one remembers them. They're like books you flip through when you're on the can, you know, it's got pictures, big typeface, and you gotta take a dump real, real bad, bam, a perfect match. Match made in heaven."

"Like, I'm thinking of including this thing about Liz

Phair's birth, just 'cause I'm thinking I should say more about her...."

For yea, Liz Phair's Father so loved Liz Phair's Mother that they lay thusly, Scepter to Darkness, and thusly adjoined in rhythm did seek to conceive. And such was the breadth of their love that His Scepter spake unto Her Blackness, unleashing adorations in multiples which advanced five hundred million strong, each as an army driven nigh by mighty mitochondria. Thus propelled madly into Blackness did the many million race. And it came to pass that solely one adoration survived to rejoice upon the egg. Thus it did occur, within the place which is named "Uterus, Base of Blackness," that a centrosome conveyed His message, migrating to the heart of the egg, dividing thusly to form the spindle such that chromosomes fused and begat daughter cells. And the heavens did spread as to unfold and a dove speckled of both black and white, grasping in its beak a branch of ripened pomegranate, did descend from the heavens earthbound. And the face of Liz Phair's Mother shone merrily and turning to Liz Phair's Father, She did say unto Him, "Behold! For you have begat unto me chromosomes numbering three and one score and I unto you an amount numbered the same and thus it shall come to pass in a space of nine months' time that an infant composed of mortal flesh will be born in blood from our union this night." And with each passing of the moon's cycle Liz Phair's Mother spake thusly unto Him to advise Him of distant occurrences (which were in lands frightening and unknown to Liz Phair's Father), as from embryo to fetus, fetus to infant, Liz Phair's Mother spake of Mitosis and Amnion, Placenta and Umbilica. And Lo! the child grew merciful and mild within her, cartilage giving way to bone as its toenails grew and its thumb was sucked. And thus it happily remained until a traveling Messenger of Life did arrive from the distant land of Obgyn and the infant was delivered unto us for all to enjoy. And as one they looked to the heavens and saw that there it was writ that just as they were spoken of as "Liz Phair's Father" and "Liz Phair's Mother" hence-

forth this infant would be known as "Liz Phair." And the infant grew, and it was good.

Pause.

"You see. Now call me a man who can't sort polyester from silk but that was sweet, baby. I knew it! I knew this about you the minute I read your name, I knew—this guy! He's the one! You know what I'm doing now? I'll tell you. What I'm doing now is wiping my glasses."

"Gabe, you know that was just a joke? You got that, right?"

"Wiping my glasses. Because that piece was so sweet, I wept, you hear what I'm saying to you. Gabriel Snell wept. You got a great instinct, Joy. Listen to me. You keep going the way you're going, you don't need to keep calling. You got a great instinct. You don't need me at all. Don't bother calling. Trust yourself a little."

"Yeah, right. You'll send the CDs, the bio stuff? Maybe another check?"

"I'm calling Federal Express the second we hang up. Goodbye, already."

"'Bye."

I think everyone would agree my friends and I formed a pretty odd group of fellas. I can't pretend to know what drew us together. Acey, with his elastic expressions and silly puns. Prendergast, with his incredibly long pauses and quick hand and darting eyes and shyly winsome grin, the perfect thief. Jimmy, stuck with that blubbery pink face and those pale plastic-framed glasses, as ugly as some melted nerd doll, always sniffling and drooling, helpless to stammer more than one or two words from that unformed mess of lips. Each of us unique, each of us pretty useless. And then Roy, perhaps the scariest of us all because he looked and acted like such a damn model teenager with his shirts tucked in and his hair perfect. Roy had this invincible air about him, the attitude of a born leader, except he was brimming with more guilt and guile and hate and hurt than you could conceive of.

As I think about it now, Roy had more movie-of-the-week, troubled-kid difficulties than any of the rest of us. His father was a paraplegic, his parents had separated early, his sister was a relentlessly hostile little beast. He was very suave and intelligent, but he also displayed all those symptoms that talk-show hosts tell us now are warning signs—hurting pets, bullying, expert lying, extreme moodiness.

One time, back right before my parents split up, I came across Roy standing in my house late at night. His hand gripped a machete. The house was dark, but by the glint of the streetlight, I could see his eyes were flat and without recognition. I asked him where in the hell he'd gotten a machete but he would not speak. We were in front of our fireplace, which held the sort of fake log everyone used to have. I was speaking low and calm to him, palms down, trying to get through. I was figuring he'd cut me and I'd bleed to death all over the fake log. His mouth made a hissing sound like the sound of a burning twig dropped into water. And then he swung with all his might. The machete whizzed by, less than an inch from my face. It wasn't a terribly sharp machete and if he'd hit me he would've instantly had some story to cover it up and everyone would've bought it, even me. He possessed that winning a presence. It's a little scary to think of it. He kept this up for about twenty minutes before his hormones settled and then he scurried out to his beat-up Pinto and drove off. Later, he didn't remember doing any of this.

Another time, he and I were driving back from the County Drive-In and he told me to jump out. I opened the door, studied the white line blurring past. How fast are we going, I asked. Fifty-five, he said, and it's easy at fifty-five. I shut the door. Nah, I said. He braked a bit. Okay come on, he said. Forty-eight, forty-seven, forty-six. Look. He pointed at the speedometer. Forty miles an hour, he said. He was really hooked on this idea, like it was genius or something. I watched the road. I wouldn't look at him. He continued slowing down, and cars pulled around and passed us and then we were alone on Plains Highway 12 at about 11:30 p.m. and the worst possible thing occurred. I began to understand his side of it. Okay, I said. Twenty-five. No faster. Thirty-five, he countered. We split the difference and agreed to thirty. But swear to god no faster than thirty, I demanded. Right, yeah, he purred. Roy was this kind of guy who could summon or dismiss you with a look and now, I was being summoned. I didn't want to do this but I could hardly back out now. He grinned impishly at me. Well, we're there, he called out. I opened the door and I jumped. Somewhere along here I realized what a sloppy death this could mean. I was thinking, of course, of Jimmy's older brother, Brock. After I tumbled to a rolling stop, I looked down at the gravel imbedded in my kneecap and the long slash in my new jeans and conceded that I had not been entirely smart to attempt this. Up close, one finds the sides of highways littered with broken glass, blown car parts, metal shards. It would not have meant one of those beautiful deaths if I'd cut a vein or snapped a neck doing such a thing. I got back to the car and climbed in without meeting Roy's eyes. Well, I said. Now at last I can say it. What, muttered Roy, so flat it sounded like he had nothing left in him. I sighed. Now I can positively say I've done every stupid thing known to man. Roy snorted, like he agreed, and drove me home.

Eventually Shaleese and I saved up enough for another vacation, our first since the New Mexico fiasco. We visited a Missouri resort, carved into the bluffs along the Mississippi River. It'd been built with old-style cabañas, Jersey-style boardwalks, hacienda-style restaurants, kiddie-style arcades.

Cliffs of granite surrounded the resort like steep Aegean isles.

We sunbathed, gambled at the casinos, drank Bloody Marys, made love totally slow. She wore my shirts and for once I was okay with it. And nights we got into studying the Milky Way—it was knotted and thick, textured like a scarf. We saw so many stars, layers behind layers, that we could not stop making up constellations. It seemed the old names were no longer needed.

We watched the clouds, too. I remember one day, we were watching a cloud shaped like a conch shell swirl overhead, its rapid dissipation making the cloud seem to expand in a swift descent. Then its misted edges dissolved into sky blue and the blue traveled down the cloud, and it became two clouds, like a series of handsome villages riven by a magnificent waterway, then the cloud was too gone to suggest any shapes at all, but from its borrowed vapors other clouds were forming, others were coming into focus as automobiles or animals or scowling faces. Waves lapped gently somewhere down beneath us, motorboats murmured in the distance. A tower clock chimed each quarter hour and we scarcely moved, watching the clouds, feeling the water, hearing the boats. Holding hands.

A young woman whose face I could not see appeared on the boardwalk overhead, leaning against a wooden banister. We calmly noted her presence. We tilted back our heads to smile at her. Some fragile link I hesitate to name was established among the three of us. It was a gradual, relaxed sort of trust, forged beyond the reach of mere words. Us in the sun and sand, her on the boardwalk, joined in a silent contemplation of nature. We felt we had been there for years, the three of us, yet the chimes had struck but once.

A knot of teenage boys hurriedly approached along the overhead walk. They were muttering softly to one another, kicking stones. They had not noticed the cloud like a conch shell transform itself into two villages. They were moving faster even than the clouds, a roiling mass. For them, the tower clock struck every minute, the boats were racing past, the waves pounded the shore like regrets. Time was running out.

The boys descended upon the young woman like wasps on soda. They positioned themselves around our young friend as if they might suddenly grab her from every side and launch her high into the air. She did not acknowledge them. She was desperate to be left alone, to be permitted to rejoin us, in silence to admire the emergence of new clouds.

"Wanna come with us?" they all asked at once. "Wanna party?" Their words raked over her like cap guns sputtering. Their hair was cut close to the scalp. They wore long baggy shorts, baseball caps, torn workout shirts. It was still the middle of the day but these boys were eager to party with this nice woman. They wanted her to come, or said they did. One wore a shirt emblazoned with a large tongue lolling lewdly from between fat lips. It was a cartoon based on Mick Jagger's mouth that had long ago become the insignia of the Rolling Stones.

She smiled weakly. As I remember this event now, it seems strange to me how unscared our young friend was. It was as if the dangers of the situation had not occurred to her. She simply desired to be left alone, and naively assumed their respect for such a wish. Undoubtedly she sensed the fragile kinship which had been established between herself and the two of us down below, and trusted that if something threatening developed we would intervene. We might have, I can't say. Those boys scared us as well in their torn workout shirts. What scared me, in particular, was how completely I lacked any sympathy for them, although I had once been very much like them.

Without warning, the boys gave up. They suddenly reformed as a group, again moving rapidly. Our friend had emerged unscathed, except that as the boys left they could not help mocking her. "Bitch!" one of them sang out, a Rolling Stones title. "Damn cold bitch." Another looked at the ground, spat a thick wad. *"At least we got friends,"* one of them shouted,

HER POPULARITY CONTINUES TO GROW!!

"You're all alone!" And they were gone, racing against time to isolate one girl who'd agree to party with them.

We could no longer find the clouds. The young woman gripped the banister with both hands, weeping now. She was upset, but not with them. She was upset with us. The boys were right. She had stupidly believed in a kinship too fragile to voice. She had thought we were friends but now saw how gullible that was, how hazardous. She knew if she had called for help we would have hesitated, however slightly. We were not her friends at all. As they'd assured her, she was alone.

That night I told Shaleese about my sister, how she'd run off when I was little, with all the guys in the world after her. I told Shaleese how my sister must have hid or caught a ride and got clean away because my parents got summoned to court, there was something about the state calling them unfit but I had never gotten the whole story straight. In talking about how much I missed my sister, I think I was trying to change the subject; but it didn't really work. It was that same subject all over again; and later, those boys in torn shirts were all we'd recall of the vacation so carefully planned. Those boys and that young weeping woman, the friend we betrayed in silence.

Franklin the Fed Ex guy just dropped by with a package. Good job, Gabe. At long last, I thought, her CDs, the biographical info on Liz Phair. Ripped it open and what did I find? *Exile in Guyville*, yes, accompanied not by *Whip-Smart* but by a bunch of pie charts, graphs, survey information for "Independent Recording Artist—Liz Phair." There was only one enclosure which was not about marketing. It seemed to've slipped in by accident. It was a paragraph from an undated Liz Smith gossip column hinting at an involvement between Rob Lowe and "rising punk starlet Liz Phair—wasn't that Lowe we saw stepping red-faced from Maxtron Recording Studios well past midnight the other night? Phair is currently remixing final tracks at Maxtron for a long-awaited follow-up to boffo *Whip-Smart*." I'm calling Gabe to complain. If I get him on the line, I'll pop the microcassette in and record the conversation.

Just hung up from his answering machine. Left a long message. Told him I'll pick up *Whip-Smart* myself, but I need the rest of the clippings and a new check. I asked him to call me immediately.

When they stake a square of string around our culture and begin gently to unearth and whisk off our remains (the women-in-rocks issue), when in a few hundred years they reassemble our meanings and aspirations while camped out in some hostile, dusty tent murmuring over a cup of boiled grime: what will they make of us? Will they find only the transgressions—the thudding repetitions, the unbearable volumes, the adolescent chemistry, the arrogant power and ludicrous stadium angst, the vast storehouse of stupidities rock and roll engenders—will such bland, buried things as apologies and sorrows and pained consciences go (like the good intentions and halting prayers of a long-dead civilization) unnoticed in the dirt alongside the unearthed gleam of genuine primitive zeal: record albums by

Black Sabbath, Judas Priest, AC/DC, Molly Hatchet, Motorhead, Aerosmith or whatever you'd pick of rude twentieth-century noise? Will John Lennon in the long run be less remembered than the madmen he inspired—the Mark David Chapmans with their personality collapses, the Charlie Mansons who desired rock-star acclaim but lacked the wherewithal to withstand initial rejection?

Now, having walked through the record store to put in my order for *Whip-Smart* (it'll arrive in ten days, the guy tells me, which is no help at all, by then my fifteen meals are up), I am exhausted by the number of young bands, old bands, undiscovered bands, rediscovered bands, so many many CDs by so many many bands I've never heard of, name card after name card of clipped sound bytes—Superchunk, Supergrass, Supersuckers, Superstar, Supernova, Superthis, Superthat—and all the bands named after television shows and bad movies and then all the JFK assassination–related nomenclature (Dallas in November, Single Bullet Theory, the Jack Rubies, the Oswalds, the Lee Harvey Oswald Band, the Dead Kennedys, the Grassy Knolls, the Texas Book Depository, Jackie's Pink Skirt, the Jim Garrison Group, the Warren Commission)—assuredly, none of it good music!

I know as much about music as anyone my age, yet I wonder how rock critics learn about every act that comes along. They can't. The deluge of bands clamoring for their attention all the time—the impression critics create is that they know them all—how can you know them all? It has to be a lie. They gotta learn to work up opinions by glancing over superficial aspects, hearing which famous people recommend this artist, gathering quotable rumors of sexual escapades, or glimpsing the cover art. Or else they gotta specialize, isolate a few of these tens of thousands of young bands, zoom in to one quiet block out of the city of sound, and comfortably explore the houses on that block, giving their fullest attention to each and every room. These latter critics—can you tell they are the only ones who approach my heart? They too love.

And when one of their specialties meets with an accident—drops out of sight for a week and is found with his head shotgunned off—this becomes their moment: the klieg lights swing their way. Switch the critic on! What good fortune to be, say, a reporter who got paid in the seventies to write studies of John Lennon, how lucky that Mark David Chapman became learned in these studies—that Chapman blasted holes in Lennon's body to provide that strange and yummy final chapter to your specialty. What chance that while still in your prime, with your Lennon knowledge at its peak, you might be asked to contribute this celebrity's eulogy, and not have to wade through decades of his pathetic grandfatherly drivel for the opportunity to bury your specialty, when each passing year would lop another paragraph off the obituary (if Lennon had lived to one hundred and five, articles about his death would be eight words buried at the bottom of the back page: "Former Beatle dead at last of natural causes.") Oh! for the tidy finality of plane crashes, the suicides and accidental overdoses that keep rock critics in mourning! There must be some part of any critic who yearns to be culturally useful that honestly gets titillated when he hears his particular specialty has gotten hooked on some dangerous drug, that grows silently pleased by stories of stalkers hunting his specialty, who even considers maybe he should himself somehow (a few threatening late-night phone calls, a mickey in the drink, why not! a swerve of the steering wheel, a sharp blow to the head!) damage his specialty once he is hired to write a book about her. This is only reasonable to assume, human nature being what it is.

When I was young, we located very little hard evidence that growing up would make our lives any better than they had been thus far. Not that there weren't a few good "things" in growing up but mostly "things" felt like they would continue to be out of our hands for the rest of our lives. "Things." We would throw around inexact words like that a lot, Prendergast and Acey and Roy and Jimmy and me, words like "things" and "those people." We'd say "Things completely suck" or "All those people are so fucked" and we'd know exactly what each other meant, even though it turns out we didn't, not really.

We would hear stories that our town had once been called Crazy Horse Junction because some evening a long time ago, along the bluffs where they would build the County Drive-In, Crazy Horse and Sitting Bull and all the other Sioux Chiefs gathered to plan the Battle of Little Big Horn. But these were probably just stories. We saw no evidence anywhere. Why honor someone for scheming to massacre your soldiers? It didn't make any sense, just like it didn't make any sense now to call it Site 3 since, as far as we could tell, there was no Site 1 or Site 2. But still, no one had been around long enough to have any expectations about continuity or permanency so no one knew how to phrase such questions. No one older than our parents lived in Site 3. No building in the town was over six years old. I think I went up until that field trip to Chicago with Roy before I saw a person over forty-five or a building older than I was.

"Camden. How come you never look at me?"

"I do."

"You never do. You shut your eyes when we kiss."

"No, I don't. I do?"

"You shut your eyes when we make love, like you're thinking of someone else. Who are you thinking about when we make love?"

"I don't know. You and me. I guess."

"Then why don't you ever look at me?"

"Shaleese."

"Why not?"

"Well, why don't ever show me any of all this arty stuff you work so hard on?"

"Hold out a minute. That's not what this is about."

"All right then, I do. I do look at you. What about that time in the motel, in your mother's motel, after we went swimming, huh?"

"You looked at me then? I don't remember that."

"I... um. I..."

"Yes?"

"Shit, my mind just went blank. I forget what I was gonna say."

"That was the very first time we made love."

"I know."

"That time."

"Yeah."

"That was years ago."

"Time flies."

"I mean it, Camden. That was years ago."

"This is so stupid."

"Okay."

"This is like my parents, the way they fought."

"All right. What color are my eyes?"

"Worse than my parents. This is like a *Three's Company* or something, an *All in the Family.*"

"Camden?"

"What, Meathead?"

"No come on. Really. Camden?"

"Yes, Edith."

"Camden, listen to me. What color are my eyes?"

"They're a sort of brownish-green, with this sort of blue-black thing that happens when you get too caught up in some ridiculous idea."

"Would you say they're closer to olive or hazel?"

"This is like, remember that series with that munchkin

kid and that other kid, the one who grew up and murdered all those people in that crack house or something? Like the way adults talked on that, on like a bad episode of that."

"Olive or hazel?"

"Diff'rent Strokes. That's what it was. *Diff'rent Strokes.* Like a really bad episode. The kind that gets a series canceled as soon as it's aired."

"I mean, if you got up right now and you looked at my driver's license, what would it say? Olive or hazel?"

"Jesus, Shaleese. I gotta work tomorrow. Jesus." I threw off the covers and grabbed my bathrobe.

"My driver's license is in my purse," she called after me. "In the kitchen. Put your thumb over the photo when you're checking or you might accidentally see what I look like."

(A fraud is someone whose identity is a composite, everything they are has been stolen from someone else. She was making me feel that way. She was making me feel like a fraud.)

Our place wasn't big enough to get away from each other. We had the bedroom and we had a kitchen, which we sometimes called the living room, and that was all. The place was so small the walls went in and out with each breath. She could hear me now in the living room, flipping on the stereo, putting on a record, just like I could hear her fidgeting in the sheets, a few feet away.

At night in Sioux City at this time—this was truly only four or five years back—you'd hear nothing but crickets and air conditioners and strangers calling hello as they passed in the street. I'm not saying Sioux City's so big, but it's a city nonetheless; now at night you hear glass breaking, dogs barking, cars turning over and over and over, and shouting matches which end suspiciously fast in silence.

I put on the headphones.

I wasn't trying to find her driver's license. I was looking for something else.

There's this moment on the *Imagine* album when John

Lennon sounds too disgusted to go on. It always made me feel good. I had to hear it. I had to hear him go "AAAAhhhh" like he was missing the Beatles, like having George Harrison playing lead guitar was teasing him to death, like he was looking over at the bass, wishing Klaus Voormann was Paul McCartney, wanting Ringo, disappointed at Alan White riding the crash cymbal all the time. Like John was sick to his stomach, vividly remembering this bad dream he had once in which he was walking towards his building entrance on New York's West Side and some reedy-voiced twerp shouted his name and squeezed off six shots at his back. *AAAAAhhhhh*. Again and again I picked up the needle at the start of side two, plopped it down into the Phil Spector–produced thicket of "Gimme Some Truth"—a nasty moment bedeviled with four guitars, piano, bass, drums, tricky dicky, mother hubbard, money for rope. I pressed the headphones tightly to my ears and my eyes wandered over her stack of journals sitting on the shelf beneath my albums.

There were seven or eight of those journals, some dainty and flowery, some clothbound, some stiff and formal.

The truth was I did have a thing about looking at her, and I wondered if it was all tied up with those journals. Not that I had read the journals behind her back. I had sorta lost my curiosity about them once I figured out what was in them. Every time she heard about anything bad a man had done, I'd see her dash to the journals and start to scribble. I figured they were like these logs of male atrocities. Some guy howls out his car window at her on the way home, into a journal it goes. Two rapes on the nightly news, in they go. Some man gives her directions so detailed he implies she's dense, some guy in a college newspaper calls a female student a "tramp," some husband gets busted for selling "favors" from his wife, some father excuses his son's rampage because "boys will be boys." All logged in, all written down, day after day. There was hardly anything I did without fearing it would somehow merit a mention in those journals, and I'd be placed there alongside those jerks.

So there was that, plus, when I was like seventeen, I remember there was a letter in a newspaper column from a distraught girlfriend. She complained her jerk boyfriend continually looked at other women as they walked down the street together, checking out their tits and butts, that kinda thing. Well, after I read that letter, you can be sure I never did anything like that in front of a woman. Instead, whenever I was walking down a street alongside any girl I liked, I trained myself to look for the boys on the street, and I studied *them*. Usually they were too busy checking out the girl I was with to notice, which worked out fine. The girl I was with ignored them, and I ignored their girlfriend. By the time Shaleese and I got together, I was entirely consumed by this not-looking-at-girls thing. And though we'd slept together every night for the last one or two years in our clapboard place on Kimball-ton Avenue, I still had never really seen her face—I know it sounds dumb, but in the daytime I was usually at work or too wrapped up in something to really notice, and at night I was flat-out forgetting to look. But also, I was terrified. I had con-ditioned myself to look only at men, at their broad foreheads, their thick necks, their ample shoulders, their muscular, hairy chests. I worked with men and I drank with men and I played music with men. I was accustomed to impenetrable gazes, bragging mouths, t-shirts and Levi's, measured responses, swaggering struts, five o'clock shadows. I was used to look-ing at men. What if I was disappointed in women now, seeing them again after so long? What if I looked at Shaleese and she was so soft-featured, so obliging, so feminine that I cringed, and this went down in her journal, or worse, she wrote to a newspaper column asking, "My boyfriend finally looked at me last night and is he gay or am I crazy or does he just think I'm ugly?" I'm not gay, really, it's only that to look at her took more nerve than I had in my life just then. I mean, I was working all day at the cannery, and nights I had this band with Acey I was working on. I was pretty tired after all that. The last thing I had time for was to meet the eye of some girl I loved just to find out she looked entirely wrong.

I listened to John Lennon and continued to look around our place. There were beautifully huge spaces on our walls, large, white areas that were just dying to display Shaleese's paintings. Of course these spaces were completely blank. In fact, Shaleese and I had positioned on our wall at this time only one thing, one framed photo, and it wasn't a photograph taken by her. It was a photo I mentioned earlier, that picture from my father's copy of *1969—The Year in Review*. Shaleese had found the book among my stuff, had snipped out the photo, mounted and framed it in an inexpensive silver frame. It was like I couldn't get away from it. Whenever I wasn't studying the photo, pouring into the task whatever was left of my mind after another long day at work, then Shaleese was. I'd come in sometimes and she'd be standing with her nose pressed against the glass of the frame, peering deep into the photo, mumbling to herself or maybe to the people in the picture. I knew how she felt. It was one of those photos that spoke, and often I felt obliged to say something back, to respond verbally to the recently broken window, the scantily clad looter; the glistening light of the window display illuminating the black-and-white night in a way that brought to mind bathysphere searchlights, silhouettes against a frozen moon, X-rays of winged creatures. Her face was turned away and her hand, the one nearest me, rested calmly in her jacket pocket, though perhaps her hand was simply invisible against the darkness of her jacket, and it still held the rock that busted the window. I couldn't say—I really did not know—though I wondered about it every single day, and I know Shaleese did, too.

So now I have heard this *Exile in Guyville* CD, listening to it repeatedly in my room until Mrs. Dannerby knocked on the door, asked if I was all right, then suggested maybe I could turn the music down a tiny bit. This CD creeps me out, it reeks so bad with majesty of impulse.

I think of all the sad participants of this life parading past in the alleyway outside, hearing snatches of this CD, their hungry, angry brains blinking *fame and riches*, each to end up a trash heap of body parts in disrepair, their minds no longer reliably there to lean on, like me, a sad sack of cravings and cruelly sharp memories. If only I had been a Liz Phair fan since Day One (what will stop the *if onlys* springing ceaselessly to mind?), if I had sought her sound to sop my heart, would I be all better now? I wonder. This CD—hearing at last her side of things—brings me understanding. If only I'd heard her debut while I was still with Shaleese—flatly impossible since Shaleese and I were kaput by then for almost fourteen months—still, if I had had this sort of passionate feedback then, who knows what kindness I might've started showing her, hope springs eternal, if Shaleese had only spoken to me as Liz Phair, capturing her words, dressing in her cloaks to better convey what she—Shaleese—meant: well, who can blame me (she can! and she does!!)…

Let's discuss the way she sings. Okay, responds my beautiful Pocket Secretary, my perfect little companion, my true love, my one friend. You do the talking, she murmurs, and I'll just lie here and drink up the genius of your observations. Let's see you earn your rock-critic wages!

Liz Phair sings with teeth gritted, vomit riding high in her gullet: not standing before us like a preachy rock star, but beside us, like a disappointed friend, looking askance at us over her shoulder. And the truth is, she does not sing her songs so much as seethe them—she seethes better than any other vocalist I've heard, male or female. To seethe requires restraint, a barely controlled fury. She seethes so well you can practically hear her eyes as they narrow, her expression as it tightens. When her voice climbs from its low seething range into a strong, clear, melodious soprano, she can sound almost like Joan Baez, but she falls back on that powerful voice only when she's getting defensive. Instead she'd rather seethe, and when she feels like trilling she combines it with a low growl to come up with a very unusual warble. Rather than singing in the voice of Joan Baez, which she could easily do, Liz Phair consciously chooses to seethe in the voice of someone who has never been trained to sing, someone unaccustomed even to voicing an occasional outburst of song. She might raise an eyebrow, pull her face back, and glower blankly, yes, sneer slightly, yes, snort often, yes, but sing an occasional song? Never. She runs out of breath in mid-line, she insists on stretching for low notes she can't possibly reach, she croaks and mutters as if she can only use what's left of her voice after screaming at someone for hours. And though we listen to this voice, all the while it suggests that her half-lidded eyes are telling the true story. Her tone of voice is carefully modulated so the neighbors won't worry; in the meantime her look is murdering us. Though she's chewing gum and acting like a hard chick, and boldly mixing her signals by dressing in hot pants and a diaphanous blouse, she still keeps talking about her feelings in tenderly worded similes.

In short, her songs are very singable, yet you cannot sing along with them. There is too often a quality to Liz Phair's voice which—like Lou Reed's voice, my favorite—can fool you into thinking she'll soon be joined by another, warmer singer. In "Explain It to Me," "Shatter," and "Gunshy," she sounds like she's singing a duet with someone we cannot hear. Hers is that calming, flat voice, often steely, calculated, and guarded, which would normally be submerged, the harmony accompaniment to counter an uplifting, brash melody. Except that, because this album is by Liz Phair alone, we don't hear the other half, we don't get the uplifting and brash segment, we only hear the dead-toned response. It would be like this if you dumped one singer out of the mix of most any duet. You'd hear an absence, frustrating and impossible to identify; something missing that is too strange to solve, and on listening to the song you'd feel lonelier for the lack of it. What Liz Phair accomplishes with this voice is to communicate not just a song but also a caginess at the song's heart; it's as if she's saying she's truly in love yet at the same time impossibly lonely. The voice of her songs pulls simultaneously in both directions.

Brock's little brother was Jimmy and the neatest thing about Jimmy was that one day Brock just died. For a time, it lent Jimmy a certain mystique in our eyes.

Death, after all. Death. What beats death? Straight flush beats four of a kind, royal flush beats a straight flush, scissors cut paper, rock smashes scissors; but nothing beats death. Kids—who understand a lot about being beaten because they feel pretty much beaten by everything—seem to be the only ones who honor death's overarching power, which maybe explains why they're so obsessed with it. It's the only passion kids have to themselves. Adults, for their part, write about teen suicide like it's some inscrutable illness, they scratch their heads and bemoan the chilliness of youth when some seemingly normal ten-year-old blows someone away. Were they never young? When I was a teenager, this messed-up kid named Johnny Moore got mad at our teacher one day; he walked out of class, went home, got his father's shotgun, went to the school playground, sat on a swing, put both barrels of the gun into his mouth, and fired. I can't tell you how cool that seemed back then. We'd all thought Moore was a retard, but dead, he was a celebrity. And those few lucky kids who had glimpsed his bloated, purplish remains splattered over the swing set, they were like heroes to us. We listened avidly to their descriptions of where Moore's teeth had landed, how his shirt soaked up the blood, the sprawled placement of his feet. Death.

We read of people who shivered with premonitions of their own deaths, which sounded familiar to us because, as I remember it, we each shivered with premonitions of our deaths every single day; some days we'd easily have five or six premonitions. We talked of suicide back then with supreme intensity, like black guys talk of their dicks or old men talk to dice at the craps table. It's not like we thought we'd live forever or that we felt impervious; on the contrary, we were all going to die tomorrow, and we wondered perpetually whether we'd look inspired or brutalized, disappointed or inanimate, transcendent or what, when it finally happened.

As for Jimmy's older brother Brock, he was in the passenger seat of a Buick Regal one night going down Plains Highway 12. I forget who was driving, I think it was George, and there were two other friends of my brothers in the back seat. Everyone was drunk. A dust storm came up. The Buick Regal had dim headlights. Visibility fell to a few feet. The music, I'm sure, was loud. And bad. They yelled at each other, debating whether to slow down or pull over—but what if a car plowed into them from behind? It seemed likely. What other options were there? No one had any suggestions. They continued. Someone got the bright idea of looking for landmarks. They started looking for this roadside vegetable stand called Boone Ranch. They all knew it was real close. They would stop there and wait out the dust storm. "Boone Ranch," they started to chant. "Boone Ranch." George or whoever was driving started pounding the steering wheel along to the chant. "Boone Ranch! Boone Ranch!" It was their mantra. But the storm was getting worse. They could now see even less. "Boone Ranch! Boone Ranch!" Finally George announced he couldn't see the yellow median anymore. He wasn't sure if they were still in their lane. Which is when Jimmy's older brother Brock became a hero. He rolled down the passenger window, and stuck his head way out. He was trying to locate the white line which runs along each edge of the highway. He couldn't. "Boone Ranch." The fact is, just then, the white line was under their car. "Boone Ranch." They were half off the road, driving far to the right. Brock looked up, squinting in the gritty air. A posted sign reading *Soft Shoulder* appeared from nowhere and took off his head.

So for a time this incident made Brock's little brother Jimmy quite appealing to us. We figured he was quiet because inside, behind those scratched lenses and filmy eyes and that inflated, rubbery, fishlike face of his, way down deep inside he was really suffering. When people made fun of sniffling Jimmy and his drowning expression, calling him "dumb" to his face, we would make fun of them to their faces. We imagined he had some superbly hidden skill, like mathematics or computers or something. Then we realized that sniffling Jimmy really was dumb. And then it just happened that we lost all respect.

The two Jimmy stories are these—how we Molotoved him by accident and how, when we were setting up the Big Bang, he was put in charge of amassing the potassium nitrate.

First the first story. Molotoving. Okay. How, you ask, did we know how to construct explosives? I don't think we would have if the IRA hadn't been so in vogue just then, with Maggie Thatcher being such a fucked-up witch. There was a *Life* magazine photo about that time, really cool, some Irish kid with a red kerchief tossing a firebomb, photographed in just such a freeze-frame way you could see how simple Molotov Cocktails were to construct. Take a bottle, any bottle, and fill it with gasoline. If you want napalm, just saturate it with Ivory Soap flakes and shake it up good. Then stuff a rag down into the neck of the bottle. It pretty quickly soaks up the gasoline, however, so don't put the rag in until you're ready to light it. Then you put a match to the rag and toss the thing. Sometimes, if you lob it high enough, the fire will actually ignite the gasoline in mid-flight. This creates a pretty sight, but since it explodes the bottle you'll have glass flying everywhere and you'll need to protect your eyes. If it's just a short toss to your target, the rag will burn but nothing will be ignited until the bottle breaks against something and spills gas everywhere. If you've added Ivory Soap, the fire will burn with a strange stickiness. Without soap, the fire dies out pretty quickly, unless you've Molotoved something that burns easily, like a car interior or a ping-pong table.

For a while, we started going out each weekend and Molotoving some place we really hated. Like the Mormon Church. Like the money machines. Like the dumpsters outside McDonald's. Like the damn city parks, closed at dusk. Things rarely stayed on fire for any length of time. At the Mormon church, the bottles crashed against the front door, but once the gasoline burned up, the fire fizzled and died.

It was that sly boy Prendergast who gave us the idea. Most days after school we were over at his place, pretending to have a band practice (Acey on drums and the rest of us on guitar), acting like we were gonna do something big and important one day. Prendergast lived with his mom in this tiny, immaculately white, thin-walled, plush-carpeted apartment. There was a cheap plastic chandelier which hung in the center of the apartment and the ceiling was so low that the chandelier was about chest-high, and we were always running into it and cursing. Mrs. Prendergast was a checkout lady at a supermarket. Since she always needed the overtime, she was rarely home. For three years now, she had been telling her son they were only staying here temporarily, long enough to scrape together some money; then they were moving on. This was a momentary stop on their journey west.

Prendergast was, as I said, a simple guy: your basic thief, lanky, cautious, with a greasy flop of hair he was forever combing out of his eyes in a very deliberate way. He didn't have a lot of clothes, so every day he wore the same outfit to school: slacks and an open polo shirt. We would huddle together and study the way Prendergast moved: he moved like a cat-burglar—cagey, watchful, alert. It had us all visualizing how easy it must be to break into homes. We learned to trust his instincts.

We were at Prendergast's when he brought out this picture from *Life* of the Irish kid with the firebomb. Prendergast had this drawl that made things he said seem italicized, and in this kinda wary way he had, he said, "I... got... this *idea*." Then we saw the photo and immediately it was like, it wasn't just his idea any more. We all knew we had to try.

I credit Prendergast, but really it was Roy who kicked the whole endeavor into a higher gear with the manifestos. You see, we wouldn't just Molotov. First we'd litter the target area with these Xeroxed messages. Then we'd Molotov. The idea being that when the cops came they would find these curious pages full of non sequiturs; they'd soberly use tweezers to lift the pages and seal them in glassine envelopes and haul them in to be studied and stamped and filed. We had fun with that, imagining the shrewd chief of police poring over our file with an immense magnifying glass, trying to riddle out what our demands were, what precisely we were protesting, the source of our complaints. Will nothing satisfy them, he would ask his staff, throwing up his hands. Or will they just continue to burn things—burn, burn, burn?

Written on these scraps of paper was a kind of pantheon of rock-and-roll moments. I don't know what the point was, really. Rock and roll barely deserved us. It certainly didn't deserve Roy's marvelous writings. I remember how one manifesto talked about what made Iggy's version of "China Girl" superior. It went something like this: *When Iggy sings "I'm feelin' tragic like I was Marlon Brando," it differs from the Bowie version of "China Girl" because in Bowie's he elongates it all romantic to evoke the sense that he's feeling tragic in the style of Brando's screen roles while in Iggy's it sounds as if he'd actually been stuck in the tragic role of that distasteful old has-been Marlon Brando.* I think that was the one that went all over the steps of the Mormon Church. I'm sure it helped to clarify an important musicological distinction for them. Then there was one which said *Creedence Clearwater Revival*, because we loved those three words together and they were our one favorite band and we all agreed their songs were almost completely made up of "moments." And there was one manifesto, this was the best, which only said *Pet Sounds*. I loved that one. It was all over McDonald's the night we hit it, tucked under the windshield wipers of cars in the parking lot, slipped into the secret McDonald's mail slot, sprinkled all over both sides of the street. *Pet Sounds*. Imagine being in the patrol car that responds to a trash fire at a fast-food joint where the only evidence you can find are two words written everywhere on little pieces of paper. "*Pet Sounds*?" one shrewd cop might ask the other, perplexed. "*Pet Sounds*? As in the Beach Boys?"

But I was trying to tell about how we Molotoved dumb Jimmy by accident. After the third or fourth time out, we had this routine, like I said. Every afternoon we'd gather at Prendergast's apartment after school. Roy and Acey would droningly recite their sarcastic litany of dead-rock-star jokes ("How many dead rock stars does it take to read by? None. You can read by the brilliance of their holy image alone. How many dead rock stars does it take to crush an elephant? None. You can crush an elephant with the weight of their investment portfolios alone. How many dead rock stars does it take to win a Nobel Prize for Poetry? None. They're all such truly genius poets that the Nobel Committee is too intimidated to honor any of them. How many dead rock stars does it take to get a girl to go to bed with you? None. No girl will ever go to bed with you, loser. Ha. Ha.") I'd plug in everything. I'd tune the instruments... or I'd try. I'd get them approximately right and then go, "Close enough." Then Acey would go, "Close enough for jazz." Then Roy would go, "Close enough for government work." Then Acey would go, "Close enough for government jazz." And then everyone would sit around eating junk food, cursing the chandelier, listening to our guitar amplifiers pick up cockpit conversations, and we'd discuss moments of the majesty of impulse and targets for our Molotov cocktails. We never drank much alcohol or were very interested in drugs; I guess this was our exciting substitute. (I don't mean to imply that me and my friends didn't do drugs. Mostly we'd inhale things, the propellant out of whipped-cream cans, the heady aroma of magic markers, spray paint, model glue, liquid paper. We were stunned to realize that almost every store, no matter how innocent-seeming, contained something that could get us off. Sometimes when we tired of the head-aches we got from huffing things, we'd swipe grain alcohol from State Liquor and get drunk and spin each other inside the dryers at the laundromat until one of us threw up. Then we'd call it a night.)

The first few times we Molotoved, we quite consciously kept dumb Jimmy on a pretty short leash. We weren't sure how he'd handle all the excitement. We sent him with Acey to spread out the manifestos, while Prendergast and I sat waiting in the car, putting on dark jackets so we'd be camouflaged. Roy customarily drove. All of us were usually out of breath and so we hardly ever spoke at this point; the adrenaline was way too intense. There was not only the increasing likelihood that eventually we would be recognized or caught but also the possibility that we would accidentally hurt some innocent someone—a topic we studiously avoided discussing, I think because secretly we were all terrified it might actually happen and we'd spend the rest of our dull little lives wrestling with that.

This was the set-up when, on our third or fourth run, we decided to let Jimmy try it. He hadn't really expressed any desires one way or the other, but we felt positive he was curious. Probably we wanted to implicate him further, I don't know. Our target that night, I'm pretty sure, was this newly dedicated garden structure at City Hall, a lacework of vines and tendrils growing up through a cross-hatch of interwoven twigs. It was an expensive arts-and-crafts project whose construction had been supervised by Spencer's father, Mr. Schwartz, and since muscle-bound Spencer was sort of on our hate list right then, we decided to burn this thing. We staked it out for a couple of nights and found there was only one security check, at 11 p.m., by a roving band of security guards. We felt assured this would be an easy one.

What I'm getting at here is that everyone that night wants to have a Molotov cocktail in their hands. It's like, if Jimmy can do it, I can do it. Even Roy is no longer content merely sitting behind the wheel. He wants to throw a couple, and so does Acey. Our manifesto that night was something I'd nominated. To my mind, it was the coolest line Tom Waits ever sang: "There's a hummingbird trapped in a closed-down shoestore." I always felt like that line said something about us there, hummingbirds trapped in the closed-down shoestore of Site 3... who cares? We wrote it in fat magic marker on top of a sheet torn from the classifieds, and went down to a copy store and ran off about two hundred 8½ x 11 Xeroxes of this page. We got together some pop bottles and siphoned a can of gas out of a car in the drugstore parking lot, and tore up somebody's old shirt to use as rags, and drove on over to City Hall. It was about 8 p.m.

Everything went smoothly until it came time to light the things. There were five of us by now, five pretty noticeable characters, quite publicly doing what is best done by one or two shadowy figures. We line up shoulder to shoulder, like we're in a showdown in a Western or something, except the enemy we're facing is Mr. Schwartz's weird wooden structure, this pathetic goodwill gesture from the father of someone we hate only because, years ago, when we were thirteen and deeply suspicious, Roy and I sensed he might betray us.

So I go first, I'm holding a bottle, and I stuff a rag in and flick this butane lighter and set it aflame and chuck the thing. We all watch its progress, it arcs real turquoise and pretty and settles on top of the arbor. The landing is so gentle the bottle doesn't break immediately, it just sits there for a time. We're all watching, waiting for the thing to explode. Suddenly Jimmy makes this grunt. We look over and, unbelievably, Jimmy's sleeve is on fire. You see, a bottle of gasoline, even with a rag stuffed down its neck, will still spray a certain amount of its contents when it is thrown. I'm right-handed, and I threw the Molotov pretty side-arm, and short little Jimmy, standing to my immediate right I guess, got a splash of my cocktail on his shirt, along with a touch of flame.

It sounds, I know, rather harrowing, but you have to realize our hyper-tense state at this point. We're all waiting to be arrested, waiting for this Molotov atop the arbor to explode, waiting, waiting, just going *crazy* with the *waiting*, and we look at Jimmy, slapping at his arm, sniffling and making little grunting pig noises, shaking his head so frantically that we watch his glasses fly off his nose, and we start to laugh. Okay, it wasn't funny, but it was funny.

"Fuck, loser," says Acey, amazed. "You're on fire. You look like the scarecrow in that movie."

Jimmy slaps the fire out, and after Prendergast retrieves his glasses Jimmy indicates he wants to be next to light his Molotov.

"Go right ahead," I tell him, backing away to give him some throwing room.

He does and it goes just sort of the way you'd expect. He winds up and throws it all wobbly, and when he lets go he's so off-balance he falls down, and afterwards his glasses have flown off somewhere else altogether and he has lit his other sleeve on fire, this time all by himself. You never realize how flammable clothing is until it's too late.

"Dumb," drawls Prendergast, letting out a low, cautious laugh. "Dumb dumb *dumb*."

Meanwhile, his Molotov is eternally gliding through the air, veering farther and farther from the arbor. It looks for a time like it may hit City Hall. But then, following some bizarre trajectory, it levels off and approaches Roy's car. Jimmy sniffles and starts to giggle, kinda nervously, still on fire.

"Oh, fuck," says Roy. "Oh, fuck, no."

"Way to go," says Acey.

The Molotov hits a grassy patch and explodes glass all over Roy's car.

"Thank you," says Roy. "Thank you very much." So now Roy steps on Jimmy's glasses, spins on him with a lit Molotov, and says, "Now run." Jimmy takes off, still battling his lit sleeve, and Roy tries to hit him. He misses, hits the lower rung of the arbor, and the thing explodes beautifully into flame.

We're all so giddy we've become nearly hysterical with laughter, but even so, Acey tries to choke out a few words. "Come on, loser," Acey, howling so hard he's doubled over, says to Roy. "That was uncool. He didn't mean it."

Roy too is laughing as he answers. "I know, I know," he giggles.

Prendergast and Acey let theirs go, and then the whole arts-and-crafts piece pretty much disintegrates under this deluge of pumpkin-colored fire. We take off sprinting, find dumb Jimmy at the car, a little shaken up but still his usual self. We hand him back his bent-up glasses, check him over thoroughly for burns. Only some hair on his arms is singed. Even his shirt sleeves look fine. Roy's car is fine, too, just a little scorched on the driver's side. Later, as we apologize to Jimmy in the car, we're still fighting to keep a straight face at the memory, him with those pig noises, his glasses sailing off into the dark, trying intently to slap out the fire on one sleeve only to light up his other one seconds later.

What sort of girlfriend *was* she? All these things I forgot. It must be some stupor I'm in all the time, that must be it. A trance. Or the glue, could be the glue, I'll admit a certain weakness for glue, even now, earlier today. One thing I can remember, throughout my life, is telling myself, "I've got to remember this, I've got to remember this," and shutting my eyes tightly and opening them and shutting them again until the image of whatever I was looking at was sealed, I felt, forever. But now I can remember only that procedure, those steps, I cannot remember any of the images. I think, in fact, I snuck peeks at Shaleese and ordered myself to remember, but soon forgot what I had seen.

And how much about Shaleese must I remember anyway, how much can any of us truly describe one another accurately anyway? do you want me hypnotized to recount the precise size of her stained molars, her skin in this light, the expletives she would never use—do you require a life-size replica rendered in painted plaster—what is the price of making her believable to you? if it is the same cost as making me agonize over her absence, *then you shall never know her!*

My mom used to think that the title line in "Free Ride" by the Edgar Winter Band was "C'mon and take a three-five." Prendergast always heard the line "Open up I'm climbin' in" from the Eagles' "Take it Easy" as "I'll open up my private inn." Monica always believed the line from the Gerry Rafferty song "Right Down the Line" was "When I wanted you to shave my legs" when the real line was "When I wanted you to share my life." Roy told me he always thought the Beach Boys sang, "If everybody had a notion/across the USA." Acey always swore the line in Steve Miller's "Take the Money and Run" was "Get it on and watch cartoons" instead of "Get high and watch the tube." In the bridge of "Every Breath You Take" there's the line "And my poor heart aches" which—given Sting's open-mouthed, fake-Jamaican style—always sounded to me like "I'm a pool-hall ace."

Leave it to the listener and we'll come up with plenty of weird interpretations drawn from misheard lyrics. Sure, I used to wonder why Sting would bother to brag about his billiards ability right at that point in that sad little song. Roy just figured that what he heard made perfect sense—if everyone in this country just had a notion, just one goddam idea, then they'd be surfing USA. Acey's mistake says a lot more about his wacked-out idea of fun than it does about his ears—paradise for Acey was gettin' it on and watchin' cartoons. Monica believed it was a very sensuous thing for Gerry Rafferty to desire his sweetheart to shave his legs. Prendergast imagined that part of "taking it easy" was to open up a little bed-and-breakfast or some kinda private inn. And my poor mom, well, I think she figured that a "three-five" was some codified something she would never get to experience, referring to an illicit substance she would never get to try or a speed limit she would never be allowed to push or a stimulating stretch of highway she'd never get to travel.

Where am I going with this?

Oh, yeah. I wanted to do a rock-critic thing on a song from *Exile in Guyville*, a song smack in the middle of the CD, the one called "Fuck and Run" (I turn down the CD when it gets here so Mrs. Dannerby doesn't get mad). It's this track that makes me miss Liz Phair. The song's premise is modest—she awakes one morning to realize she is in bed with the wrong guy, the kind of guy who would fuck and run. Now, if this was an event sung about by some quasi-folkie, we'd hear a breathy waif telling us of her good intentions and her broken-hearted excuse—maybe she was too drunk when she met the guy and she lost her judgment and now she feels a little victimized. If this was something sung by a brawny, brawling, punk girl group, we'd hear women screaming about abusive men and date rape. But that's not what interests Liz Phair—in Phair's version the first thing she feels is "sorry"—she's angry too, but mostly at herself for being stupid enough to do this again. "Almost immediately I felt sorry. I just didn't think this would happen again." The only accusation she levels against the male is that he can't help being who he is—but she *can* help it, she believes, although this was one more time she didn't. So maybe she's just as stupid and weak as he is. Which is when she begins to plead, "Whatever happened to a boyfriend? The kind of guy who tries to win you over? I want a boyfriend. I want a boyfriend." Interpreted this way, this song devastates. There is no way your heart won't go out to her, no way you won't feel guilty. You feel you're watching someone accustomed to singing flowery, sensitive singer/songwriter paeans going over a truly horrible event for the very first time, like you're about to see Janis Ian puke all over her flower-print muumuu and open-toed shoes. Of course, like the rest of the CD, "Fuck and Run" is also melodically perfect and expertly produced—the voice and instruments on the song, particularly the drums, give off a sound a recording engineer would term "dry" (meaning stark, smacky, tight) as opposed to "wet" (lush with echoes and reverbs, with lost spirals and eternal signals). "Dry" versus "wet"—in this song especially Liz Phair makes you work with what the engineering nomenclature connotes. I imagine her telling a sound man she wants the snare to sound as tight and dry as a woman it hurts to fuck, a woman so dry she virtually cannot be fucked.

What I'm getting at here is that there is a lyric in "Fuck and Run" I couldn't understand, despite the fact I love the song so much. What is it she mumbles after, "I want a boyfriend. I want all that stupid old shit of..."? Of what? I ask you who are hearing this—whoops, sorry, reading this—I ask you right now to hum the song to yourself and tell me what you think that line is.

Well, I'll tell you, all I could get out of it at first was "feathers and sodas" or maybe "leathers and sawdust." That stupid old shit of feathers and sodas? Of leathers and sawdust? Then I got to the point where I listened to that and thought, *why yes, how perfect.* For this is what I was thinking: you know how in relationships a few stupid things, a few "stupid old" shitty kindsa things attain heightened poignancy, like inviting someone you adore to shave your legs or to join you in a three-five, whatever, the secret codified euphemisms getting indistinguishably tangled up in the romance of the affair, rendering it all the more impenetrable and mockable to your cynical, doomsayer friends? How better for Liz Phair to illustrate this than to sing of missing "feathers and sodas" (or "leathers and sawdust")—a slap of complete nonsense, a reference we can only guess at—which could mean anything to us and evidently meant everything to Liz Phair?

Well, I congratulate myself on what a truly fine interpretation that is, but I just realized it's much simpler than that. Feathers and sodas, leathers and sawdust? Nah. "Letters on sweaters," that's what she's singing. As in, wearing your sweetheart's athletic letter on your high-school sweater. That's the stupid old shit she's missing. Which is an interesting irony, for the connotations of "letters on sweaters" are not those we think of as supportive of an independent woman like Liz Phair. It's as if the thing she's saying in that song is not only that she wishes she didn't have to sing this, but she wishes this were a world in which they wouldn't even let her sing it. It's a daring notion, that women were better served in the past, back when the behavior of men was bound by chivalry and honor, and women were left with even fewer choices than they have now.

Among the people I grew up with, Acey was the first we ever heard using the word "loser" in a greeting, as in saying "Hey, loser!" and meaning it affectionately. My friends and I checked into it and after some research became convinced that Acey himself was the origin of this usage, that he was the father of the sarcastic "Hey loser" and "You're such a loser" and "Man, loser—you're something else!" We worked to convince Acey of this and though he seemed to believe us and accepted the credit, my point here is that he never took the proper steps legally to protect himself, he never copyrighted "loser," never registered it with the Library of Congress as a fond denigration employed between friends, and so ultimately surrendered all claim to it. This turned out pretty lame because then all Acey could do was to remind us, "I invented that," whenever it came on the television or the radio or whenever we had cause to say "loser" among ourselves. But he never made a nickel from his invention.

Acey was kinda like our clown. He told a lot of jokes, made up a lot of lies, did imitations, put on funny faces. He could do all our voices, all our mannerisms. He always kept us laughing. Like, for example, when we were working at McDonald's together, Acey would swipe the strip punch every day and make himself a new name tag out of totally random letters and symbols. Sometimes when McDonald's got busy they'd ask Acey to work one of the registers in front. Up he'd go, with this name tag that read *Hello! My name is JlJjkfloi9&8!* (or *Kijqplui* or *ReReRe-9* or *Hamfartz*) *May I Please Take Your Order?* His customers would always get these pained little expressions just trying to read his name. Some of them would choke in attempting pronunciations, or tearfully apologize to Acey for what "our people" had done to his people.

Acey would also start calling back orders for impossible amounts of food ("I need a half billion filet o' fish pronto on the double!!!") or, when he was at the grill, would send up hamburgers with bites taken out of them. He and I didn't know what lay ahead for us, but it didn't look good, so we figured at least we should keep laughing.

This was when the girl first showed up at McDonald's, the one who was always ordering an iced tea then easing over to sit in that same booth, day after day. Acey insisted on calling her "No Face." "No Face" because she had, as far as we could tell, no face. Always she was slouched at the shoulders, head down, writing in her journal. When she walked anywhere, it was with her hair slung before her, masking her face from view.

"Hey here comes No Face," said Acey one day. "Let's snag her notebook."

"Nah."

"C'mon, loser. It'll be a blast. Really. She won't mind."

He went down the aisle nonchalantly wiping things, acting bored, until he got to the girl's table. He slapped the wet rag on her table. She recoiled just enough. In one motion he yanked her journal away and sent it Frisbee-ing across the dining room and over the Mayor McCheese statue to me. I think he expected her to look up and cry or something but she did nothing, she just turned away and looked out the window. I walked the journal over to Acey and told him to return it to her. Let's read it first, he said, snickering. I think he expected it to contain standard teen-diary crap like who at our high school had a cute butt and who was stuck up. He opened it, but his expression changed. He looked a little pale. He placed the book back in my hands. You give it back, he mumbled. Tell her sorry. What'd it say, I asked. He shrugged. Weirdnesses. Something about eating a goat. Here, I told the girl, I'm sorry about my friend. He's sorry too. Here's your book back. She said nothing. I said sorry. I promise we won't do it again. Okay? Okay, she whispered. I'm Camden, I said to her. Welcome to McDonald's. She chuckled in a truly sweet way. Hello, she whispered. My name's Shaleese.

My twenty-first birthday came at me like a funnel cloud moving slow and deliberate across the prairie. I could see it approaching from months away, I could turn and run but never get away. It would descend on me no matter where I hid, suck me into its black, junk-filled swirl, and deposit me in some stupid land of grown-ups where I'd be obligated to spend the rest of my days, where everybody voted and behaved responsibly and spoke with the utmost sincerity. Considering all the dangerous things I'd done and all the stupid chances I was willing to take, it bummed me out that I was still around to turn twenty-one. I felt I deserved to be dead or at least to be celebrated as if I were dead. Acey and I were still doing our band thing, as we'd been doing for the last thirty thousand years since man first walked upright: playing loser bars where people pretended their heavy hands hurt too much to applaud, playing student rec halls where kids our own age winced at us like we were freaks from outer space. We were constantly looking for a really good bassist, and constantly settling for less. As my twenty-first birthday neared, the only things that started sounding good to me were minor-key dirges and so that was all I would play. Our rehearsals began to sound like funeral marches. Acey drummed along obediently, though with an expression of distaste.

Once I waved a song to a halt to ask, "Do you know what the Rolling Stones were doing by this time? by the time they turned twenty-one?"

"Ummmm... No."

"I don't either, okay? but you can bet they weren't sitting around here in nowheresville."

Acey nodded, clicked his drumsticks, and we started up the funeral march all over again.

Suddenly we just stopped rehearsing, stopped gigging. It wasn't doing us any good at all. Plus, now that I was turning twenty-one, all my free time would probably soon be taken up by PTA meetings and income tax protests and feeding squirrels in the park and trying hard to hobble my rickety way across the intersection while cars zoomed past barely missing me with my walker.

"Listen. We need to talk." This was Shaleese speaking. I was at the kitchen table, looking sadly at my plateful of scrambled eggs. "Listen. I need to be alone today. I hope you can understand."

"So?"

"I was wondering if you could go out."

"I guess."

"Until five or so."

"Five? Oh, great. What, you got someone coming over or something?"

She jumped at that, and stammered, "I need some, I have some art I need to finish up, really. That's all."

I nodded, like I believed her, like I was totally calm with it, and glared at my fork. Something was wrong, something was going on. And now the soap opera begins, I thought. It suddenly made sense why she insisted on being so secretive about her "art." I grew up in a house run by an unfaithful woman, I was plenty familiar with the suspicion that something was afoot, some anticipation in the air, some secret plan. Shaleese's voice was full of remorse, as if what she really meant to say was, "Camden, you might as well know, I'm sleeping with someone else," as if she had come as close as she could to confessing, had said everything but what she meant. The more I sat there, casting barbed looks at my silverware, the more certain I became that what she meant was that she wanted me to leave her alone in our house so that she could invite over her new guy. "So you're having an affair," I wanted to say, and I felt a momentary twinge of perverse pleasure as I thought about adding, "Great—I mean we're not married or anything, you know?" or "So—you think I care?" I wished I could then say "Yeah, me too" but I was not a good enough liar nor did I have enough time to have an affair. Then the twinge subsided and I just said, "Shit. Your art. Okay. Whatever."

I hardly heard her ask me if I promised, if I really, really promised to stay away because if I came back early I'd spoil what she was working on and blah blah blah. I just crossed the kitchen and headed out the door, feeling only disgust that my life was already being overtaken by adult concerns like failed relationships and broken commitments. Next would come the PTA, the tax-protest leagues, etc., then me almost getting flattened by kids in cars.

I met Acey at the bar downtown, this place called the Downtown Bar. The Downtown Bar was always open and had no qualms about serving under-age folks as long as we had the money to buy drinks. Not that I was under-age any longer—hey, I was an adult now!

I ordered a Long Island Iced Tea, a Black Russian, a whisky shooter, and a glass of red wine. I alternated sips between the four. I figured that together they might shake up my system and make me feel at least a little something.

In typical fashion, Acey didn't question why I'd called him down to start drinking at ten in the morning, he just ordered a pitcher of beer for himself and sat there beside me, making wisecracks, doing imitations, being the fucking truly invaluable friend he was.

"Hey, today's your birthday, right?" He toasted me with his half-emptied pitcher. "Well hey, happy birthday!"

"Tell me what screwing Lily is like," I murmured to him craftily. He'd been dating a waitress from the Nighthawk for a few months. She was still in high school, had this perfect little aerobics body. "Seems like she'd be awfully hot."

"Well, she's... No, I can't. Okay? It's not nice."

I shrugged, lifted the shot glass to my lips, and slurped. "Do you do her like you did Monica that time?"

"Camden. That was you."

"Spank her ass and all that shit. Make her swallow after you've been in her ass. Bastard."

"That was you."

"No. That was you."

We drank in silence. We were entirely alone in the bar but for the baseball game on the television and the bartender way in back.

"You seem all weirded out about something, loser, and I'm not even gonna ask, all right?"

I repositioned myself on the barstool. A plan came to mind, a little vengeful perhaps but nothing my girlfriend had not earned. "You know," I said, clearing my throat, "Shaleese told me she's Brian Jones' daughter."

"Who's that again?"

"Brian Jones. One of the original Rolling Stones."

"Really? Man. How am I going to remember that? Okay. I know how. Jones rhymes with Stones. Rolling Stones, Brian Jones. Okay. I'll remember. How come I never heard of him?"

"'Cause he's dead."

"Oh."

"She's weird about it, doesn't like anybody knowing."

"Okay."

"Do you want to know what it's like screwing Brian Jones' daughter?"

"I think I can imagine."

He looked at the television for a time, and started to comment on the game, but I jumped in. "Shaleese likes it difficult," I said. "The more pain for her, the better. She fights the whole way, but that's just an act. Interrupt her while she's putting together some artwork, tie her up so she can hardly move, it's not enough. Fuck her ass and come all over her face, it's not enough. You know? She pretends to be hating it while it's going on but she wants nothing but total humiliation."

Acey took a long swig of beer, his eyes glued to the baseball game. Beads of sweat were starting to break out on his upper lip.

"You know that choking thing?"

He pretended to ignore me.

"Acey. You know that choking thing?"

"Um, no. What choking thing?"

"She likes to be choked while she's being fucked. It's like a lack-of-oxygen thing, it heightens her pleasure." I held my hand to my throat in display.

He nodded at me, swallowed a few times, his eyes lit with this awful, hungry glint.

I wasn't sure how to play my next move. I decided to come right out and ask: "Is Lily at your place right now?"

"I don't know. I just don't know, Camden. She had a late shift last night. She might be."

"Shaleese is still at home. She's working on her art, I think, or she might still be in bed. I should probably get home to her, but I'm kinda tired of all these... these sex games. I can't keep roughing her up. Sometimes I want it slow and gentle, you know? I bet Lily knows what I mean. Slow and gentle."

"Watch yourself, now."

"I think you should go see about Shaleese. See if you can help her out."

"Camden, now—"

"And I'll go pay a visit to Lily, one slow and gentle visit, that's all."

"She's not even home, Camden."

"But she might be."

"She might be."

"She had a late shift. That's what you said. 'She had a late shift last night.' She might still be in bed."

"I think this is a bad idea."

"What about it's a bad idea?"

"Can't we just sit here like other people and enjoy our drinks and celebrate in honor of your big birthday, do you have to go around mucking everything up?"

"What about it's a bad idea?"

"We'll never pull it off, Camden."

"Acey. C'mon. You and me? Friends like us not pull this off? Give me a break."

Acey took out his keys, slapped them down with a sharp crack on the Formica in front of us. "Spend the afternoon at my apartment, then, if that's what you really want." And then he added, almost as an afterthought, "I know Lily thinks you're okay-looking."

"Yeah?"

"Yeah, and um..."

"Yeah?"

"And I'll... I'll do what I can to help out Shaleese, you know?"

I said nothing for a full minute. I glanced at my watch, pretended to become engrossed in the game, craned my head to look around the empty barroom. Acey stared intently at me the whole time. He looked flushed with lust after all the lies I'd just fed him.

"Well," I said at last, "Well. Okay."

Acey lived in this colorless box on Dwight Avenue, a few blocks away. His was one unit among many. Across the street was Sioux City's oldest building, a faded red-brick thing built in the 1880s as a Salvation Army hospital. Occasionally, through the years, it had served this or that official function, housing state militia, that sort of thing. Now it was a firehouse. I plopped down on the front stairs of Acey's building feeling sloppy drunk. The sunlight came down heavy, illuminating the firehouse in a gorgeous blast of whiteness. I was breathing hard and trying to keep my mind off throwing up. The firehouse door was up and I could see the firemen inside, polishing their fire engines to a blinding gleam. "Oh you fucking brave hero soldier boys," I muttered at them. I rose unevenly to my feet, intent on making my way across the street. I decided I would ask one of them for a match and if they gave it to me then I would turn right around and burn their goddamn firehouse down. I tottered into the street and halted. A car was coming. It slowed, stopped, honked at me. I waved for it to go on by. The driver shook his head, motioned for me to go first. I refused. I wouldn't budge. We continued looking at each other. Finally, the driver backed up, pulled a three-point turn, and drove away from me. I shook my head. Already it was harder for me to cross the street and I was merely twenty-one. It would only get harder. I looked up and saw every eye in the firehouse turned on me. "You okay out there, friend?" one of them called. I waved at them, my legs heavy, my coordination unsteady. "Just great," I called back. "You got a bathroom?"

Inside the firehouse the air was damp and cool. They slapped me on the back, steered me up some stairs. "Isn't it a little early to start hitting the booze?" one of them wanted to know. He had a mustache and a disarming grin. As a matter of fact, they all had mustaches and disarming grins. "Oh," I muttered, "Oh man, you wouldn't believe the day I've had so far." It was the brightest, most orderly place I'd ever seen. Everything was hung up and utterly spotless. I brushed past the helmets and fire-resistant coats hooked along the wall, each bearing the owner's name in masking tape, and I locked the bathroom door behind me. It was the whitest, most porcelain-heavy place I'd ever seen. I got down on my knees and waited. Eventually the

HALLOWEEN REMAINS LIZ PHAIR'S FAVORITE HOLIDAY

IN 1974 LIZ WENT AS FIDEL CASTRO

IN 1975 SHE WAS HELEN KELLER

IN 1976 SHE CAME TO SCHOOL DRESSED AS THE STATUE OF LIBERTY'S TORCH

IN 1977 SHE WAS AN AMC PACER

IN 1978 SHE SHOWED UP AS MICK JAGGER

dizziness focused in a little and I puked my guts out. Afterwards I washed my hands like the sign told me to do and I earned more slaps on the back. They offered to drive me home. "No," I said, "No, really. That's okay." I could see our friendship escalating to a point where they'd be asking me to lend a hand helping a cat down from a tree. *No thank you.* I staggered back out into the blasting ache of the sun and headed home, my plan a shambles. Even imagining Shaleese back home preparing herself for a special visitor—not the stirred-up rival I was sending to pre-empt him—even with the gorgeous Lily full in my mind, there was no way I could make myself head back to Acey's place. I just couldn't do it. I would snuggle up to her nubile young body and she'd wake, dreamily look up at me. "Oh, you're that okay-looking friend of Acey's," she'd say. "I guess I'll sleep with you."

"I'm not sure what I'm doing," I would say. "I'm an old man now and I don't know if all the parts still work like they used to." My penis would shrivel in a drunken daze. My mouth would reek of fresh vomit. I could see some definite problems developing. It was all too sudden, I should have seen that back at the Downtown Bar. I could not fuck Lily just like that. I would need to fit her into my story somehow, talk with her until she began to believe I had always wanted her or until I sensed enough resistance that I could see her as some sort of challenge. I could not make it that abruptly with a virtual stranger, even for revenge. It was not that it didn't square with my sense of romance or that my conscience would balk—it was simply that my penis would not accept it.

So instead I went home. Down the sidewalk I lurched, the ground tossing me like a ship at sea. I kept tasting acid and spitting. When I looked down, the only thing in focus was my right shoe. When I looked up, believe it or not, the trees shifted their limbs slightly to smother me—I had to keep jumping back to avoid falling into the grasp of branches.

All I could hope for was to catch Shaleese and Acey or whomever in some compromising act. I would swing the door wide, disgusted by the sight, delighted at the fright I'd cause. I would begin to beat them across the head with a broom handle I kept near the door, and they'd be too vulnerable to fight back; then they'd lie in my bed an unconscious bloody mess, and I could do absolutely anything I felt like to their bodies.

I tiptoed up my walk, onto my wooden porch, its paint peeling and covered as usual in oak leaves and bird shit, and put my ear to the door. There was no sound. I quietly turned the knob. It was unlocked. I swung the door wide, reached for the broom handle.

"What the hell's going on here!" I screamed.

Lily looked up in horror. She was splayed across the floor amid a pile of balloons. She was fully dressed. "Oh, god," she said. "Shaleese!" she called out, even though I could see Shaleese standing right over her.

"I gotta go," Shaleese said into the telephone and hurriedly hung up.

"Well," I accused her. I was pleased by the thought that at very least I had ruined her phone call.

"That," she said quietly. "That was your daddy."

"Sure it was."

"He won't be able to make it to your party."

I nodded, as if I understood what she was saying. "My party." I looked around at the balloons, at the streamers, at the stack of presents on the table, at the banner which read *Surprise!*

"And your brothers can't make it, or their wives, or your nephews. I'm sorry."

"Hey, Shaleese," said someone, and in from the other room walked Roy, home from school, dressed in a suit and tie like some professional basketball coach, "Well hey, look who came home early. Hey, man." Following on Roy's heels came Prendergast, grinning and shyly waving to me.

And there was Acey, too, crouching to help Lily tape balloons to a large piece of flexboard. He'd been there all along, I'd just failed to notice him. Acey looked up and shrugged as if to say, *oh well*. Shaleese came up from behind, wrapped her arms around me, kissed my cheek. "I'm so sorry. All I needed was a few hours. Darn. You must have heard us talking about you, is that it? Were your ears ringing?"

"Burning."

"What?"

"I heard you talking about me so my ears must have been burning. Not ringing. Burning."

"You know," Roy advised me. "That's some girl you got there."

"Yeah."

"This was no easy thing to organize."

"Sure."

"It was really nothing." Shaleese snickered in embarrassment. "I just wish I could have kept you away a little longer, is all. Happy birthday, sweetie." She kissed my cheek again.

"Yeah. Thanks. I think I'd better sit now, if that's okay."

"Camden Joy there?"

"This is Camden."

"Ah, the big-shot journalist. Well Joy, what is it? I must have ten thousand phone memos from you here, you calling morning, noon, and night. This may surprise you, Gabriel Snell does other things too, he don't just sit around waiting for the fucking phone to ring."

"I only called you once."

"Tell me you were calling to say you got the Fed Ex package and everything is sugar sweet. That's all I want to hear. Tell me you're fine, the weather's great, and you got this whole Liz Smith book almost ready for me. That's all I want to hear. Is that too much, Joy?"

"Um."

"Yes?"

"Well, the weather actually sucks. It's hailing."

"Great. Well, it's been swell chatting with you, Joy. Call me with some good news sometime, can't you?"

"I got the Fed Ex stuff but there's no information about Liz Phair. There's Gavin stuff about her sales figures and her charting on various V-1 radio stations, but there's no information about her... as a person."

"Yes?"

"So this. This doesn't help me. I need to know about her influences, about her ambitions, about her education. Why did she leave? Where has she gone? That's the kind of stuff that people picking up this book will want to read. That's what I would want to know—"

"Hold it."

"—if I picked up a book about whatever happened to Liz Phair."

"Hold it, I said. I got another call coming in. Hang on a second."

Click.

Pause.

Click.

"You there?"

"I'm here."

"Okay, listen, Joy. Don't sweat it. Get this—I'm working on getting you a meet with Liz Phair. Calling in a few favors, nothing special. Nothing you wouldn't do for me."

"Great."

"Then you can fire away with all these questions you think are so red-hot important, find out from the gift horse when her next release is scheduled."

"The horse's mouth."

"What?"

"'Straight from the horse's mouth,' that's what you mean

to say. You're confusing it with 'Don't look a gift horse in the mouth.'"

"Look. When I say fuck off kid, you understand what I mean to say?"

"Sure."

"Good. See what you can find out about how much longer we got to get this book out before she does her splashy comeback thing."

"Okay."

"So get a car—"

"I don't have a car."

"You don't have a car. At this time you are saying to me that you do not have a car, is this what I hear you saying?"

"I could borrow one maybe."

"Borrow one, rent one, see what I care, get a car and go on into Chicago and meet with her. First tell me this—I got all these phone memos from you—tell me—you finish dictating any tapes yet?"

"Yeah, sure."

"'Yeah, sure,' he says. Okay, smarty-pants. You gettin' any ideas on what to call this book?"

"I figured it would be *Liz Phair—Her Life in Photographs— Where the Hell Is She Now?* or something. *Her Life in Nowhere.* You're not saying I really get to decide the title?"

"Maybe."

"Well. In my head I've sorta been calling it *Vomit in the Camera.* I call that my working title."

"*Vomit in the Camera?*"

"Yeah, you want to know why? It comes from this time I heard about when Bob Dylan was riding around in a limousine with John Lennon—"

"*Vomit in the Camera?!* Gotta love it!"

"—and they were both high on amphetamines and heroin or something—"

"Gotta love it! It's a coffee-table photo book and we call

it *Vomit in the Camera*! I won't even ask! You just gotta love it!"

"—and Dylan was getting kinda sick to his stomach and kinda sick of being filmed and so he says to John, 'I've been photographed doing everything else, I might as well just—'"

"You see in the trades about this new marketing strategy, it's the new thing, you sell something by insulting it and this ups the integrity indicators, you start to see numbers climb right off the fucking map, lights go on all over the board."

"So you like that, *Vomit in the Camera*? I mean, as the title of this book?"

"Oh it's so smart, you don't even know. I been seeing in the trades about these baby-buster kids, and that's who this'll grab. Age group eighteen to twenty-nine. Attributes: parents divorced, intelligent, sarcastic, mistrustful of mainstream advertising, big *Speed Racer* fans, overeducated, underemployed, big TV watchers of the seventies, make references instead of conversation—"

"I see."

"Right, right. It's a title from heaven, you ask me, very Gen-X."

"Very Jennecks? Who're the Jennecks? Are they some seventies television family?"

"Gen-X, I said. Two words. Like 'ass hole.' Gen. X."

"Oh. Them."

"Right, right."

"Us."

"Yep."

"Me."

"That's what I said."

We all attended a public high school which got $5 a day from the state for every pupil they could verify was in attendance. Thus a premium was put on trapping as many kids as possible on the grounds and then shuttling them into whatever class-rooms were available. We were kept in trailers because no one would give the school money for permanent school structures. The grounds were lined with barbed wire, and called a "closed campus," which meant no one could leave during school hours without written permission from the principal. The majority of kids figured they had it pretty good. They'd waste themselves in the parking lot before first period, and then sneak in enough weed to zone out again after lunch. That way school felt like a dull TV show.

Of course, there were still kids at our school who were normal American brats, kids who enjoyed fist fights, joined the Scouts, carved things on tree trunks, played sports, snuck ciga-rettes, ran paper routes, made crank phone calls, all that quaint, old-fashioned crap. But we scarcely noticed them. Many of them even had first and last names, but we never bothered to learn them. We were all the time digging out history books to see if we could locate kids who were more like us, and most of the time we could. Like not many people know this but in Hitler's Germany there were highly efficient youth gangs who sabotaged railroad lines and for a long while evaded arrest. These gangs named themselves after American Indian tribes. There were the Sioux, naturally, and there was even a fifteen-year-old named Klaus Hauptmann who called himself Crazy Horse. From the mo-ment we verified Hauptmann's existence we knew that no matter what they told us, we didn't live in Site 3 at all. As far as we were concerned, we still lived in Crazy Horse Junction, and we knew who Crazy Horse was.

So the fact that we never heard of other kids performing acts of vandalism like ours did not trouble us. No civilians living in the Third Reich knew about the war role of the Sioux, either. Even kids in our own town had no knowledge of us. Our activi-ties went unreported in the newspaper's Fire and Rescue column (I checked each time). We read history books and were encour-aged, and figured that teens everywhere in America during the mid-eighties were playing with matches and performing similar actions, and were as little known for it as we were.

Shaleese was playing the electric guitar I'd lent her, practicing the chords I'd taught her, teaching herself how to sing. At first I had to plug everything in for her. I'd tune her guitar... or I'd try. I'd get it approximately right, hand the guitar over, and then go, "Close enough." After a pause, I'd go, "Close enough for jazz." After another pause, I'd go, "Close enough for government work." At last, I'd sigh and go, "Close enough for government jazz." She'd nod, strum the guitar, and go, "Yeah, well. Close is what makes hand grenades." Then she'd ask to be left alone with the guitar.

Pretty soon, what I overheard sounded good. She would stop playing as soon as I stepped into the room, so I had to eavesdrop on her progress while staying out of sight behind the doorjamb. Considering her other feats of artistry, considering her heritage, the strength of her material did not surprise me. It was in her blood or something. I was right behind her, encouraging her to get out there and play coffeehouse gigs. She could take the car. I would say that. I would say, you can take the car and I'll walk to work. She made tapes on my four-track and sent them out to people in cities, and soon enough she had taken me up on the offer, she was using my car—we called it "our car" now, though I was still making payments on the thing—to drive herself hundreds of miles in various direction to play at clubs. I never resented the way I had to work all day applying adhesive to labels at Maccoby's cannery, to pay the rent on our place and buy us food and pay for our car and her car insurance while she got to go out singing. She'd be gone for days at a time, and I hardly missed her.

You ask how could that be, for I did adore her immensely, and I must confess it was mainly because our sex was still not worked out all that well. This may sound weird, but after all the experiences she and I kept having I often wondered if sexual intimacy wasn't actually a contradiction in terms, because sex only worked to distance us more from one another.

Shaleese wouldn't go on the pill for fear of cancerous side effects, and I couldn't wear a rubber because I would lose the erection, so our sex was a festival of interruptions and disappointments, always it was my semen spilled on her pale stomach and neither of us speaking very much. Sometimes, when we felt really daring, we would fuck while she was having her period and she would whisper that it was okay if I came inside her because there was absolutely no way she could get pregnant then and I would do this but the entire act would leave us slathered in menstrual blood, like mercenaries in action-adventure movies covered in mud, gun in hand, eyes wild and hearts unfeeling. With us there was never any oral stuff or unusual positions. She had early on confided how her very first boyfriend would make her give him blow jobs while he read hardcore porn mags and she wore satin lingerie. The scenario thrilled me too (wouldn't it anyone?), but I was so disgusted at the crude, exploitative, dominating, narcissistic way it sounded that I swore never to gratify that side of myself with her. So I did not come once in her mouth nor ask to see her in lingerie nor reach for smutty material during intercourse; nor did I get jerked off by her hair, or fuck her behind the knees, or come between her feet; instead always on her belly, that alabaster belly. Because I wanted to be talked about later as a fair guy, a decent fellow. I suspect this did not happen, that she in fact hates me more than she ever hated her first boyfriend, which is why I am now bewildered as to exactly what did occur between us.

I can't really speak about *Whip-Smart*, but *Exile in Guyville* is a story dismantled into a hundred pieces—shards that, shuffled into the proper sequence, would add up to the entire story of a relationship. To make sense of what she is singing, one would need to listen to the CD in another order.

First you would hear "Explain It to Me," "Soap Star Joe," "Six Foot One," and "Fuck and Run." These are the songs of a single woman, suspicious, wary of men. A relationship is like plunging your "head underwater," she sings in "Explain It to Me," like being made to "kiss the gravel." She is at a loss why she should willingly go through such hell again. She's had previous relationships, been burned, has trouble trusting anyone. She has turned to a friend for help but, in the end, nothing her friend says makes any sense—"You never could explain it to me," she tells her friend. In "Soap Star Joe" and "Six Foot One," she advances this line of critical thinking, scoffing at the link she recognizes between the seductive games of both hypersensitive males ("I bet… you sell yourself as a man to save") and macho men ("He's just a hero in a long line of heroes, looking for something attractive to save"). Finally, against her better judgment, acting out of loneliness despite what she knows, she beds down with one of these types and, unsurprisingly, awakes the next morning thoroughly disgusted at her own lack of willpower ("Fuck and Run").

Just when you figure nothing will satisfy such a difficult person, she begins—in "Glory" and "Flower"—to grant herself a certain vulnerability. Perhaps this last guy, she thinks, perhaps he wasn't so bad after all. In the cold, sober light of day, she goes back over her reasons for fucking him. "He's got a really big tongue it rolls way out snaking around in the cloud it slicks you down." She begins to fantasize, playfully sings a porn ditty as if it's the bridge of "Somewhere over the Rainbow"—"I want to fuck you like a dog. I'll take you home and make you like it. I want to be your blow-job queen. I'll fuck you till your dick turns blue."

Their relationship takes off. The boyfriend knows nothing of her reservations. He is completely in the dark; when he gives their relationship any thought at all, it's only to congratulate himself, since evidently she liked fucking him enough to come back for more. Meanwhile, she is hoping her original instinct (which was to despise this guy) will prove wrong and he'll be a better choice than he initially seemed. But none of it comes easy. As their time together increases, more and more faults emerge, more and more ways in which she recognizes how completely wrong they are for each other. He obliviously fails to observe any of this, fails to recognize when she is testing him, fails even to notice when she is mocking him to his face. And worse, the two of them are now hardly ever alone. The boyfriend is now perpetually surrounded by his crude, rude, and lewd pals, who do not always treat her so well.

In "Shatter," she works to separate the boyfriend she likes from these sleazy friends of his whom he apparently loves. In "Help Me, Mary," she has lost not only her boyfriend to these sleazy ones but her home as well. In "Canary," she is left alone—no doubt the boys have gone out drinking together—and she uses the occasion to open a beer and mimic what these boys apparently want from her—that she keep her mouth shut, "come when called, clean the house, put all your books in order..." In "Never Said," her drunken boyfriend returns in a foul mood, accusing her of all kinds of impossible things. "All I know is I'm clean as a whistle," she tells him, and she's feeling a bit tipsy herself. "I never said nothing." By "Dance of the Seven Veils," he's passed out and she's wondering about the argument they just had. How did it happen? She works to retrace it in her mind. "Get out of the business," she sings to him softly. "It makes me want to rough you up so badly," meaning she wishes he would stop being so damn self-obsessed and taking her for granted and acknowledge the value of what they have together. She begins to wonder if it's maybe a little bit her fault—"I'm a real cunt in spring"—but by the end of the song she looks at his sleeping body, realizes that he has been sleeping not just through this whole song but through this whole relationship, and concludes—from the way he's snoring—that he's "already dead." In other words, by the end of that awful night, she knows the relationship is dying.

By "Girls!Girls!Girls!," she can almost speak this truth aloud, though merely to herself. "If I want to leave," she practices, speaking to the mirror, "You better let me go." Her temper climbs, her voice drops into a low and murderous pitch. "Don't you know I'm *very happy*," she intones sarcastically in "Mesmerizing." Then she stops, scared she might be going off the deep end, talking all this talk entirely to herself, and she arrives face to face with the prospect of breaking up with this guy only to be lonely all over again, which is not what she wants. "I want to be mesmerizing," she admits with difficulty, "Mesmerizing to you." Still standing alone before the mirror, she sighs. How to save this relationship? She tries a new tack. "The fire you like so much in me," she calmly argues in "Strange Loop," "is the mark of someone adamantly free." Then she rubs her eyes and speaks the only words with which the clueless boyfriend is thus far familiar—"Baby I'm tired of fighting," she wearily concedes. Then she storms away from the mirror. The separation for which she's been auditioning finally takes effect in "Divorce Song." True to form, neither of them is ready for it when it happens. It's a divorce in concept only—it's clear they haven't been together long enough to marry, but have only been sharing a house for perhaps a few years. It's a divorce initiated through a misunderstanding, accomplished without argument, and largely achieved through awkward silences. Neither is being terribly forthright, and both respond too late.

"It's true that I stole your lighter and it's also true that I lost the map," Phair acknowledges, though you know that's not what this is about at all. "But when you said that I wasn't worth talking to... I had to take your word on that." You're a drag, he finally answers her, thinking of all the complaints she has kept to herself and is only now beginning to reveal. "Oh," says Phair, unable to control herself, her voice caustic and hushed in that same ominous way we heard her use before the mirror in "Mesmerizing," "You've *never* been a waste of *my* time. It's *never* been a drag." When the boyfriend wearily explains that's not what he meant, and pleads for her to understand his side, it's far too late. He can say whatever he wants but she's not about to give him a chance. "Take a deep breath," Phair counsels him pitilessly, half-enjoying what she's doing to him. "Count back from ten. And maybe you'll be all right."

The last three songs in this reordering would be "Johnny Sunshine," "Gunshy," and "Stratford-on-Guy." They are the songs of a woman attempting to make sense of a breakup. She is once more disappointed ("I've been taken for everything I own") and bitter ("Sea monkeys, do monkeys—story of my life. Send three bucks to a comic book—get a house, car, and wife"). She is losing the context for what happened, unable to remember why she let herself be drawn into a doomed relationship. Finally, it comes to her. Flying into Chicago at night, watching the city and sky trade places as the plane banks, she is led to some resolution inside herself. "Once I *really* listened," she later recalls of the insight, and she's referring not just to the roar of the airplane in descent but to all the clatter and unsortable agony of her life lately: "The noise just went away." It's not a complete epiphany, no thunderous revelation, just an acceptance. She is at last positioned to return to the days of "Soap Star Joe" and "Six Foot One," ready to circle back on the insanity. The listener returns to the top of the order to hear the whole story start once more.

Monica grew into a leggy, tawdry, self-confident head cheerleader. Until about junior year she and I never went on a proper date, we were just always fucking. We'd fuck in the bucket seats of her Volkswagen in broad daylight, still wearing our clothes, pants down and underwear pulled aside, her squatting over me, parked at the far corner of the drugstore parking lot. She liked to make it in dangerous spots, in public. Some afternoons we'd go into the back of the supermarket where the employees had their shower rooms and lockers, and ask to use the bathroom, then fuck there. We fucked in the Philosophy aisle of the local library, lying down on the carpet, even though to my mind it wasn't really risking getting caught because no one ever read those books. We fucked on Site 3's bare runways as airliners took off and landed a few feet away, so close we would've been unable to hear each other scream in ecstasy, if we'd been all that much into screaming, or in all that much ecstasy. Once we even snuck into the police parking lot, laid down a tie-dyed bedsheet, and fucked on the cement there, amid the silent vigil of black-and-white patrol cars. She was responsible and used birth control, so I never had to use a condom, which got me used to the juicy experience of sex and spoiled me for life.

When things started to go wrong between Shaleese and me, there was little hope I would ever find out what it was. Always she and I missed each other's meaning, like we did not come together or I praised the book *American Psycho* (Shaleese wanted the book banned while my only complaint was that it didn't go far enough) or she ridiculed me for crying over *Tender Mercies* (a videotape she felt was sexist and antiwoman) or I ridiculed her for crying over the videotape of *Frances* (I said Frances Farmer got what she deserved—you can't piss off that many folks without expecting some payback), or I'd make a little drawing for her and she'd mistake it for something else and offhandedly insult me. Maybe I wasn't some great talent like her or some great articulate guy like my friend Roy but I still had feelings. Anything she said that had some substance to it I'd interrupt to ask, "Now you don't really mean that, do you?"—but only because she did it to me all the time. This went on for years. Missed cues, bad timing, the red tip of the inflamed clitoris, the belly with crystallizing semen, us with our stupid, movie-size, Saran-wrapped hearts, unintelligibly beating out the most important words of our lives.

"A woman called," Mrs. Dannerby yelled in a painfully shrill voice as I was stepping onto the plastic runner, heading up the carpeted stairs to my room. "She didn't leave a name."

"Huh?"

"I don't like that, Camden. I've spoken to you about our house rules here and I intend to put my foot down. Gabriel Snell calling, this I will let pass, but I cannot sanction a whole harem telephoning you night and day—"

Devil! Devil! piped up a sudden squeal in my head. *Witch found slain by hero's hand!* I almost said what I thought to Mrs. Dannerby but caught myself in time. "I'm sorry" was all I said, muttering it against a great aching clamor of voices calling me names which rose with the rush of the glue I'd sniffed outside moments before.

She twisted where she sat, turning to speak to me over the top of her corduroy armchair. "I don't want to have to think that I come home one day to find the house filled with your lady friends, like what happened in that disgusting movie, you understand what I mean?"

"She called me?"

"Yes, she did. Don't act so shocked."

"I'm just surprised."

"I hung up."

"A woman? It couldn't have been. I haven't given anyone this number except Gabe. His secretary? It was his secretary. Or the record store maybe, calling about my order? Did she say she was gonna call back, did she leave any message at all?"

"I hung up. That was all. You telephone your lady friends from outside the house, that's the rule. I can't have the phone ringing all hours. So long as we understand each other."

I stood at the bottom of the stairs for a moment, nodding, awaiting clarity, then I turned around and headed back out.

In the end, I find, things will only get so clear. There's a time to be brave. Like right now. I had better just go and do it.

By the time I was seventeen, I was no longer living at home because we no longer had a home. Once Daddy realized no one was coming back to this suddenly big house of ours—realized my mom and my brothers and everyone but me were pretty much lost for good—he informed me we were gonna move. But after checking the rents for places large enough for the two of us, he decided it would be cheaper to rent us each a little apartment. So he got me a place tucked in the back of one of those high-security stucco complexes. The complex "boasted" a pool and a laundry room and several rows of tall black fences. You needed a key to get into the complex, of course, and you also needed this magnetic card, which I was always forgetting. I got to be a nuisance for the manager, because he was always having to hike down the stairs to let me in. Finally, he told Daddy he'd evict me unless I wore the magnetic card on a chain around my neck at all times.

So I did, and though at first I felt humiliated, the card with all its mysterious holes dangling at the end of the chain started to look kinda cool to me in the mirror and I began wearing it outside my shirt, decorating it with ribbons and stickers and feathers and graffiti. I slept on a fold-out sofa that came with the place; all in all I suppose I was pretty happy. Monica came by quite often, and between the pool, the laundry room, and my workplace, there were all kinds of exhibitionist possibilities that delighted her.

I'd recently gotten a job as a pump jockey evenings and weekends at a service station a block away. There was an incident around that time with one of our frequent customers. He always had two kids with him who acted like maniacs, playing war games, dodging bullets and screaming victoriously, sliding over the seats and slipping around like rodents inside the station wagon. The guy would insist on pumping his own gas, and would always pump a little more than he could afford, then claim he'd been too busy watching his kids and it was an accident. You can't crucify someone for an honest mistake, he'd claim. I let him go the first few times. I talked to the other pump jockeys and they said he pulled the same crap with them; they also let him go. It wasn't worth the hassle.

One day, after filling his tank, he maintained he'd completely forgotten his wallet, left it at home. I live just down the street, he told me, vaguely waving at some far-off buildings. Just let me run right home, lickety-split, I'll be back with the cash. Honest injun. I'm real sorry about this. But hey, it was an accident, big guy. You can't crucify someone for an honest mistake. Well, I don't know, I answered. I don't know about that. Look, he proposed. Here's what we'll do. I'll leave you a deposit. For instance, you can hang on to my— He poked his head into his station wagon, looked around. You can hang on to my flashlight. He got it from his glove compartment and held it out to me. Here. Keep this, I'll be back faster than Jackie Robinson. Good as a promise, since you've got my flashlight. I need it all the time, I'll have to come back.

I don't know, I said. I don't think that'll work. Well look, he said. He ran a hand over his crewcut, opened his palms to me. I got nothing else here to offer. Except my kids. You want my kids? He called them out of the car, put a hand on each of their shoulders. This is Camden, the guy told them, reading my name off the patch on my uniform. He'll be looking after you for a little while. Camden, this is Josh. Hi, said Josh. And this is Jake. Say hello to Camden, Jake. Hi, said Jake. I said nothing. The kids were quieter than they'd ever been. The guy clapped his hands together. Great, he said. He whistled a few notes. You're a real salt-of-the-earth kinda guy, Camden. I'd never actually heard anyone use that expression before. I'd only known "Salt of the Earth" as a Stones song, the last song on *Beggars Banquet*. I think it was the first song on which Keith Richards sang lead.

He climbed behind the wheel of the station wagon, turned the ignition. The engine whined, over and over, but would not catch. I think it's your battery, I announced. I think you need a jump. The guy hopped out, went around the car, and from under a tarp in the back of the station wagon he pulled out his jumper cables. I directed Josh and Jake to get back in the car. They silently obeyed. Then I gave their father a jump and told him I was keeping the cables as a deposit on his tank of gas.

But it's just a deposit, I said. We don't really need more jumper cables here. We're a service station. We got plenty already. Just go home, I ordered, pointing firmly at the far-off buildings. Grab your wallet, come right back, and square your bill with us. I shook the cables at him. Then you can have these back. For several minutes the guy argued with me, saying his battery might die on the way back or something and then how would he get a jump without his cables? I shrugged. Have to tell you I hate the idea, Camden, he told me at last. Yessirree Bob, I do not like it at all.

Look, just come right back, I said. They'll be here waiting for you. He sighed, shifted into drive. He looked at me. Take my kids, he softly suggested one last time. Just take the kids. Leave me the cables, okay? You're a nice guy. Show a little mercy here, big guy. C'mon. I shook my head. Just come back with the money, I said. There won't be any problems. The guy rolled up his window, gave me a discouraged look and drove off. Of course, he never returned for the jumper cables. I told the other pump jockeys and they said he had stopped coming around altogether. Of course, we all wondered whether he would ever have come back for his kids, if I had accepted them.

Shaleese's trips got longer and longer, her phone calls less and less frequent, until finally I lost touch with her for several weeks in May and began to panic. I called her mom then, the German woman, still running that motel back home; she said yes, "Chalice" was home and resting but could not come to the phone now. I got some mail from Shaleese soon after. I imagined her writing it sitting in that booth at McDonald's, beneath a sky filled with colored lights and screaming metal birds. Shaleese's letter implied we were still together, just going through a rough period of separation. "This morning I got up and took a pill for you," she wrote, which was said I think to reassure me we'd be together soon.

I took a pill for you. How had it become such a thing, so manipulative a complaint, how had I done it to her? I hadn't come in her mouth, but I'd made her take a pill every morning. I felt heartsick reading this, and it also made me horny, but she was sixty-five miles distant, with my car, and I could get no closer. All her stuff was still hanging in the closet and folded in the dresser and sitting on the shelves in the little clapboard house with me. It stank of loneliness. I ached for her and I wasn't even sure what her face looked like. One night I got very drunk on sloe gin and tried to reach her by telephone. I knew she was at McDonald's, the clown who answered the phone there basically admitted as much, but he wouldn't go to her booth and tell her she had an emergency phone call. I got really mad and threw the receiver, then drank a bit more. Finally I decided to help myself to one of her damn precious journals, to review her log of male atrocities and see exactly what she'd written about me.

It turned out they were not journals at all. They were stories. My name didn't appear once. How dense I had been! What I heard as male atrocities I guess she just heard another way, as something that inspired her to write. They were stories she'd once begun to read to me, only I'd been too lame to comprehend, and so she'd trailed off and never started up again. I'm sure she would've told me, that day in the bookstore, if I hadn't been so busy being a regular riot, interrupting her, making her chuck her book behind the cabinet.

In these stories, I plainly heard the voice of Shaleese, speaking clear as could be about why, when we were growing up, she was always sitting in that same booth at McDonald's. Apparently she believed she was destined for stardom. Not because she was the last daughter of the dead Rolling Stone (in fact, this was something she'd concealed to protect her mom), but out of some twisted faith in justice, in cosmic retribution for the man taken from her mother, the father taken from her. All she had to do to satisfy this faith was settle into some seemingly nowhere spot and wait, and she would be found. The way Malcolm McLaren discovered Annabella of Bow Wow Wow in a London laundromat, the way supermodel Claudia Schiffer was discovered in a Berlin discotheque, the way Roman Polanski discovered Nastassja Kinski in the last place you'd expect.

I read all her stories that night, then sat down and wrote Shaleese a long letter. I said how much I missed her, and begged her to return. I told her I supported her, I truly did, and wanted her songwriting talent to be discovered as much as she did. But, I asserted, it was a lot more likely in Sioux City than Site 3, a lot more likely in a music club than a McDonald's. Please, I said, please understand it's not that I don't want you to get famous. I just need you here with me now. I'm falling, I'm stupid without you. I need you so I can laugh. And really Shaleese, I wrote. Really. Come on now, we're all adults, let's be honest. You put out tapes and tour to support them, that's how it works. If you're related to someone famous, all the better. People don't earn record contracts through faith or desire, or believing in cosmic retribution, they don't get signed for sitting in the right booth at the right fast-food restaurant. That's not the real world, pumpkin. It's only because I love you that I tell you these things.

I never mailed the letter. Once I was sober, I glanced through her stories again and saw, written in a margin, something that looked like *If you would just talk to me I wouldn't have to hurt you.* There were other scraps of words, written even more sloppily, which appeared to say things like *You left me nothing* and *Explain it to me* and *I never said nothing.* But all these things were written so sloppily I couldn't tell if it was her handwriting or mine. And besides, here I go saying I read all her journals that night but they weren't even all her journals anyway. I realized there was still one left, one I'd watched her throw away at Adventure Books, the "library book" I kept meaning to go back and get. I'd lost my nerve. When we finally did get hold of each other on the telephone, months had passed. Things had gotten confused in my head because women I thought looked just like Shaleese had repeatedly fooled me. I'd be on my bike or on the bus and they'd cruelly distract me into following their lead, following their car, following them home, and though I know it doesn't make any sense I'd sometimes end up really far away and the cold cannery bastards started to dock my pay. Shaleese was in Chicago, recording for some guy, some record executive. This guy had heard her demo, traveled to Site 3, stopped at McDonald's, and lo, discovered her there, waiting, like Annabella gazing out the window of a laundromat, like Claudia Schiffer wiggling her hips in a discotheque, like Nastassja Kinski patiently posed in the last place you'd expect. It was the miracle she'd always believed would happen. She had faith, she believed. I didn't. Shaleese was calling to explain that she and I were breaking up though she wouldn't call it that, instead she was advising me how to meet girls and saying I wasn't keeping up with her changes and how much better it would be for me to stay in Sioux City.

"Shaleese," I whimpered.

"And they don't call me Shaleese here," she said, her voice chilly.

"Elisabeth?"

"My name's Liz now."

When we hung up, I was very unclear what this "Liz" person wanted me to do with what remained of Shaleese's stuff, the stinky stuff still in our house with me, hanging, folded, sitting, the black v-neck sweaters and dropped-waist, floral-print dresses and black tights, reminding me that somehow I'd done something wrong though I couldn't say exactly what, and I tried to stay to keep watch over her belongings, but the rent went up without anyone asking me if that was okay, and finally I took off. I had to.

From Shaleese to Liz—of course. This *was* a record company she worked for now, the kind of people who invented spin control. Behind the CEO's offices, they have whole departments hidden where they reinvent the artists on their roster, make up legitimate-sounding credentials and brainstorm the most appropriate résumés.

The compromises would not stop with renaming her. Public relations would see to that. There'd be no mention of former boyfriend Camden Joy or Sioux City or Site 3 or anything related to Iowa. They might even agree not to upset her mom, they might not have to exploit the Brian Jones angle (besides, how could it be checked? who could confirm it?) if "Liz" would, in turn, assent to a whole new past—parents (two of them, a mother *and* a father) in Chicago, say, a big-city art-school background, no real interest in fame, absolute surprise at any suggestion that her song titles rebuke the Rolling Stones, complete wonder that her CD should precisely mock the song count and title of the first Rolling Stones masterpiece recorded without any input from Brian Jones. They'd work to make her genius appear pure, irreproachable, untarnished, the insights of her songs less the product of pedigree and more a surprise inspiration, a thoroughly lucky accident. Believe me, I know how record companies lie, how they delay a release until the right moment, how they make the artists roll over and play dead and retrieve the ball and lick their keeper's hand, all on cue (don't ask how I know!). The god-damn record companies invented the idea of selling us things we do not need, that's their game. A new name, a new past is nothing to them. I imagine one day I'll probably see one of Shaleese's albums, except it'll be by Liz Somebody and the songs will be rewritten and so polished there will be nothing about her that I recognize or admire and it'll be just like when Winston Smith and Julia pass at the end of *1984* with nothing but ice in their eyes.

Adventure Books was still there, like always, that same familiar layout, like slipping easily through a dream, still cozy enough to haul up a truckload of painful memories, and yet weirder, even weirder than that…. Do they never clean their store? How could such a thing remain in place after so long? Calmly I strolled over to what she and I used to call the celebrity cabi-net, currently the home of *Tracy Chapman—Where Is She Now?*, *Suzanne Vega—Where Is She Now?*, *Nina Hagen—Where Is She Now?*, *The Shaggs—Where Are They Now?*, and putting all my weight on one foot I leaned on the cabinet's side and tugged it towards me. The cabinet scooted out just far enough—and there, yes! Still! The library book, she had called it, the little liar. Her journal, as I suspected, the last one, the only one I have yet to read. I promised myself (and now I've kept that promise!). But god, the door this opens: after so many years, to finish all the journals requires yet more strength—too much like devouring her, skeleton and all. I mean, once the journals are completely exhausted, Shaleese will most truly be gone. She will be "Liz" and there will be nothing at all to look forward to.

When I went to leave, the guy at the register beamed at me just like old times. But he looked thin and no longer so jubilant, probably because his pet project had moved on. He asked where I'd been.

"I don't know," I replied. "Around."

"You just missed that... what's her name? She was just in here about half an hour ago."

"Who."

"You know that girl I used to see you in here with?"

"That was a really long time ago. Shaleese."

"Yeah, but that's not her name."

"It wasn't her."

"I'm positive it was her. But dude, that's not the right name, is it? I'm pretty sure this was her."

"What did she look like?"

"Oh, dude. I'm never good at that. You describe her to me."

I looked at him for a time. "I... can't."

"Me neither, man. She's just, you know... what could you say, this certain type."

"There's a lot of times I think I see her but it's only that... She's just become that kind of girl."

"There's a lot of girls like that, man," he sighed. "Just a fuck of a lot."

"I don't understand how this could have been her."

"I must be wrong, you know? I am not at all into mind-fucking you, dude."

"This," I shrugged, "was not a problem."

I waved Shaleese's journal at him, meaning it as good-bye but also so he could see it was not something I owed him money for, and I ducked out.

When I finally suggested to Monica we should go on a formal date, it was pretty late in our relationship. She was dating two other guys that same week that I knew of—one being the most popular guy on campus, the other being Hank Paulsen, a star linebacker from the local community college. It was Friday night. We drove to Sioux City, an hour away, to see some old foreign film, something she'd never done before. It was this confusing British thing called *Performance*, which showed a lot of people dyeing their hair and a lot of gangsters talking on telephones and a lot of Anita Pallenberg's breasts. It was Mick Jagger's first film role, and since they'd modeled the set after Brian Jones' old apartment and hired Brian Jones' ex-girlfriend as the lead, Jagger had decided to act the role as if he were Brian Jones. On the way home Monica fell asleep in my lap while I drove my daddy's Toyota Corolla hatchback. I took her home and kissed her goodnight and for the first time in what felt like forever we didn't sleep together. The next morning she and Hank went to see the Rolling Stones at Comiskey Park in Chicago. She told me later they got up real close to the stage and she sat on Hank's shoulders through a lot of it. She said Mick Jagger was foxier in the movies than he was in real life.

Two weeks after our first date Monica won Homecoming Queen. They spelled her name out in fireworks on the football field at half-time, the "i" dotted with a heart. Her parents clipped the huge photo of her from the next day's front page and attached it to the kitchen refrigerator with magnets painted to resemble lady-bugs.

A few weeks later, she stopped coming by. I rarely saw her in school anymore either, except when she performed at a pep rally. She was getting kinda famous at our school. I guess I was happy for her, though I felt a little forgotten. I was astonished at how much I began to miss her. It was like out of nowhere came this window of longing for her, and sweeping past the window were the sweetened-up memories of our various fucks. I recalled things so detailed I'm sure I was making them up. I even remembered how once she had boldly confessed to me all her fantasies of taboo sex, after first making me absolutely promise that I would help her indulge each and every one of them. In the years that followed I failed to help her indulge any but her most voyeuristic ones, and she never brought up the subject again.

But after Monica forgot about me, one of her fantasies began to haunt me. I remembered her phrasing it this way: "And then also, I want to be fucked by someone I can't see and be like all, whatever. Y'know? Like, I'd be so okay with that. Really! Like, I think every girl if she's honest with herself would admit she wants to be *raped* by a *stranger*." I started thinking about my responsibilities to my old friend Monica and contemplating how easy it would be to accommodate this fantasy of hers. I was sure she'd appreciate it because I knew a lot about fantasies: I knew that when they lie there unfulfilled they start to simmer and can really mess you up. It's best to simply act them out. *Every girl if she's honest with herself...* I'd have Prendergast break into her bedroom, blindfold and gag her, then silently haul her out of the house. There were all kinds of strange windows and little rooms in Monica's family's house that were rarely used. She could be slipped out of there quite easily. We would hot-wire a Postal Service van, something we frequently did, and put Monica in back, roped at the wrists and ankles to some cinder blocks. We would drive around and around, disguising our voices to stay anonymous, while my friends and I took turns obliging her fantasy. Bound in that position, surrounded by that many guys, quite a few of her fantasies could be indulged.

I don't mean to imply, by the tone I use to speak of it now, that we didn't actually perform this service for Monica. It was done, the fulfilling of her fantasy, the blindfolding, the kidnapping, the diligent rape in the roving van. It's just that I got pretty detached about it and I don't remember the night with all that much fondness. I think we all got a little motion sickness from the van. Maybe the ventilation didn't work right or something. Plus Acey went a little overboard with Monica, baring her ass, hurting her. It wasn't even funny, the way he was doing things, and I can't really defend it. He undid her gag and did some awful things to her mouth as well. "Take it, you," he said in a low voice. That was Acey, always way over the top. Come to think of it, maybe it wasn't him, maybe it was Roy. It was dark and we were all kinda queasy and this was a while ago and I can't really remember all that well. It seems kinda more like something Roy would do. Then again, maybe it wasn't even Roy. Maybe it was me, who knows. I suppose I'd be clearer about all this if we had been arrested. Then it would've been straightened out which one of us performed which violation. But since we were never charged with anything, all I remember for sure from that night is being giddy then hesitant then cold and numb which, since, is how I've always imagined it would be to sleep with a celebrity. The whole night kind of served to change my opinion about helping other people indulge their fantasies.

I just got off the phone with Gabe. I am usually holding hands with my Pocket Secretary so that I can flip out her microcassette and pop it into Mrs. Dannerby's answering machine to tape Gabe's calls. But this time I had left her in the other room—it was a lover's quarrel, you don't want to know the details—so I am forced to recall the phone conversation now from memory. It was a short conversation anyway. One thing worth mentioning about these calls of Gabe's—I'm not sure if it comes through when I tape them—he's always on his cell phone, there's always some frantic business going on in the background. One time it was all splashing sounds and echoes and men rumbling in foreign accents. Another time I distinctly heard dance music and a bullhorn in the background encouraging gentlemen to come upstairs where there is a live show every twenty minutes. This last time he was whispering. There seemed to be a contest of sorts, a loud, authoritative male voice with another voice interrupting to cite objections. Gabe just called to say that my interview with Liz Phair in Chicago is set for tomorrow. I'm to meet her at a Chinese restaurant on Wabash Street between East Wacker Drive and Lake Street at four in the afternoon. Gabe said I could ask her anything I wanted but that I should be rather circumspect about this book. Better yet, he felt I should represent myself as "some smarty pants magazine writer" and not even let on about the book. He implied there are copyright problems attached to the use of her childhood photos, some release which "her fucking legal weasels" have refused to allow her to sign. Assuming it gets published the book may have to appear without photos, a possibility Gabe refuses to accept since it's so anathema to his so-called aesthetic. Now the book has become like a crusade to him. He's determined to "get it out and get that bitch" by which, I gather, he means he'd like to profit from Liz Phair, since her lawyers have him outmaneuvered.

One night right around when the guy offered his kids in exchange for twelve gallons of gasoline, Spencer's father, Mr. Schwartz, called me. I was at home practicing with Acey. We were trying to nail down some majestically impulsive riff. Acey's shirt was drenched in sweat. I answered the phone still wearing the guitar around my neck. While Mr. Schwartz and I talked, Acey stuck his drumsticks up his nose and folded back his eyelids. I nervously played guitar leads with the volume turned off. All I could think was that he was calling about the City Hall arbor—that somehow he suspected we were the ones who'd burned down his expensive arts-and-crafts project.

Don't get me wrong, I liked Mr. Schwartz fine. One night in third grade, he drove me to Parent/Teacher night when my parents couldn't make it because they had couples counseling. He substituted really well as my father. He was very tall and blushed easily. He was also my Little League coach one year. After I'd gone three games without getting on base, I heard you got to go to first base free if the catcher interferes with your swing. So I grabbed the longest bat we had, backed up as far as

I could in the batter's box, reached way back and swung as hard as I could. The catcher caught it in the back of the head and fell in an unconscious heap. Someone called an ambulance. I acted stunned, like I couldn't believe it. I asked the umpire if I got to go to first base now but instead he told me that I had done it deliberately and had to go to the dugout and I was out of the game. Mr. Schwartz came unglued, blushed terribly, got really mad at the umpire and promised to lodge an official protest. I didn't have the heart to confess I *had* done it intentionally, so I opened my mouth like I was amazed and said nothing. I could no longer precisely recall what I had done. I started to feel justified, like the umpire was picking on me for no reason. I felt I deserved first base. I heard Mr. Schwartz tell the umpire I was a good kid, a real decent fella, that I would never purposely hurt anyone, much less hit a kid in the head with a bat. Then I heard him say I had family problems right now, a mother and a father at each other's throats, a sister in some weird legal limbo; that I needed attention and support instead of yet another reason for kids to make fun of me. I was impressed by all this. My own parents had always tried real hard to keep things from hurting us kids: they never fought out in the open or brought up the subject of my sister. Here I had been trying to get to first base and instead I got to hear adults pore over my family's secrets and talk about me like I wasn't there. It was great. I tried hard to act the part of the kid he described. I made my eyes go vulnerable. Give me attention and support, my expression said: I would never purposely hurt anyone. But the umpire wasn't buying it. He made Mr. Schwartz walk me to the dugout. I hung my head low, dragged my bat loosely, carried the batting helmet in my free hand like it weighed a hundred pounds.

So my thoughts of Mr. Schwartz were in no way unkind. I just couldn't figure out why he would be calling so many years later. Unless he was gonna try and trick me into confessing that I smacked the kid intentionally and burned down his twig sculpture. I couldn't imagine why else he would call.

"Have you had any recent contact with Spencer?" was the first thing he wanted to know.

I told him no. I made small talk with the exaggerated jocularity we all used when speaking with adults. I gushed about how nice it was to hear from him, how often I thought of him, asked about his pets and his wife. It always surprised me that adults never seemed to catch on to what we were up to. It was so exaggerated it could only be sarcastic—unless, that is, we were the happiest teenagers on earth. Evidently, Mr. Schwartz was of the latter opinion: he answered my questions in a sweet and serious way.

"Well, Camden, I'm a little worried about Spencer. He left home several hours ago and he was pretty upset about, about some things, and we, we haven't seen him since."

I made small mutterings of concern. If Mr. Schwartz was laying a trap he was doing it rather weakly. So I decided to let down my guard, maybe give him a chance to catch up. But it didn't help. Not a word about Little League, not a mention of his arbor. He went on and on about his son's disappearance as if it was his sole concern. And maybe it was. Mr. Schwartz hung up after making me promise to call him if I heard from Spencer. I never did call.

The story with Spencer was that he had grown into a huge boy and a terrible student. Too bad for him, our school required athletes to get above a C average. After he was cut in his junior year, Spencer went from star varsity linebacker to doper in one week. From there, I guess, he was looking to sink even lower. The only gang left below the jocks and the druggies was my gang: Roy, Acey, Prendergast, Jimmy, and me. Suddenly the oft-ridiculed Spencer was back among us, joining us after school at Prendergast's, dropping by during my shift at the service station to chat. He liked to drink beer and he liked to talk about dynamite. We endured his presence because we seemed stuck with him, and because for us he was a textbook case of adolescent rebellion. That's how it felt anyway—as if compared to us

143

he was the norm. We probed him with elaborate surveys every time we wondered how a certain action would be received. And we tolerated his presence because of his strange fondness for dynamite. It seemed to come out of nowhere. We wondered for some time if he had simply heard some jock mention it once or something. Then he told us about his brother-in-law's cousins.

A year earlier, in what had threatened to erupt into one of Site 3's biggest scandals, Spencer's sister, who was extremely pretty and therefore I suppose widely regarded as town property, had married a Samoan. That's right, a pretty white girl marrying a Samoan. Well, you wouldn't believe the commotion this stirred in our little town. Before that I doubt they knew a "Samoan" was anything other than a kind of Girl Scout cookie. It was as if no one had noticed that Pacific Islanders were admitted into this country. Anonymous death threats were delivered to the newlyweds in ordinary envelopes. The groom requested help from a few menacing cousins, and Spencer fell in with them, and this was where he learned about dynamite.

I am not the one to ask for help in making tomorrow shinier. I came down to the breakfast table today to read in Mrs. Dannerby's morning paper of a blond teenager gang-raped in a barley field by five assailants whose faces she couldn't see.

"Terrible, isn't it?" remarked Mrs. Dannerby.

"Yes," I said. "Yes."

The paper ran a picture of her leaving the hospital, a photo taken from behind so as not to reveal her identity. I looked at her hair spilling down her back, her rayon pants suit, her funky hat, her platform shoes, her beaded purse carrying... god knows. A fake ID? A library card? A couple tampons, a package of fertilizer, some match heads, a fuse? An unsigned note from one of her assailants apologizing for the rape? I considered this on the front page, excused myself from the breakfast table, took the front page into the bathroom, applied Mrs. Dannerby's hand cream to my penis, and massaged myself until I came all over the girl's photo. I found that come dissolved much of the photo and, in blurring the inks, partially erased the girl. I raced upstairs to bury the paper in my desk before returning to my breakfast. Do you truly want a man like me on your side? I address this to my Pocket Secretary but she does not respond. She seems pleased to withstand any humiliation for the sake of companionship. How dare you, I tell her. How shameless you are.

The planes were still falling out of the sky pretty regularly, docking at Site 3, but there were fewer of them now. Ever since the strike and its mysterious halt (after the chickenshit compromise of my father's union), the whole town was off-kilter, spooky, unsure. Planes would arrive in bunches or not at all. The rhythm was off. A criss-cross of contrails settled permanently over the city like spiderwebs. Even though each plane landed as ever seemingly only to disgorge a whole new set of pretty cabin attendants, foxy women delivered down from the heavens for our naughty perusal, still something was on the decline, you could feel it. There were daily denials from the airline that they were building a Site 4 in West Texas but the rumors persisted, until finally they were no longer denied. Then the rumors congealed into something approaching fact. Site 3 was hailed in flowery language, deemed "an historic experiment" and "a grand contribution to aviation knowledge," and then slated to be closed in just shy of a year's time. Which was probably best for everyone concerned. We had given them our weather, they had given us their stewardesses. And then, a month after the fate of Site 3 was sealed, during some regular awful day of my senior year in high school, an unusually swift front moving cold air down from Canada met a hostile updraft in the skies

145

above us and, despite repeated assurances that such a thing was impossible, the airline's ballyhooed instruments failed and there was a midair collision, the first in Site 3 history. We were sent home from school early, following an explosion that rattled our windows and a notice over the p.a. of an "unprecedented atmospheric tragedy." Pieces of debris were scattered all over town. The airline announced rewards for everything that was turned in to them. They promised to pay by the pound. For months, we were still turning up odd scraps of seat material and chunks of shining steel. After that, we in the town felt relieved that the airline was leaving us, even though there was truly no future without them.

Fortunately, we were old enough to figure out how to get going ourselves. Roy had been accepted at some Ivy League school back east. Acey and I were gonna move out to Sioux City, get gigging with this band thing of ours. Prendergast was staying in Site 3 for the time being, because his Mom at last just about had the money together to move them west, or so she said. None of us bothered to find out what dumb, sniffling Jimmy planned on doing with the rest of his life, though we all spent a great deal of time together over at Prendergast's deciding how to bid adieu to Site 3. We all agreed that whatever we did, as Roy put it, we had "to liberate those people from all these fucking things" though again, who or what Roy meant by "those people" and "these things" was left to our own interpretation. It had to be loud, it had to be violent, it had to be terrifying. But what was "it"? Then we all looked at Spencer. We asked if he could really, truly, honestly get us some dynamite. We waved a wad of bills in his face and he assured us that yes, it could easily be done.

Well, he lied. All he came back with was a recipe book called *Ka-Bloom! The Real Thing*, written by some explosives consultant to the Jordanian secret police. It told us how to make tamper-proof bombs, package bombs, booby-trapped doors, auto traps, sound-detonated bombs, pressure mines, that sort of thing. We thanked Spencer with tremendously artificial gra-ciousness, then looked at each other, rolling our eyes. Except for Prendergast, who picked up *Ka-Bloom! The Real Thing* and started flipping through it.

"You know… this looks pretty easy," drawled Prendergast, pointing to a recipe in the book. "We… empty a bunch of bullets into a sealed pipe… dump in powdered sugar and potassium nitrate… which"—he flipped back and forth between a couple of pages to confirm this—"you can get from fertilizer. That's all. That's it. Or here's one… that's even easier. We fill a bottle with match heads… and light a fuse." He looked up. "Hey… I never even thought of that. You know… Spencer… this is pretty cool."

We leaned in close to read over Prendergast's shoulder.

"I can get the fertilizer," sniffled Jimmy. We were astound-ed. It was just about the first grammatically correct sentence dumb Jimmy had ever articulated in our presence. We looked at him, shocked. Finally, Roy spoke.

"That'll be great, Jimmy. Great. You do that."

And that's how the Big Bang began.

I was pulling out early this morning when I found my way blocked by a huge white, purple, and orange delivery truck. It didn't appear to be moving. I stepped out of the car, went to look in the truck's driver side. No one there. I didn't want to wake up Mrs. Dannerby by honking the horn. After a few minutes, Franklin the Fed Ex guy materialized out of a near-by house, his uniform wrinkled. It was a foggy morning. The streetlights were still on from the night before, dappling Frank-lin's face, highlighting his scar handsomely. He claims to have gotten the scar one night at a club after he complimented the wrong woman. I can only imagine what he was up to in my neighborhood, so early in the morning. I don't think he lives anywhere close. "Whoa now," Franklin said, swaggering up to check out the luggage in Mrs. Dannerby's car. "What all you got going on here?"

I playfully adopted a stuffy accent and informed him, "I... am going to Chicago."

"You going to Chi-town? This ain't your car. What the hell you doing with this car?"

"It's a loaner. It's okay. Mrs. Dannerby gave me the keys."

"It's okay?"

"I hope so. Sure."

"Well, this would have to be the first time I have heard absolutely anything of this. Why the secrecy? You running from the law, hunh, that it?"

"No."

He grinned slightly, wrinkling his scar. "Yes, you are. I see it in your eyes. You're scared about something. And this fancy automobile. Something does not fit into our little picture here. So tell me—which route you going to take?"

We turned together to address Mrs. Dannerby's car, as if inviting it to join in our conversation. "Uh. I was thinking I'd take eighty straight across."

Franklin shook his head slowly, put a leg up on the bumper of Mrs. Dannerby's car, leaned a full hand down on the hood of Mrs. Dannerby's car. "That's not what you want to do."

No one else on my street was even awake. We were just two fellas out in the road at dawn, talking traffic. We could be farmers, could be anyone. "Why not?" I asked.

"That's not what y'wanna do!" he insisted. He looked at me incredulously. "You wanna avoid the speed trap outside Des Moines, all them truckers coming off the scales, you gotta hook up—" (he motioned at my back) "—with Lakeport over there, follow it right out to twenty, button-hook down on three-eighty at Waterloo, and straight out into Illinois on thirty."

"Oh." It wasn't that important to me. Whatever route got me to Chicago in time. "Then that's what I'll do."

He folded his arms solemnly, faced me full-on with that scar. "For reals here."

"Okay, okay. Thanks." I was a little exasperated with him, taking this stuff so seriously. I had assumed we were joking.

"So really now," he jerked his chin at me. "Why you running away to Chi-town? You can tell me."

"I have to talk to this woman. I'm writing a book about her. It's supposed to tell everyone where she has gone."

"No, c'mon." He obviously wanted to horse around a little. "For reals now. You can tell me."

I was anxious to get on the road. I was also getting a little cold, standing in the fog with Franklin. But something kept me from breaking our conversation to pull my jacket out of the car. I guess I was glad for a little conversation. All this dictating, this endless monologue, is kinda getting to me (not counting Mrs. Dannerby's interruptions, which are no interruptions at all but usually simple requests to help her bring in groceries from the car or dry the dishes tonight or her calling out for me to remember to wipe down the shower walls after I'm done in there). So I tried to think up some great lie to heave at Franklin, but I really couldn't come up with a thing. I should have explained I had Mrs. Dannerby in the trunk, sliced in thin strips. Instead I eyed him suspiciously, like he wouldn't be able to handle the truth. "Oh, yeah?" I said.

"Yeah. You can tell me. I might have some real good advice for you. After all, you have before you—" (he turned both hands upside-down, ran his fingers through the air as if harp strings hung from his arms) "—a man who's done it all, baby. Whites, blues, reds, uppers, downers, inners, outers... Quiz me. Go ahead. I've done every stupid thing known to man."

"Oh, yeah?" I smirked. "Ever jump from a speeding car?"

Franklin blew through his lips like a horse. "More times than I can count." He ran up a sleeve to show me this scar, a pants leg to reveal that one. "That the best you can come up with this morning to challenge our mighty man here?"

"Well, okay." I rubbed two hands together, blew on them. "Here's one. You ever taken somebody, sexually, I mean, against their will?"

"Sure." Franklin shrugged casually. "I was in Los Angeles a while back, man, and the things we'd get each other doing... you wouldn't believe. We take them ladies out to the beach late at night, get them drunk, this, that, the other, feed 'em all kindsa bullcrap about my brother jus' dyin', this and that, we'd have 'em down in no time flat. Couldn't hear nothing with them waves crashing all around you, neither." He stopped, ran a slow tongue under his lip. "Why? You runnin' from a rape charge?"

"Not exactly, no," I said. "How 'bout this—you ever stalked someone, like someone famous?"

"Someone famous," Franklin muttered. He scratched his scar thoughtfully. "Well, no. Well. Well, I followed my ex–old lady a good long time, she was this travel agent, I used to have to spend thousands to keep up with her, charter flights here and there and everywhere, Miami, Texas, Palm Springs."

"Nope," I said.

"Man, but oh, she was something, you know? I swear to you, you will never see a lady this fine. Used to be I would see her leave in the morning, I just couldn't let her go."

"Nope," I said. "That doesn't count."

"She even slapped me with a restraining order, bam, bam, bam, this, that, and the other thing. No phone calls, a two-hundred-yard perimeter, all that sicko shit."

"Nope," I said. "I said famous, they have to be famous." He looked at me curiously, and I elaborated. "That's what it's all about, man."

He nodded. "Well, you go talk to that woman, then, if that's what it's all about," Franklin said. "That's what you gotta do." He held out his hand, so I could give him five. "I wish you luck. But you come back soon, now, you hear. They got some chilly pussy in the windy city. Break your teeth, you go chompin' on it. Better you should turn right around and head on home, you hear? And remember what I said—Lakeport to twenty, button-hook on three-eighty. Trust me on this. I know this one."

"I know," I said. "I will. I do trust you."

But I started to tell you my second story about Jimmy and look where I wound up. This story, as I mentioned, concerns Jimmy's promise to deliver fertilizer on the night of the Big Bang.

And now as I drive Mrs. Dannerby's car (I don't think she'll miss it) across the breadth of Iowa following the path plotted for me by Franklin, I wish I could report to you as a war correspondent might, that Iowa viewed from the length of Interstate 20 is a state in absolute, botched disarray, that the eye of the Hawkeye State is itself blinking and blinded from the smoke of ten thousand fires, that ravenous hogs, inadvertently raised on toxic slop, have attained a near-human form and fled the hog farms to sail the mighty rivers and control the waterways like pirates, that the sky is afoul with malignant insects and forked lightning, that the people retch from an unfamiliar pestilence and the head of each and every corn stalk in Iowa has mysteriously burst into holy flame and burns eternally, lighting each farm by night like a ghostly field of tiki torches. And I wish I could see the effects of a children's crusade in which the youngsters, having risen up to confiscate the implements of authority, are closing schools and blowing up TV towers and seizing radio stations while they issue demands and denounce rock and roll as "stupid grown-up stuff."

But this is not what I see and not what I hear on the

radio. On the contrary. Dropping south on Highway 380 to pass through Cedar Rapids just now, the city looked healthy and happy and unmarred by apocalyptic incidents, and my radio picked up—of all things—a nationally syndicated food critic kindly praising a restaurant in San Francisco. San Francisco? This is what the teens of Cedar Rapids want to hear? Well, it got worse: at one point the critic elaborated, "—and you know what kind of place this was, you know who I saw there? Do we have any rock-and-roll fans out there, raise your hands, yeah, I see you, quite a few! You know who I saw there? You remember Johnny Rotten? You remember him, the Sex Pistols, Sid Vicious, all that—you remember? Like twelve, fifteen years ago? Well, sitting at the table next to me there's Johnny Rotten, except he's John Lydon now and his band is Public Interest Limited, bet you didn't think I knew all that, hunh? So at this restaurant, there's Johnny Rotten, and one booth over is the bassist of the Rolling Stones, just hangin' out, bein' guys, eatin' hamburgers."

I flip the station to a call-in talk show, a woman seeking advice on a difficult breakup.

"It was like, there he was, always so nice and, you know, considerate, and here I am, you know, trying to be compassionate, and we're just like, not listening."

"He was leaving the toilet seat up, that sort of thing?"

"No, no, nothing like that. It was more... structural than that. Well, first of all, I should say, Gail, I'm a career woman, I should point that out. Some men have problems with women who want a career, I know that. I know that. At first he seemed to want for me what I wanted but then..."

"Then it changed."

"Not at first, but then, I don't know." The woman started to weep. "I've met so many jerks since then."

"Sounds like you miss him very much."

"Uh, yeah. Of course! Christ, I haven't seen him in so long."

"Have you tried telephoning him, calling him, talking to him about what went wrong?"

"He hasn't, I don't know where he is anymore, you know, Gail. I mean, I found this number but when I dialed it this other woman answered and hung up—"

There's no mistaking her voice.

It occurs to me I've done this before, gone to Chicago in search of her and... Was that...?

Jesus, give me distraction. I would welcome any sort of uprising at this moment.

A few incorruptible rock-and-roll moments so subtle and rich that they could never be co-opted—these were, after all, what was left to inspire us, a kaleidoscope of song snippets and music fragments we wove into one delightful pattern after another. You may suspect this came from loving Bob Dylan far too much for far too long, that such an affection turned us judgmental and gave us unrealistically high expectations. But still, listen to that great early stuff by Al Green and then see how so much other music of late pales by comparison. Then tell me how unrealistic me and my friends were. Listen closely to that beautifully sad Beach Boys song "Don't Worry Baby"; hear the story in it, how it's all just about some messed-up guy so crazed with insecurity that he requires constant reassurance before he can drag-race, and then dry your tears and tell me honestly there are a lot of popular songs these days that are as touching and yet as weird. Or dig out the Velvet Underground's "Ocean" and listen for the lines, "Insects are evil thoughts/thought of by selfish men. It nearly drives me crazy... In the Himalayas/ they have small rubber dolls/ recording all our actions. And here... come... the waves." How often do you hear lines that strange and powerful that are available in most every record store? I'd like to see you call us too harsh in our dismissal of contemporary rock and roll after you hear what Van Morrison did with a wistful guffaw (in the late sixties) in "Slim Slow Slider." Until you hear these things, I don't think you will begin to understand how significant rock and roll can be. Until you've heard these things, you should not begin to mourn.

On Interstate 30 now, east straight to Chicago. I've picked up a powerful Chicago radio station that keeps broadcasting Rolling Stones songs. Makes me wonder when the Stones last saw America this way, from the height of a highway. Must have been in 1966, for by their next tour—three long years later, in 1969—they were transported to most of their gigs by private jet. The American landscape had changed since their previous visit. Oh, if they had only made it across the Atlantic just a year earlier, touring in the happy, hazy hippie days of '68, then their tour would have been wonderful. Instead they waited until the good vibes of Woodstock had faded, until the police riots at Chicago's Democratic National Convention had fragmented the Left, waited until the benevolent spirit of Brian had left the scene. Then they released a single saying the poor can't lead a revolution but can sing in rock-and-roll bands, a dope-headed sentiment that still managed to inflame the aldermen of Chicago so much that "Street Fighting Man" was banned in Illinois until after the conspiracy trial of the Chicago Eight was concluded. The Stones had long internal debates about the correct political path now that antiwar sentiment in America was turning so mean and militant. After all, the Stones, of all people, were supposed to be the junkie vanguard of the counterculture. They were obligated to stay one step ahead of this crowd in terms of controversy. But if there was ever the possibility that rock and roll could incite a street revolution, it would have had to be in 1969, when everyone was ready for anything. Those were the only days when the crowd's juice was high enough and yet you could still hear the singer.

But the Rolling Stones did not land in 1969 to deliver a revolution, they arrived in private jets as (let's admit it) war profiteers. Once onstage, the Stones couldn't even decide whether to give the power salute or the peace sign. In Berkeley, Mick Jagger gave both and was resolutely booed both times. Then, attacked as price gougers by the Left because their tickets cost so much, the Stones got the bright idea of staging a free concert at a speedway and, smarter still, asking Hell's Angels to guard the stage. Later, after the murder at Altamont, Keith Richards said something, I'm trying to remember exactly what it was, something like, "In America in '69, you got the feeling they were trying to completely suck you out." Yeah, thanks a bunch, Keith. I'm trying to feel sorry for you.

I brought along that journal I spoke of, the one I found yesterday in Adventure Books, the last journal. I haven't read it yet. Do you see why it scares me so? Can you explain it to me? It's on my dashboard right now, baking in the sun. I like thinking I'll confront Shaleese with it, or something, if I happen to run into her. She might want it back.

I should probably try to prepare some questions for Liz Phair.

And still this Chicago station continues to play Stones songs. Now that the fate of the Chicago Eight has been safely resolved, I guess the aldermen are no longer concerned.

The radio is playing "Shattered."

Something occurs to me.

It's inconceivable that any aware pop musician today could title a song "Shatter" without having in mind the Rolling Stones song "Shattered." So we'll accept it as indisputable that Liz Phair meant something significant by titling the thirteenth song on her debut "Shatter." The thirteenth song, commonly the final cut on any album. "Shattered," of course, occupies an identical position as the last song on the second side of the Stones album *Some Girls*. And both songs, just when they appear about to end, briefly jump back to life.

That established, we look deeper for parallels which might shed light on the intentions of Liz in so titling her piece.

At first listen, these songs appear to have nothing in common musically. "Shattered" is an abrupt dance song while "Shatter" is a slithering and meditative piece. "Shattered" is very much about NYC of 1977, the island city beset with blackouts and bankruptcy which hosted Jagger's early Studio 54 cocaine days. "Shattered" sounds like the product of a binge night in which Jagger can't keep straight what he wants—"sex" or "success" (each repeated four times in a row), going "up" (for which we can safely substitute cocaine, "up" repeated five times in a row), compliments ("flatter" repeated seven times in a row), or sadistic thrills ("tough" repeated eight times in a row). To Jagger, Manhattan is an Atlantis sinking beneath the weight of its bloated decadence—and though he enjoys it all immensely he does not trust his friends (they're full of "flattery"), he does not trust the city's leaders (they're "money grabbers"), he envisions himself whoring ("I can't give it away on Seventh Avenue"), imagines getting shot ("Brains... splattered all over Manhattan"). There are rats on the West Side, bed bugs uptown, and Jagger is losing it—"What does it matter?" he repeats throughout the song, alternating this with "Look at me!"

Time and again in the song, Jagger returns to speak of "the street." "They're still surviving on the street," he sings, referring to love and hope and sex and pride and joy and dirty dreams. This reassures him things are not so bad (though such a reassurance could become lazy and fashionable: he sounds despondent, recalling a "cocktail party on the street.")

But if "Shattered" is cocaine, then "Shatter" is Quaaludes. For two-and-a-half minutes (roughly the length of "Shattered") the narrator is so broken up and benumbed she can say nothing. We hear guitar and droning feedback and nothing else. Then she breaks her silence, in a voice lower than Jagger's, and it's eerie to learn what compels her to speak after so long: "I know that I don't always realize how sleazy it is to be messing with these guys but something about just being with you slapped me right in the face"—her throat catches, for to actually speak of her face hurts so much the words come out in a croak. Then she finishes: "nearly broke me in two." She goes on, trying to hint at what she wants but so scared she can only trail off, "Honey, I'm thinking maybe... You know, just maybe..."

While Jagger vacillates between "Look at me" and "What does it matter?" Liz Phair is worrying, "I don't know if I can fly a plane well enough to tailspin out your name or high enough not to lose control completely." While Jagger looks through tinted limo windows, pitying the poor and praising "the street," Liz Phair (who clearly holds her liquor better) has been recruited to do the driving. Excusing herself early on for any mistakes she may make, her tremulous voice leaps an octave as she humbly free-associates an apology to the passengers: "I don't know if I could drive a car... fast enough to get to where you are... or well enough not to miss the boat completely."

Listening to the songs in tandem, it grows obvious that "Shattered" is sung to a roomful of rowdy men, while "Shatter" is muttered to oneself. When Liz sings "how sleazy it is to be messing with these guys," she is undoubtedly referring to the Rolling Stones. Surely both songs depict the same event—Liz Phair has just come home with Mick Jagger. They are both pilled up and flooded with anguished visions. But Liz cannot squeeze a word in edgewise. She finds herself unable to voice uncertainties until Jagger has concluded his own rant. He stands at the penthouse windows, railing, idly jotting down parts of his tirade that seem brilliant to him. Picking up the phone, he barks at the concierge to ring the other Stones, then boasts to them how this rant he's on can be worked into a hit, something called "Shattered." Liz feels it is better not to interrupt the master at work. Finally, in desperation, she steps into the coat closet, shuts the door behind her, plugs her ears, and—in a scarcely audible moan—mutters a song to herself. This song, the song of the closet, the song of frustration, I think we can agree, is what she came to call "Shatter."

Once we had the Big Bang laid out, we got pretty fanatical about covering our tracks. We worried about the cops being able to trace the explosives, so we scattered our purchases wildly over neighboring counties, we wore costumes and adopted misleading accents and switched license plates. Then we decided to come up with alibis for the night of the Big Bang, under the assumption that after meeting up with someone we could slip away unnoticed for an hour to detonate bombs, then return without being missed. Spencer, for example, made plans to take his father out to dinner, then pretend he'd forgotten his wallet and had to rush home. This would have left his father at the restaurant, still officially busy with Spencer and certainly willing to cover for him, while Spencer would actually be driving out to the airplane hangers of Site 3 on the most dangerous mission of the Big Bang, lighting the fuses on each of the charges, and then turning around to race back to the restaurant. Acey's alibi was to ask "No Face" out on a date for that night but after I informed him that her name was Shaleese not "No Face" and that I had the same intention, he bowed, said "Be my guest, loser," and then implied that a ten-dollar bribe would send him looking elsewhere. So I paid him. After our alibis were set up, it seemed nothing could go wrong and everything was settled and safe except for the lingering possibility that one of us, if arrested, would narc. Our primary concern was Spencer, who once admitted to Roy and me that he would rat on us under pressure.

That had been years ago, but we had long memories and seldom forgave. We confronted Spencer, who assured us of his loyalty and asked if we wanted to test him and we said yes and he said okay, fine, strap me down, do anything to me, I won't confess. So we belted his arms and legs into a weight-lifting press and Roy started dropping weights onto Spencer's rib cage and putting matches to his feet and after a while I got bored and told Spencer fine, we believe you. But in fact, despite the broken ribs we'd given him, Roy still didn't truly trust Spencer.

The mission Spencer had was the most dangerous. I think Roy may have assigned Spencer the mission of blowing up Site 3's airplane hangars with huge amounts of improvised explosive because there remained the likelihood of grave physical injury and Roy still wanted to test him. The explosive Spencer would detonate was extremely unstable, being little more than a home-made fertilizer concoction. And this was where Jimmy entered the picture.

Jimmy had told us he would take care of getting the fertilizer and hell if that wasn't what he did. We had told him we were gathering all week to put bombs together in Spencer's sub-basement, so Jimmy showed up there with a wheelbarrow full of steaming steer manure that he'd been shoveling all morning and had pushed one mile across town to deliver to our door. Jimmy later returned with another barrowful. Meanwhile the sub-basement began to reek of manure and Jimmy had this earnest expression and a sweatshirt visibly covered in shit. He helped us fill plastic sprinkler pipes with steer manure, then load these shit-smelling things into Roy's Pinto hatchback. This was the Thursday night before the Big Bang. We were going to sneak around and put the bombs in place that night so that Friday night would be limited to darting around and setting them off. By the time we finished the loading, Prendergast, who had rigged the pipes with detonator wire and fastened the electrical components, had already gone home. It was just the four of us and Jimmy, still in that sweatshirt so gross-looking we laid newspaper down on Roy's upholstery before we even let Jimmy get in. As we pulled onto Plains Highway 12 and headed into town, sniffling, dumb Jimmy was sandwiched in the back seat between me and Spencer and we each had our hands over our noses, all but gagging over the filthy stench of this boy. Acey and Roy were in the front seat and were just beginning to trade a new series of dead-rock-star jokes when, from nowhere, bright red lights went on behind us.

"Shrewd cops at six o'clock," I said. I was suddenly aware of Jimmy next to me, gnashing his teeth and softly whimpering.

"Now it happens," said Spencer. He punched his own hand. "Here we go."

"Nobody turn around," Roy barked as he glided us over to the side of the road. "Nobody say a thing."

"We could take 'em," said Spencer, craning his head to peer past the cop's high beams. "They got two, we got five. Even with my cracked ribs. How 'bout it, Roy?"

"Shut up, Spencer."

"We could eat 'em for breakfast."

"I said shut up."

"He doesn't understand how they operate," I said to Roy. I was, of all things, suddenly very sad. I turned to Spencer. "You just don't know." In the rosy glare of the cops' lights, I was having this kinda cosmic moment. It was like I was seeing us all together for the first time and suddenly realizing how pathetically wrong we were for each other. Hearing Spencer's bravado, hearing sniffling Jimmy express terror in his typically timid, rodentlike way, hearing Roy take charge, hearing Acey obey. In the depths of my cosmic moment, I felt terribly alone. These were my friends, the ones I did battle with, yet here they were, suddenly so selfish and petty in their concerns, Roy worried about how this could ruin his academic career, Spencer worried he'd be perceived as weak, Jimmy and Acey scared they'd be locked up, trying to imagine what they could tell their parents. I was sure in that moment I was positively the only one who was

160

frustrated, because now the Big Bang would never come off and we'd never get to say good-bye to this place and we'd never get to achieve anything.

"Just don't compromise," I heard myself saying to Roy.

"Whatever that means," Roy replied.

"You're kidding. That's what this whole Big Bang thing's against, isn't it?"

"Acey—"

"Answer me, Roy."

"Acey, I want you to turn your head very slowly, look in your side mirror, and tell me if you can see which guys these are."

"The cop getting out on the driver side is Nanker."

Roy nodded, his face blank. "The shrewdest of them all."

"And the passenger is... uh-oh. Spencer'll love this. The passenger looks like Durant."

"Hot damn!" yelled Spencer. "Come and get it, Durant, you big jerk-off."

"Let it go, Spencer," I murmured to him. "It doesn't apply here."

"What does Spencer care?" asked Roy.

"Fuckin'-a it doesn't apply here."

Roy had lowered his visor so he could use its compact mirror to watch the cops approach. "Acey. Give it to me quick. What's Spencer's problem with Durant?"

"I'll tell you what my problem with Durant is," spat out Spencer, before Acey could begin. "He's a prick son-of-a-bitch, that's what my problem with him is. He dated my sister for a while, and I guarantee you he was one of the ones threatened my brother-in-law."

The cops were advancing with slow inevitability, each step signaled by the jingling of keys and cuffs and the leathery creak of their bullet-filled belts and gun holsters. Now they were close to our car.

"Okay Spencer—here's the deal. If you open your mouth

we're all going to prison, so keep your goddamn trap closed and I'll see if I can talk our way out of this." Roy rolled down his window. "Evening, sir," he said.

Nanker shone the flashlight in Roy's eyes. "Roy."

"Officer Nanker."

"What are you boys up to tonight?"

"Oh, you know. No good. Just driving around. Sir."

Nanker nodded, paused, stroked his chin thoughtfully.

"Just try and catch us," called out Spencer. "We're evil!"

"Spencer!" I said sharply. Nanker stuck his flashlight through Roy's window to shine it at me. My cosmic moment was gone. These were my friends here. "What he meant to say," I continued lamely, "was 'We're evil, sir.'"

"Evil," said Nanker. "What was it Chekhov said? 'Evil and suffering shall drown in mercy.' Wasn't it something like that?" he called across to Durant.

Through the back window I turned to see Durant nod. "Then there's 'Evil is easy and has infinite forms,'" he tossed back to Nanker.

Nanker shrugged. "I give up."

"Blaise Pascal. 1653."

Everyone was waiting for Roy to reply. "Help me, " he whispered out of the side of his mouth at me. "I'm dying here."

I leaned forward, put my lips to his ear. "'Evil is putting bombs in people's shops,'" I told him softly.

"'Evil is putting bombs in people's shops,'" he declared with tremendous sincerity.

The cops exchanged curious glances. "Well," said Nanker. "Okay, we're stumped."

"Mick Jagger," I said proudly, so everyone could hear. "1969."

My friends smiled. Yes, my cosmic moment was definitely shattered.

"Hmmm. I hadn't heard that. Sounds pretty reasonable."

"You boys are gonna have to get out of the car now," said

Durant in a high-pitched voice. "I want you all to get out, keep your hands where I can see them, and we'll just keep right on talking, that's all."

"Fuck you, Durant, you son-of-a-bitch," Spencer snarled, scrambling forward over Acey and out of the car.

"Oh that's good, Spencer," muttered Acey. "Real good."

The rest of us got out, quite subdued, and leaned up against the side of the Pinto, arms crossed, while Spencer stomped up to Durant and spat at his shoes.

"Spencer," I whined.

The car doors remained open, the fertilizer fumes seeping into the evening, the bombs barely hidden from view. As soon as Nanker got around to lifting that sheet in back, we were gonna be dead busted.

"It's too bad about your sister," Durant said faintly to Spencer. "Her with all those gangster losers."

"Hey," said Acey. "I invented that! 'Loser.' Tell him, guys. Tell him I invented that."

"Yeah," I confirmed. "That's Acey's word. You owe him a dollar or something."

Spencer had his chin jutted and his arms curved along his torso like Charles Atlas. His fists were flexed. "Right now, Durant. Come on. Even with two cracked ribs I can take you. Right now." They stood nose to nose, locked in one another's glare for several seconds.

"This is sure dumb," said Acey. "Did we do something illegal, is that why you pulled us over?"

Nanker coughed. "You feel the world owes you something, is that it?"

"Not at all, sir," answered Roy quickly. "On the contrary."

"Because when I was a young man, I know I felt that way. I felt—"

"Excuse me, Officer Nanker," Roy piped up.

"Yes?"

"How old are you? If you don't mind me asking."

"Me? Thirty-three."

"Well then, I hardly think it's fair to say 'when I was a young man.' You're still a young man, you know that? You could live another sixty, seventy years."

"Good point," I said. "That's a very good point, Roy."

"Yes, well." Nanker got a faraway look, scuffed at the asphalt with the tip of a police shoe. "I guess I was just an unhappy boy."

"Go on," urged Roy.

"That's all. That's it to that story."

A wide-body plane screeched in low overhead. As perhaps I've already said, this was such a frequent occurrence at Site 3 we didn't bother looking up, even though the plane seemed only a few yards over our heads. After all the mandatory schooling in aircraft we had received, after all the flashing colored lights in the sky and requests for permission to land that came broadcasting out of every damn surface, having long since lost our claim to private telephone conversations, we'd become pretty sick to hell of any damn thing that could fly, dead tired of these regular interruptions when everything grew so numbingly loud we'd be forced to freeze mid-gesture, sometimes mid-sentence, and go on looking at each other, holding our thoughts, holding the same expression almost without blinking.

Durant used the interruption to detach himself from his staring contest with Spencer. With the rest of us standing like wax dummies, Durant stepped over and borrowed Nanker's flashlight, then turned to shine it into Roy's car. He appeared to grow very interested in what he saw there. After a minute or so, when conversation was once again possible, Durant suggested to Nanker that they go through the Pinto. Nanker, however, was not interested. He had this soft look about him, suggesting he wanted to get home and hug his kids and tell his wife how much he loved her.

"But I saw whipped cream in there, Nanker. A whipped-cream can and some liquid paper and some magic markers."

"And," Nanker said, "I suppose that proves something?"

"We—" Roy began to explain.

"You shut up, you," Durant said. Nanker still had this glazed, dopey expression. "They're drug users, Nanker. Listen to me. These kids are the ones, I can feel it, they're those arsonists who're putting all those coded ransom notes out and everything. Wouldn't be surprised to find out they're the creeps who raped that poor li'l what's-her-name girl, too."

"What could make you think such a thing?"

"They just are. I am absolutely convinced of it. Let's run them in, sit them down. They'll come apart in nothing flat. C'mon Nanker. It's them. The Mormon Church. McDonald's. The money machines. God knows what's next."

Nanker shot Durant a look of amazement. "You're insane."

"I'm not insane."

"So now you're telling me it wasn't the Samoans. Everybody knows it's the Samoans. But you're telling me it wasn't the Samoans. You're telling me these boys, lacking any motive whatsoever, these boys here did those acts? For what, for the fun of it? Because they're bored? Do you know how you sound?"

My friends and I exchanged wide-eyed stares. Could the shrewdest of the shrewd cops be such a sappy fool? If this was their best, where would we ever find an opponent worthy of us?

"Something," said Durant, with an angry shake of his head, "just smells awfully shitty here to me."

Could it be there were no shrewd cops at all, that that was just legend? We began to wonder—what if we toy with them?

"Something does smell shitty, yes, sir," said Acey. "It's Jimmy, sir."

Even Jimmy was in on the game as he stepped forward, nodded. "It is me."

Durant sighed heavily. He pointed Nanker's flashlight at each of us in turn. "It's them, Tony. I feel it in my bones. Let me ask you, kid, have you ever inhaled glue or paint or… anything along those lines?"

"Never," said Acey, barely containing his smirk. He could tell these supposedly shrewd cops weren't even listening. "Those things give us headaches." Acey could've answered in gibberish and it wouldn't have fazed the cops.

"You see," said Nanker, as if that settled it. He took back his flashlight, methodically clicked it off, and refastened it to his belt.

"Okay, all right," said Durant, motioning with exasperation. "That's just fine. We're outta here."

Nanker strolled back to the patrol car, keys and cuffs still ajingle, leather holster still creaking, his reputation shot. "Hey," we heard him softly ask Durant. "You think next we could maybe stop by the house? I could say hey to the little giant."

"Yeah, sure, right," Durant bitterly agreed. "Whatever you want, Nanker."

And thus the Big Bang went on.

I am in Chicago.

Must I tell you what just happened, following my arrival?

I suppose so.

Two hours spent waiting at the Chinese restaurant on Wabash between East Wacker and Lake, racking my brains to remember what Liz Phair looks like (I looked and looked and swore I'd remember, and now look). Two hours asking every young white woman who entered the place, "Excuse me—are you Liz?" and then rushing to tell them, "Hi. I'm Camden." Two hours watching these same young white women back away from me nervously, every single one of them. Two hours listening to an older couple in the next booth discuss their imminent breakup ("What things do you still blame me for?" he asked, and she said, "What does it matter, you'll just say it's not your fault," and then he said, "It's not. It's not my fault. It's absolutely not my fault. Nothing's my fault. I just wondered what you still blamed me for. I didn't think anything you said would make any real sense," and then she said, "Well, I blame you for the paint chips, for what happened to the paint job. I'm speaking of the condo," and then he said, "The paint job was lousy. He used lousy paint. That's not my fault," and then she said, "Miguel does not use lousy paint, you just didn't treat it the right way," and then he said, "He used lousy paint. That's not my fault. You can't blame me for Miguel's piss-poor paint," and then she said...). Two hours sipping tea and munching those dried Chinese noodles. Two hours blaming Gabriel Snell for saying there would be a meeting, blaming Liz Phair for never realizing that this nonexistent meeting was to take place, blaming Miguel for his lousy paint job, blaming my parents for having me. Finally I ordered some shrimp in garlic sauce. It's my fourteenth meal of fame (only one left). I got it to go.

I ate it in my car, grateful for silence at last, staring the whole time at the sidewalk pay phone outside the restaurant. A guy came by, asked if he could wash my window, asked if I could spare anything. I shook him off. A series of dogs raced by, all unattended, apparently headed somewhere important.

When I finished eating, I went to the pay phone and stood for a time. Then I picked up the receiver and asked directory assistance for Liz Phair. "Liz Phair," I said. "Where is she now?" They told me no one by that name was listed. There is a question whether she even exists, in a constituted form of fleshy being which can be met and interviewed, as something apart from a collective project sponsored by a record company. I hung up confused, kicking the cement for ideas. Then I remembered! I remembered the Liz Smith column Gabe had sent me, the one about Rob Lowe, the one that said "Liz" was finishing her next album at Maxtron Recording Studios. I called back directory assistance and this time they very kindly offered me not only a number but—after I lied a little—also an address for Maxtron, on Clark Street.

I got to Mrs. Dannerby's car, took out my map, attempted to navigate my way down to Clark Street. Maps, you will notice, don't tell you which direction these fucking one-way streets flow. Clark is one-way, then it becomes two-way, and it's cut every which way by one-way streets which take turns running in opposite directions. Twice I pulled u-turns in one-way streets, each time causing a wide line of cars to honk and squeal on their brakes. It was like a chase on some TV cop show, though I can't say what it was I was chasing. Big-city driving. Big fucking city drivers. I feel my head going. Tell me again why I should live in a big city.

I made it onto Clark eventually, even managed to be heading west, where the numbers seemed to be growing in the right direction. I passed McDonald's, the Hard Rock Cafe, several multiscreen theaters: junk food of the body and spirit.

Maxtron Recording Studios. It came up on my left after a few miles: a squat, beige little nothing of a building with discreet neon lettering over its front entrance and no other doors or noteworthy features. Though it was only seven or eight in the evening, everything on the block—all the fancy-looking skyscrapers—appeared abandoned. Nothing was open for business but a shop across from Maxtron called Guns & Ammo. I eased up to it and parked.

I just now went to Maxtron's front door. There was a buzzer and a piece of scotch-taped cardboard with a felt-penned arrow: RING BUZZER. I did like the sign said and rang the buzzer, but no answer.

No problem.

I can wait. Have some glue.

I've waited this long.

A man pushing a wheelchair approaches from the east. He is three blocks away. He appears out of the horizon as if coming from the end of the world. He walks from the world's edge pushing an empty wheelchair. He stops every ten feet, looking carefully in both directions, motions people into the wheel-chair, then continues. There is no one else on the street but for this tall man, stooping to his task. If there are people stepping into his wheelchair, I cannot see them. He behaves as if he is advancing down a hospital corridor, inviting those in the rooms he passes to join the pile of people riding in his chair. Perhaps it is just one specific figment, who persists in climbing out of the chair every fifteen steps; each time, the man has to motion this figment back aboard. With very little effort I'm sure I could imagine everything that could be occurring in that man's mind. Moving this way, in stops and starts, he seems to get no closer.

The bracelet came off finally. I was working on it non-stop for the last fifteen minutes, twisting, stretching, twisting, stretching and at last I could fit it over my wrist (yeah!) and close it up in the glove compartment of Mrs. Dannerby's car.

I have the "Liz" story with me, at least that last journal, the one I haven't read. It occurs to me that I brought it to give back out of good will, though now I'm thinking to confront her with it, to see how much of it she remembers writing. In this way we will see just how far Shaleese has left us. I want to wave it at her like Gregory Haldz did at sixteen when it was McDonald's, extending the journal just beyond her reach, taunting her with her secrets. Or maybe that wasn't Gregory Haldz. Maybe that was me. I admit that I would do this with every single thing she left in our old house, if I could. I would show her objects she left years ago in the medicine cabinet, things she abandoned in the closets and bookshelves. I would test their value in her eyes and then make her jump for them, make sure she couldn't get them back. This journal will be used to blackmail back a small, cruel measure of self-respect. And then it will be used as a voodoo totem, so that hurting it will be just like hurting her.

Still the man with the wheelchair approaches. Probably

ten minutes have gone by with him in my sight and he is still a block and half off. He leisurely passes garbage pails, ambles in and out of pools of streetlight. This sure is one very long hospital. A car scurries by, something is yelled. He does not notice. Imaginary figures continue to climb in and out of his wheelchair. When he is a block from me, he veers into a parking garage and disappears from sight. The garage has a lit sign saying *Park*, but there does not seem to be a park around for miles. I hope the man is not disappointed.

A slow-cruising patrol car just went by, the occupants shining flashlights at me as they passed. What am I doing here, what am I doing parked here, waiting? What am I waiting for? Might be best for me to go in the store, into the gun shop. I can watch Maxtron from there. I can look out the heavily barred windows and past my car and quite clearly spy the front door of Maxtron at the corner of North Avenue and Clark Street, observing who exits and enters.

The corner of North Avenue and Clark Street.

Stepping from my car, locking the car door, looking up, that's when it hits me.

North Avenue and Clark Street, site of the North Federal Savings Bank.

Once an army did battle here, an army of soldiers dedicated to Bob Dylan. Once they were my heroes. They formed a revolutionary cadre, lived communally, built bombs, insulted everyone else in the Movement as "right-wingers" and "creeps," exercised around the clock, named themselves after a line in "Subterranean Homesick Blues": "You don't need a weatherman to know which way the wind blows." The Weathermen have gone down in history as overeducated, sexist, privileged white students, as truly not worthy of going down in history. In many respects, the criticisms of the Weathermen work for Dylan as well—they were all unfriendly, elitist, selfish, arrogant liars, and they were tremendously lucky.

I examine the outside of the gun shop, detailed with precisely painted brand names: S&W COLT RUGER BERETTA BROWNING HK. TAURUS MOSSBERG DESERT EAGLE GLOCK. I'm remembering Weathermen accounts of 1969, how they speak at length about Dylan's *Nashville Skyline*. It was a simple album of almost plain songs. It included a duet with Johnny Cash. It was an album sung in a weird, low voice that Bob Dylan never again used. The Weathermen didn't understand it. They assumed *Nashville Skyline* was a message of some sort, a coded message none of them could crack. The Weathermen couldn't figure out what the album meant, couldn't guess what he was trying to tell us. They wandered the grim, romantic streets at dawn in their sunglasses and heavy boots and carefully pressed proletarian work clothes, going back and forth over lines like "Love is all there is/It makes the world go round" and "Lay, lady, lay/Lay across my big brass bed." They tried to do to *Nashville Skyline* what Charlie Manson had so admiringly done to the White Album: to apply a sort of sociopathic cryptography to unravel the clandestine revolutionary tactics Dylan was recommending.

I put my head down and step into the store.

I expect to be alone. I expect to enter the gun shop and for it to be like in a movie, for it to be all silent and tense and dark, for it to be a little embarrassed with itself, like a movie theater that shows porno films. It isn't. I've experienced more moody intensity in an auto parts store.

The gun shop is brightly lit and packed with customers: wives in burgundy sweatshirts and matching burgundy sweatpants helping their husbands try on soundproof headphones, husbands in open-collared shirts and gold chains showing their wives how to steady a pistol by gripping the wrist of their firing hand. There are customers of every variety pointing enthusiastically to this or that, hefting rifles, flipping down scopes, squinting knowledgeably, squeezing the trigger of each unloaded gun while softly murmuring *"pop."*

I mean to hang out unnoticed here, but this is not to be.

I remember reading how Dylan hated the Movement, the hippies, the protesters, just as he hates most people. In a 1966 press conference, he was asked what sort of protest he might organize. He ad-libbed something to the effect that no one would carry slogans; they would carry signs with question marks or the faces of playing cards. It was a sorta funny thing to say, but not that funny.

In similarly absurdist, rather unfunny fashion, the Weathermen organized an action in 1969 to "bring the war home." They called for high-school youth to invade Illinois on the first anniversary of the police riots at the Democratic Convention and to "tear up and smash wide-ranging imperialist targets such as high schools, draft boards and induction centers, banks, pig institutes, and pigs themselves." There were to be no demands: they would only destroy. There were to be Four Days of Rage.

"Yes, sir," says a salesman in a blue vest, whose name tag instructs me to shake his hand and address him as Earl. "How can I help you today, young man?"

The Days of Rage were stupid, self-defeating, pointless, alienating, and I can see exactly what they were doing. They were, to be honest, no more silly than most revolutions appear to be at their inception. Only three hundred Weathermen showed up in Chicago on October 8, 1969 to participate in the Days of Rage—October 8 being my birthday, and also one day after Montreal's streets erupted in wildness and miniskirted looters got themselves photographed from behind.

I grunt in response.

"Looking for something?"

"Okay. Sure."

The Weathermen charged Chicago's blue-helmeted police with nightsticks and railroad flares, wearing crash helmets and dungarees and leather jackets adorned with Vietcong flags, "shrieking," as the *New York Times* said, "in the ululating whoop of rebel Algerian women." Exactly here, where Guns & Ammo now faces Maxtron Recording Studio, at this corner of North Avenue and Clark Street some twenty-four years ago, they veered south, using rocks to smash the high plate-glass window of the North Federal Savings Bank, and then before me they scattered, some suddenly swinging east to run along Goethe Street, others continuing south onto State Street. I can almost see it. They savage parked cars and beat up people with lead pipes, paralyzing a businessman from the neck down. When they're tired they retire to the Methodist Church in Evanston and sleep. They regroup in Grant Park and run wild once more, regroup in Lincoln Park and again run wild, regroup as undercover peaceniks marching in the heart of the Loop, then burst through police lines and yet again run wild.

"Right," the salesman replies agreeably. In a small, open garage on the Near North Side, rampaging Weathermen come upon the bleeding bodies of two of their own—a Hartford boy, a Seattle girl—blasted with buckshot, left to die. "Now that would be something in a handgun, something in a rifle?"

"Well…"

Within days, the Weathermen are badly beaten, arrested and released several times. The action is termed a "major victory," then they jump bail, rename themselves the Weather Underground, and spend the next fifteen years—the years I'm growing up—as fugitives. Around the time they start to apologize, surfacing to surrender to authorities, Roy and I first hear of the Days of Rage and start admiring the Weathermen's glorious stupidities.

"Would this be for recreational or defensive purposes?"

"Um."

"You need some more time to look around, see if anything grabs your eye, you come get me. I'm Earl." He begins to walk away.

"Something in a handgun," I say to Earl suddenly, and

what I guess I should point out is, at that moment I mean it very seriously.

Do you have any idea how hard it is, faced with an oncoming orgasm, to pull from the wet embrace and come into the chill, open air, onto a belly which cares so little? You have no idea. Your body recoils from the betrayal. It is to step instantly from everything to nothing. And always your body is urging you to term it a mistake, to call it unnatural and to stay inside, to come inside her no matter what she says, no matter how much she begs for you to stop. Each time it takes the sheerest sort of willpower to do as she asks. Your reflexes have to be a good guy's, even if your brain is screaming from the delight of screwing, even if every tingling nerve from toe to scalp is calling for you to stay where it is warm and welcoming—still the good guy pulls out, comes on her belly, struggles to maintain dignity. The good guy shrugs off losing her as if he had merely misplaced some pocket change. The good guy goes on, undeterred by the interruption—good and decent and scarcely affected by her absence when all along it was the good guy who lost her, who came on her belly and then lost her. Would she have dared leave me if she had felt the force of my love like a choke hold, if I had ignored her frail wishes and done as I wanted, blasting her insides with come? I was always too nice for my own good. Here the whole time I was never even a good guy—just always thought I was.

"And your price range, young man?"

She will emerge from the Maxtron Recording Studio, stepping from the sidewalk to a gutter filled with trash and urine and there I will be, ready and waiting for her.

She thought she could just leave me behind, cast me the fuck off like a v-neck sweater or a dropped-waist, floral-fucking-print dress or a fucking pair of fucking black tights. "If you would just talk to me I wouldn't have to hurt you," she had written, or I had written, and some bullshit excuse about not keeping up with one another's changes.

Like I need her goddamn advice on how to meet girls.

I can introduce her to my Pocket Secretary, the little black girl who pays rapt attention to everything I say as if everything I say is gospel.

"Sir? Your price range?"

I can almost see it now.

"Look out!" someone standing beside me yells, another Liz Phair fan who is also standing ankle-deep in the piss of the gutter. "Look out—he's got a gun!"

Liz Phair pivots in her huge platform shoes and sprints off and I go chasing after her, watching her straight dark hair bounce with each step, bouncing high and shining like a beacon every time she passes a storefront, the glistening light from the window display illuminating the night, the girl, her vinyl jacket, her micro-mini-skirt, and the bare length of her lithe legs...

"Oh go ahead and run, Liz!" I yell. "Just go ahead and run. Fuck you. How shameless you are. Run like your mother did, go ahead, sleep through the hard parts, then run from the scene of the crime, you heartless bitch. Liz! You want to be the last rock star, don't you, Liz?"

Gaining on her, gaining on her, gaining on her, near enough to squeeze off a shot at her back. The sound of the gunfire staggering her. Abruptly she halts, not at all out of breath, stunned, slowly turning, and her jacket falls open, a hint of large breasts, her other hand calmly in her jacket pocket, and her face is I can see her face and her face   is

and her face   is

"Do I know you?" she asks, and she is unafraid to confront me directly, and her face looks and her face   looks

"How do I know you?"

"That's not the part that matters. It doesn't matter if you know me. It's that *I* know *you*."

175

"What?"

"When I was young," I say, "I was this dangerous kid."

"Yeah? When I was young I hated the world."

"And now the world misses you."

"The world? I don't think so."

"I do. I'm serious. The whole fucking world wants you back, Pumpkin."

"Sir?"

"Hunh?"

"Yes, sir, I was inquiring as to what your price range might be."

"Do you have a gun like... like one of those Dirty Harry guns?"

"A Smith & Wesson Model 29? Why, yes. Naturally a very prized weapon. Such things don't come cheap."

He slides it across the counter with a terrible scraping noise, smiling broadly the whole time, sliding it with the grip away, the barrel politely pointing at himself, sliding it across the counter to me. I pick it up and the weight of it is too much, my wrist immediately falls to the counter. It shocks me, the weight of it. It looks just like the gun Clint Eastwood shoots people with but it weighs about as much as... well, it feels like ten pounds of metal. I don't pick it up again.

I ask Earl if they sell ammunition for this thing. Oh yes, he says. Of course. And there's no waiting, I ask, seeking clarification. I mean, I can buy this thing tonight, ammunition and everything, right now. That's right, Earl says. Assuming that's cash. Cash, I say back to him. I repeat the word several times. Then I slowly reach inside my jacket and I see Earl lean back a little nervously. He watches me remove a black-handled weapon from my inner pocket. He continues to lean away from me, holding me steady in his gaze. How about a trade-in, I say to Earl. I hold out my Pocket Secretary. Will you take her in an even exchange, I ask. Earl's whole expression changes. His face tilts to one side, and he winces oddly.

"Her?" He grabs my Pocket Secretary, rattles her carelessly in one hand. Then he begins to chuckle. "You are too funny."

"Look," I say. "Let's just forget it, okay? No harm, no gain... no foul... well, however that runs."

"'No harm, no foul.' That's the phrase. It's basketball. The other one you're confusing it with is 'No pain, no gain.' That one's weight lifting."

"But don't you think it's better when you say—"

"We get a lot of people in here who confuse those two."

"Oh."

"I thought you'd appreciate the help."

"Yeah. I mean, thanks. Thanks a whole bunch."

"Say, you're a funny man. It was my pleasure."

I return to Mrs. Dannerby's car without a gun, return to continue dictating this for you, Gabe, as I sit here outside Guns & Ammo, watching the unchanging façade of Maxtron Recording Studio, midnight approaching, waiting for some sign of life.

Don't lose it now, buddy. Keep thinking how it's happening again, all over again, and I have to watch myself. Gotta be mistake-proof this time.

But the upshot of the story with the fertilizer bombs is that, of course, after all that hassle, they didn't go off. The Big Bang still managed to deliver plenty of thrills and chills, because we had other sorts of explosives in other parts of town that were constructed out of gasoline and gunpowder and so on. But the fertilizer bombs we'd worked so hard to prepare, our big attack on Site 3's airplane hangars, those things did not work. Call us dumb hicks from the Hawkeye State, but being from farm country we assumed that if the recipe called for fertilizer, manure was even better. This was wrong. Evidently what the recipe required was a form of potassium nitrate found in packaged fertilizer. That kind of potassium nitrate was present in steer manure in trace amounts only. Our research was admittedly slipshod, and it was all Jimmy's fault, but we didn't come down too hard on him—we didn't want to guilt-trip him for what happened to Spencer as a result. Spencer, after all, had agreed to take on the fucking suicide mission. We didn't twist his arm. He had the chance to drop out like he'd dropped out before when Roy and I were thirteen and Spencer damn near ratted on us. And maybe it was better that Jimmy's fertilizer bombs didn't work, because if they had then Spencer might have been badly hurt. Instead he was simply the only one of our group who was caught. The police arrested him initially for trespassing; then they sniffed out the undetonated, shoddily made fertilizer bombs. After his arrest, Roy was still worried that Spencer would narc, but I trusted Spencer and this trust was justified. Even though the town had been damn near burnt down in the Big Bang, and the police were given the green light to do anything that might extract the identities of the terrorists, they only had Spencer in custody, and so they only had Spencer to work with. They did not even attempt to riddle him into shame by hammering him with shrewd questions. Instead, they recracked his ribs, chipped several of his teeth, and repeatedly pummeled him into unconsciousness. But Spencer would tell them nothing. Then the cops declared their firm belief that Spencer worked alone and single-handedly did all the bombings and fires and phone calls that night. When the grand jury failed to buy this, the shrewd police next turned around and started arresting Samoans—first Spencer's brother-in-law, then the brother-in-law's cousins. Spencer was the only one arraigned on charges of reckless vandalism and willful destruction of public and private property. He was tried and convicted and sent upstate for forty-five years. Through all the publicity and trials, Mr. Schwartz continued to defend Spencer, claiming his son was with him that night, that Spencer had taken him out for a special meal and had only just stepped out of the restaurant when he'd forgotten his wallet. To the very end, Mr. Schwartz treated me like a friend, like someone who'd exerted a positive influence over his son.

And yet, ask me to reduce the Big Bang to just one fragment, one moment, and that's got nothing to do with the image I recall. What I remember, out of all the wondrous chaos and smoke of that evening, beyond the false alarms and the manifestos and the motel stuff with Shaleese, is the sight of Monica's Volkswagen aflame. It had been left parked in front of some store, had caught a lick of flame that soon billowed out. I paused for a minute to appreciate it. People were racing every which way. Monica was nowhere in sight. The insides of the Volkswagen burned and burned; just when the fire seemed to be settling down, the gas tank blew. That was okay. In fact, I think it was the one event that truly felt like something to me that night.

At last a woman emerges from Maxtron Recording Studio. She pushes through the thick door, which is covered in plywood and carpeting and is so big it scrapes the sidewalk, and stands there like she's waiting for a delivery person or something. Hands on hips, she looks up and down the street, glances across at Mrs. Dannerby's car. It is the newest car on the street, the only one on the Guns & Ammo side. I think it draws some attention to itself, being shiny and all.

I make it a point to scrutinize her, to study her face as closely as possible given that I'm slouched in my seat so she won't be able to see me.

She is tall, maybe five-eight, with long, straight, reddish-blond hair scooped dramatically off her face with a wide yellow headband. She wears a short-sleeved Chicago Cubs jersey, some pointy black boots, and a pair of holey, oversize Levi's cinched tightly with a wide black belt.

And her face is...

Well, beautiful. Something about her face jars me though, seems a bit too familiar. The little pert nose and little ears, the freckled cheeks, gentle eyes, reddish brow and lashes. I frown, reach up and re-adjust the rear-view mirror, take a good look at myself. Pert nose, freckles, reddish eyebrows. Something a bit too familiar.

What is she doing out on the sidewalk all alone? I reach for the door handle, am preparing to step out and confront her, when suddenly the front door of Maxtron Recording Studio again scrapes open and some guy emerges. She doesn't turn to look. It's as if she expected him to follow. He takes out a cigarette and lights it up, leans against the Maxtron wall, exhales, and they exchange chit-chat while she continues looking up and down the street, waiting, hands on hips, still not turning to face the guy with the cigarette. I roll down my window just enough to hear what they are saying as he laughingly points at the RING BUZZER sign, then indicates to her where the buzzer has been disconnected above the door. They take turns pressing the buzzer and snickering. Finally, he takes hold of the RING BUZZER sign and yanks it off the door frame, rips it up, tosses it into the gutter, and heads back inside, calling to her that they'll all be finished in just a few more minutes.

And I am beginning to remember Shaleese's fantasies of taboo sex. Something, I remember something about how she wanted to be fucked in a big car like this one, being grabbed from a sidewalk and dragged, kicking and screaming, into the back seat of Mrs. Dannerby's car, its upholstery still minty-new, and she wanted to be taken as if in protest, screaming all the while for help. And I hate the idea of indulging her fantasy, yet I still do adore her so much.

I would approach her quickly, one hand snatching the back of the Cubs jersey, the other hand sweeping across her front to restrict both arms and snap her off-balance. At first she'd be too stunned to fight but then, as I'd haul her back across the street, she would come alive, kicking until her boots flew off, biting at my arm, bellowing at the top of her lungs, clawing with her nails and pleading with me to have mercy and let her go. And into the back seat I would toss her like some ripped and difficult bag of groceries, into the back seat and onto Mrs. Dannerby's upholstery, and her wide black belt would come apart in my hand like something made of melted chocolate and she would be screaming for help, exactly the way she wanted, her fantasy precisely fulfilled.

I don't mean to imply, by the tone I use to speak of it now, that this is a service I do not actually intend to perform.

With a swift and sudden motion, I pop open the car door and race across the street.

"Shaleese?" I ask hurriedly.

She peers at me. Her brow is furrowed with recognition. "Excuse me?"

"Elisabeth?"

She shakes her head. "No," she says. "Sorry."

"Are you Liz Phair?"

"Me? Oh god, no. She... already left. She left a long time ago. She... had like some interview at a restaurant or something." She continues to peer at me, then at last, very gently, she asks, "Camden?"

"Yeah..."

"Is that really you?"

I have never heard her voice before in my life. "I'm sorry. Am I supposed to know you?"

"You don't remember me, do you?"

I shake my head. I think back, back through Liz Phair and Shaleese and Monica and my mom and everything, and then I gasp, "Oh. Jesus."

She nods. "Is everybody still okay, back home? What about Daddy, is Daddy okay?"

I am speechless. I can't stop thinking about how close I came to dragging this particular woman into the back of Mrs.

Dannerby's car and translating her pleas for mercy into moans of ecstasy. "Oh fuck," I say at last. "Wow."

"Wow is right."

"Long time."

"Very long time."

I swallow hard. "So—what are you doing here?"

"Well, that's what's so weird. I was in there because I'm going out with this guy, Leroy, he's Liz Phair's bassist you know and they're going over and over the same little part—it gets really boring, but anyway... And I start getting this feeling like... Well, this is weird but I'm looking at the front door and it's like, there's this feeling that there's this someone, you know, on the other side of the door. And it's like, do I have the ability, you know, the nerve or whatever, to go through the door and meet this someone."

"Yeah."

"This is really weird, right?"

"All right."

"Like I'm looking at the door wondering what is this feeling, who's out there, is it some ex-boyfriend, you know, or is it like someone, I don't know, someone famous, you know. This is just so weird—"

Maxtron's thick door suddenly scrapes open. Four guys step out, the last one shutting off lights and locking things up with a big ring of keys. They are talking among themselves and don't even notice me.

"Because here you are!" She turns to one of the guys. "Leroy!"

He kisses her deeply, picks her up and hugs her.

"Leroy, wait. I want you to meet Camden."

He puts her down, glances at me, flicks his chin. "Hi."

"Hi."

She pats his chest happily and tells him, "Camden's my brother. I mean my real brother. From my biological family and all that."

"No shit? From Iowa?" Then Leroy's voice lowers. "Hey, but I thought… Didn't you say you hated your family?"

"Oh I do, but not Camden. C'mon—he's my little brother."

Leroy shrugs, turns up both palms. "I didn't know, okay? I didn't know."

"Camden is… He never did anything wrong. He's a little angel. He's a total innocent, aren't you, Camden?"

All the guys have turned to look at me and I can feel myself shrinking in their gaze.

"Oh yeah," I say, putting on a lopsided grin. "Yeah. That's me. Just a complete and total angel."

All us guys have a good laugh over this.

I am introduced to the rest, the guy with the keys named Casey, the soft-spoken guitarist named Henderson, the sharp-featured drummer whose name I don't catch. The drummer says that well, he is hungry, and everyone else agrees that they are damn starved as well. They all decide on piroshkis at this Russian place down the street. We have walked around the side of the building to Henderson's car before I think better of it. My fifteenth meal. I am running out of time.

"Shit," I tell this crowd of new friends. "Shit, I gotta, I gotta do some things first. I'll be there in like, half an hour."

"Camden," says my sister, and I feel it in my stomach. "Promise?"

I look her straight in the eye and nod. "I promise. I'll be right there. I just got some things I gotta do first. Okay?"

So here I am back in Mrs. Dannerby's car.

Gabe, your tapes are almost full. I estimate about twenty or thirty minutes are left on this one cassette. I figure it to be my last cassette.

It is time I finished with her. Be brave. If this cannot be done face to face, perhaps it can be done in spirit. I am opening her journal. It begins with Elsa. *"Elsa,"* it says, *"came awake."* I am going to finish this damn journal now.

I can see the mailboxes from here. You'll get these cassettes, Gabe, just as soon as I'm done.

But first, I offer this parting benediction.

"Elsa came awake," it says. This is how it begins.

Elsa came awake to the braying of an alarm clock, the morning sun upon her. For once she awoke relieved: 6:45 and still in bed.

It had been a very long time since she had slipped through the night entirely asleep and out of reach of terrible memory. Elsa was accustomed to observing the city before it rose. Sunrise usually found her peering out the window as a photographed woman might from a billboard: mesmerized by the loose dogs jangling through the quarter, captivated by the melancholy sight of Mont Royal in the silverish glimmerings of dawn, entranced by the forlorn beacons rotating atop Montreal's sole subterranean shopping center as the beams dimmed to nothing in the daylight. With her elbows propped on the sill, Elsa would watch, half-dreaming, the aimless streets, the wandering animals greeting her.

"Six-forty-five." She said this aloud to herself. She put the heels of her palms against her eyes and pushed, lowered herself back into blackness, then spoke more English. She counted the numerals one to twenty-five, yawned, extended her arms, opened her eyes. She went through the days of the week, the months of the year, today's date: "October 7, 1969." She briskly rubbed a forearm, blew at the faint down on her arm. A dandelion.

In Heidelberg, her brother had been a conjurer in the marketplace; when Elsa turned twelve she became his "lovely assistant." She looked past the audience once to see dogs bounding about in the cobbled square beneath the cathedral, their pale coats picking up the colors of the sixteenth-century stained glass, and it occurred to her then, for no apparent reason, that she would no longer recognize the sound of her dead mother's voice. Her father had adored Elsa, surrounding himself with marionettes he had built to resemble her, loose blond hair and proud upturned faces. "Mein Löwenzahn" was his name for *her.* My dandelion; my lion's tooth. *Stacked-up versions of herself looked down from the bedroom shelf wearing Elsa's own wooden gaze.*

Elsa went briefly to the window. She peeked at the dependable blue mist of rush-hour traffic, at the consistent gray sheen of the St. Lawrence River, then drew the blinds.

She had class in a few hours—a class in History & Manners held every Tuesday, Wednesday, and Friday at McGill University—followed by nannying from noon to evening. Elsa could not recall the last time she had exerted any influence upon the course of her life.

She had gone to Morocco because of a man, to England too. After escaping from Cotchford Farm there had been another man, at the German consulate in London. She stood in a room before him. He talked on the telephone to a rich woman in Canada named Kathryn Martin. The conversation seemed to center around Kathryn Martin's discovery of her husband's affair with their dark-haired French au pair. Elsa had nowhere else to go. She could not help eavesdropping on the man's conversation. Kathryn Martin was apparently boasting of how she had threatened the au pair with a firearm.

The phone was suddenly handed across the desk to Elsa, otherwise void of prospects, keen on fleeing England. The ensuing transatlantic job interview was extremely brief. "Are you French?" were the first words out of Kathryn Martin's mouth.

"No, Missus. I am German."

"Yes, I can hear that."

"Yes, Missus."

"Perfect."

Then, as an afterthought, Kathryn Martin asked Elsa if she was good with children.

Elsa was wired several hundred pounds, flown out

to Montreal. The money, it was emphasized, was only a loan; it would be deducted in installments from Elsa's monthly earnings. But when Mrs. Martin met her at the airport terminal, she greeted Elsa's handsome appearance with a disapproving groan. "Of course, you understand," Mrs. Martin said, shaking her head, presumably addressing Mr. Martin's weaknesses, "This will most likely be only a temporary arrangement." Elsa said nothing, indebted now, and helpless.

Elsa submitted with reluctance to a physical examination conducted by the Martin family physician. She was weighing, in her mind, the consequences of one awful night at Cotchford Farm. What would Mrs. Martin make of a pregnant servant—the morning unreliability, the growing clumsiness? But the battery of blood tests confirmed only that Elsa carried no communicable diseases; nothing more was revealed. She kept secret her suspicion—most likely this job could be only a temporary arrangement, after all. In the meantime, she had hundreds of pounds to pay back.

Aside from these complicating factors—Elsa's unwelcome youthful beauty, her undisclosed condition—the new job went (in Kathryn Martin's favorite commendation) like clockwork. Arrangements were briskly finalized for Elsa's morning classes and checkups, and every afternoon she arrived at Westmount to watch the twin boys and the girl, while their mother went off on her own errands.

Elsa listened to Radio Canada, repeating what she heard as part of her English pronunciation drills. After pulling on a black miniskirt and ordinary white blouse, Elsa filled a frosted glass with orange juice, brewed some spearmint tea, and scraped the black off her freshly burnt toast.

"Channel 10 this morning reports that investigators associated with Montreal's bomb squad are still unable *to name those responsible for last Monday's bombing of Mayor Jean Drapeau's residence and are prepared to suspend their probe indefinitely."*

"Probe indefinitely," Elsa obediently echoed, through a mouthful of toast. "Indefinitely. Indefinitely."

"A bundle of dynamite, estimated at fifteen sticks, was exploded outside the Mayor's two-story home in the East End. Though the house was utterly leveled, the Mayor was not at home at the time and there were no injuries."

"Utterly. Lefeled. Injuries."

"Evidence originally pointed to the Maoist organization Front de Libération Populaire, but subsequent inquiries are said to have unveiled a myriad of likely suspects, including several unspecified political foes: labor extremists who were angered by Mayor Drapeau's tough line on the budget deficit, social agitators alarmed by the Mayor's involvement with new restaurant Le Vaisseau d'Or, separatists aroused by the belief that Mayor Drapeau has flagged in his efforts to make Montreal a unilingual French-Canadian haven, and social fanatics who feel that the Mayor and Prime Minister Trudeau are not doing enough to obstruct America's colonialist efforts in Southeast Asia."

With a lavender ceramic plate held low under her toast to catch the crumbs, Elsa stepped to the windows. She twisted the blinds open slightly to squint again at the morning routine. The bridges from the nearby islands were crowded with commuters as usual.

"And on the subject of Southeast Asia, Tom Seaver, the New York Mets' starting pitcher for Saturday's first game of the World Series, today joined the growing ranks of those opposed to the Vietnam War."

"Seafer. Tom Seafer. Vorld Series."

"Seaver, the twenty-four-year-old Californian who electrified the baseball world by winning 25 games for

the Mets—including a shutout against our Expos here just three weeks ago—promised to take out a full-page advertisement in the New York Times *saying: 'If the Mets can win the World Series, then we can get out of Vietnam.' Seaver is in Baltimore in anticipation of the start of the best-of-seven series."*

She moved about the apartment without lifting her knees, finishing her spearmint tea while figure skating about the carpet in bare feet. "Seafer. Best of sefen."

"The current time is 7:25.

"Expo 67 saw the Policeman's Brotherhood going along with a city request for labor peace, accepting a contract many termed disadvantageous. At the time, the Brotherhood promised this would not happen again."

"Vould not happen again, no, no, no. Oh no no. Not again." She was filling the sink with hot water and soap, as she did every morning at this time, and easing in the dishes.

"Since then, they have been quite vocal in their quarrels with Mayor Drapeau's administration, which has refused to acknowledge the Brotherhood's argument that Montreal patrolmen commonly sustain three times as many injuries as Toronto police despite earning considerably less. Guy Marcil, president of Montreal's Brotherhood, has repeatedly characterized the city's proposed salary increases as 'public garbage.'"

"Garbage." Scrubbing each dish with a scouring sponge, rinsing it in warm water, placing it to the side on the drying rack.

"Eleven months of costly negotiations, conciliation, and arbitration ensued but now, this morning, Marcil acknowledged that the Arbitration Board has at last informed him of its findings as they pertain to police wages and other contract issues. The police are to gather in the Paul Sauvé Arena at nine a.m. where Marcil will

189

share with them the Arbitration Board's findings."

There was a pause. The headlines began over again, this time in French.

"Ici," said the announcer abruptly, "Radio-Canada." As he spoke this last, Elsa washed the juice from the frosted glass and—recalling Kathryn Martin's lazy phrase of anglophile disdain, "If God had wanted me to be bilingual he would have made me French Canadian"—her hold on the frosted glass slackened as she lunged for the radio, and the glass shot free, sailing into the dirty water to hit the bottom of the sink with a muffled smash. It took a second, leaving Elsa to stare, mortified, questioning her next move as she stood frozen in position, craning her head at the murky sink water.

"Il est huit heures moins vingt-cinq."

She unplugged the radio. Her mind spun with nebulous solutions. Snatching up a clean fork from the drying rack, she turned to the sink full of water and broken glass, gathered a burst of courage, then utterly lost her train of thought. What is it I am doing holding this fork? Her hand hovered over the water, then returned to her side. What was she to do? If she could tell where the frosted glass had hit, she might brave probing with two fingers for the largest shards. If something were to float to the surface, it could be skimmed up.

But nothing stirred in the soapy water. Elsa was stymied. If she could locate the proper implement, she might unplug the sink, drain it, and clean up the mess, but the proper implement was... what? She grew terrified of what lay submerged in her sink this morning.

She had begun walking in reverse, one slow step after another, her eyes glued to the sink while she backed herself from the linoleum to the carpet, and against the sofa; now she was sitting down once more.

"Ach, Brian!" she cried. This surprised her. She had actually been thinking of her father, thinking of Heidelberg, how great it must have been once. She had not had Brian in her thoughts for weeks. Elsa sat with closed eyes, her hands laid over her slightly bulged belly. She indulged herself with remembrances of the British superstar: his piggish, misogynist ways; his loathsome obesity; his sublime, moving aerograms; his drunken, destructive mannerisms; his moronic blond giggling stupid joyous rude maddening brilliant wasteful courteous narcissistic wonderful swagger, and how she loved him beyond reason, and how very dead, how very, very, very dead he was.

"Ach, Brian..." she said once more. "Dandelion Brian." It relieved her to speak his name, as if by speaking it she was assured this was not simply some concoction of madness but something that could be given voice and explained in words. Though naturally Elsa had no illusions about Brian Jones reclining in some glorious heaven, it was also true that she could not surrender a longing for some sign from the dead man she loved, a sign, a whisper of wind, a soft whistle, anything. It need not be fraught with supernatural significance. It need not display Brian Jones' projected image hovering in the clear autumn skies over Montreal, communicating romantically to her from the mysterious beyond; it just had to be there, indisputably there, perhaps very early some morning when she stared hard into the arc lights of the Place Ville Marie, when the looming mountain at the center of the island writhed in the water's reflection so unnaturally as to seem nearly alive, a sign from the superstar saying to her, "Yes. I'm here. Yes, Elsa. It happened as you remember it. Yes. You'll be fine." That was all she wanted, to be comforted without having to return to Heidelberg or to confide in Kathryn Martin. All Elsa wanted was a message confirming she was still alive, still capable of courage, still able to laugh,

and not just given over to functioning like clockwork.

When she stood to check again, the kitchen sink had partially emptied. Visible were three jagged circles of glass, lying in a few shallow inches of suds like lethal bracelets. Elsa carefully dropped all three into a paper sack and, clenching the head of the sack tight in one fist while shouldering her bag of schoolbooks, she eased the apartment door shut behind her.

The usual man, Timothy, was not in the fruit shop. There was instead a strange, short man with close-cropped hair and wire-rimmed glasses standing proudly posed behind the register.

"Gut morning," said Elsa with a shy dip of her head. She entered this shop every day at this time in the exact same fashion.

"High-Low," Timothy always enthusiastically replied. "High-Low," followed by a quick appraisal of her, head to toe, and some impudent bit: "Well, well, Elsa, about the daring shortness of these miniskirts of yours," or, recently, "about this new hair color of yours." Goodnatured freshness. This new man seemed unacquainted with such habits. This man nodded warily, folded his arms. "Salut," he responded at last.

"Timot'y is…?"

"Il n'est pas arrivé ce matin," he snapped with irritation. "Alors," he pointed at several leather-jacketed figures busy in the back of the shop, "On a ouvert pour lui."

She looked at him without expression for several moments. She set her paper sack down upon the counter. The loose shards of glass settled with clicks and scrapes, like seashells. Elsa cautiously tucked one side of her long hair behind an ear. "Yes?" She had understood none of what he'd said.

The man smiled tightly, stomped around her to

straighten a display of tangerines. Several had rolled to the floor. The man blew off dust, gently buffed them with a sleeve, replaced them. He went on to join the others at the back of the shop.

Elsa was enthralled by the vivid color of the tangerines. She took up several in her hand, the skin of the fruit cold against her skin. Pour les fruits, payez ce que vous voulez, *read a new sign over the miniature oranges. Elsa's hand came down in exasperation, nearly upsetting the display once more. Yesterday, just yesterday, prices had been clearly marked in English.*

She carried her tangerines to the back of the shop. "Excuse me?" she timidly interrupted the man.

"Oui."

"I vas vondering... t'e cost."

He motioned in exasperation to a man in a gray sweatshirt. Gray Sweatshirt grinned at her, strode jauntily over to the sign hanging above the fruit, and read aloud while pointing out each word to her—"Payez... ce... que... vous... voulez."

"Yes."

"Yes," Sweatshirt repeated with a French accent.

"I do not speak French."

Sweatshirt and the rude man broke into rapid French, voices clouded with amazement and distress. Sweatshirt shrugged theatrically, gesticulated, shrugged again, then tsk-tsked Elsa, shaking his head disapprovingly. "C'est dommage, Mademoiselle Trop Jolie." Then he laughed heartily. "It says to pay what you like."

Elsa did not enjoy his joke. "Please name t'e cost to me."

"How much do you feel is fair, Mademoiselle Trop Jolie? Pay what you feel is fair, no more."

"Where... is Timot'y?"

"The usual fellow? He did not show up this morning.

Because he was scared. Well, I am certain you have heard. About the police."

"I cannot understand you! You must please name t'e cost to me," Elsa said.

"Le magasin ne march plus comme ça," Sweatshirt said softly, with an easy chuckle.

"Stop laughing! Stop laughing at me!" She scooped a few loose coins from her purse, threw them at his face. "Here!" Her eyes welled with tears. She stormed towards the front door, spun and glared in the direction of the men. "You may keep t'is," she shook a finger at the sack on the counter. "It is my present for you!"

A block away, three cars clung together like metal sculpture at the intersection of Maisonneuve Boulevard and Metcalfe. There was none of the sense of crisis that usually accompanies an automobile accident. The drivers of the cars—a pale green sedan, a white Buick Riviera, and a red and black GTO—stood together in the street, exchanging laughs, sharing cigarettes, patiently waiting with arms folded. It seemed an unimportant inconvenience to them.

A small sports car appeared, turning very fast in the wrong direction on the one-way Metcalfe. As Elsa watched, tangerines in hand, the sports car failed to negotiate its turn, clipped the tail of a parked car, spun uncontrollably, slammed into the side of a slow-moving taxicab, and came to rest quite close to her.

One day in Heidelberg, for no apparent reason, Elsa had stopped believing in her brother's magic. She no longer possessed confidence in those switches which spirited her mysteriously from a locked trunk to emerge from a lead-lined booth atop the funicular station thirty feet away. She doubted that her appendages would be successfully reattached after her brother had sawed her, pulled her *apart, opened her up.*

Just like that, the tricks began failing. Elsa was no longer eerily elevated above the statue of the Virgin Mary, no matter how much sweat her brother poured into the incantations. When he called "Eins—Zwei—Drei!" Elsa, crouched in the locked trunk, went nowhere. No longer were light objects waved into miraculous weightiness with a swish of the wand and a tossed-off "Abracadabra." Elsa screamed when the cold teeth of her brother's saw touched her flesh. The lovely assistant could not continue.

"Oh, Elsa, please, it's magic!" implored her brother. "You didn't really feel it. It's not a real saw. You just imagined it." But Elsa was too busy losing faith to hear him.

Years later, in Montreal, cars crashing serenely all around her. Passersby idly pointed, a few shook their heads. Steady things turned erratic and smashed-up vehicles became sculptures. Men stood in the intersection snickering.

Elsa turned to observe three men wearing ski masks calmly enter her local branch of the City & District Savings Bank. Though it seemed suspicious, other pedestrians treated it with nonchalance.

This must be a movie, *she thought:* no one appears in the least concerned. *She'd learned about sleight of hand. You lose your faith and it's all just illusion.* They are making a movie. *She thought this even as a bank alarm went off, followed by the blast of a shotgun, and the three men stepped out of the bank carrying a bag of money. They strolled away.*

Elsa shrugged. The movie camera must be hidden away. Perhaps it was filming from a very high vantage.

Elsa entered the underground lecture hall through a door in the back. She could see the professor at the front, fidgeting with the podium, attempting to lock its wheels. She took a seat in her usual place, below a vast imitation of a once-famous painting.

The professor straightened his tie, opened his attendance folder, and looked blankly over the lecture hall filled with students. His hands gripped the sides of the podium. He seemed to drop into a trance. The ringing of the class bell animated him. He began to speak.

"Historically we observe that Man periodically forgets his true nature—he deludes himself into believing he can attain the impossible—he embraces naive notions of common property while leaving human nature to guard itself—he attempts to achieve that state of noble savagery lauded by Rousseau—the imposition of complete economic equality from without—has that ever succeeded, can it ever succeed?"

The professor patted his pocket as if in search of something, then remembered. "As you read this week, pages 145 through 230 in the text...."

Elsa toyed with a resemblance she had just this minute observed between Timothy and her professor. Their faces looked nothing alike—Timothy's round, unclouded face, Timothy teasing her, versus the gathered creases of her professor's face, a dark frown, the unhappy folds of his chin. But their bodies were of a similar stocky character. If her brother had sawed them in thirds, for example, and exchanged their torsos, there would have been little effect on their overall contours.

Elsa made out the sound of something approaching from across the campus. "Drapeau au poteau!" people were yelling. "Drapeau au poteau!" A mechanically repetitious sound grew and echoed through the subterranean lecture hall—the sound of marching feet. The students raised their eyes to the ceiling to watch the lighting fixtures sway. The protesters' feet could be heard on the *pavement above.*

"Close your books now, students," the professor was saying. "Let us turn to what delightful Agnes Morton has written of etiquette and the visiting card. Now then. Who can delineate for me those cases in which personal card-leaving is required?"

Hands went up throughout the class.

"Mr. Nyems," the professor called out.

"After a first hospitality, whether accepted or not; on calls of condolence; and those after-dinner calls necessarily performed with cards."

"Very good, Mr. Nyems. You may sit down."

"Thank you, sir."

"Miss Watnick."

"Sir."

"On to questions of the graceful greeting. A lady and a gentleman meet and are duly introduced. Well, Miss Watnick—"

"Sir—"

"Do tell me. Who may bow first?"

"That'd be the fellow, I imagine."

"'The fella?' Tact, Miss Watnick, if you please." The professor raised an eyebrow, made a mark upon a sheet on his desk. "Class?" he grandly implored.

"It is the lady's privilege," Elsa's classmates thunderously responded, "to bow first."

"Very good, class," sniffed the professor. "Has it been rendered crystal clear to you now, my dear Miss Watnick?"

"Yes, sir."

"Indeed, my dear. You may retake your seat."

"Oh, thank you, sir."

"Do you know," Elsa asked Kathryn Martin several hours later, "What film is being making today?"

Kathryn Martin, dressed elegantly and smelling of hyacinths, was standing before the full-length mirror in the entryway, shaking out her long rolls of hair, attempting to flatten a few golden curls onto her high, tanned forehead. "Hmmm?"

"What film?"

"Whatever do you mean?"

"I saw strange t'ings. T'ey are making a film." Elsa tried to think of how best to phrase it. She wanted to say that everything felt wrong today. Just now, walking from class to the Martins' house at Westmount, she had witnessed more reckless drivers, more accidents that had not been cleared off. When a car with a police siren at last appeared, it was unlike any police car she had seen before, painted orange and brown instead of blue and white and moving with tremendous uncertainty, as if the driver were lost.

"Oh, my dear girl." Wetting one rigid finger to trace her crescent eyebrows, Mrs. Martin momentarily turned to Elsa. "You and your silly ideas."

"Yes, Missus."

Mrs. Martin smacked her lips together to spread her lipstick, once more examined herself thoroughly in the mirror. "How do I look then, Elsa?"

"Beautiful, Missus."

"I shall be back at five-thirty, no sooner. Remember that we have the symphony tonight, so I shall need my outfit prepared. Once Peggy returns from school, the children are to play near the statuary on the side lawn for a minimum of forty-five minutes. At which time they may, if they have behaved to your fullest satisfaction, watch the television set."

"Yes, Missus."

"How was your class today, Elsa?"

"Fine, Missus."

Kathryn Martin was studying her severely.

"Yes, Missus?" asked Elsa.

"Oh, Elsa. It's simply that I still have not gotten used to that new hair color of yours, my dear. As a brunette you seem so much more... do take this the right way, my dear, but so much more... well, French."

Elsa said nothing.

Kathryn Martin smiled prettily, blew her a kiss, then turned the doorknob and swept out, exiting in a stiff wiggle.

The children were playing a game from her childhood that Elsa had taught them. She translated it for them as Ball and Sticks. Peggy, the eldest, held Graham David in the circle with her stick while Gordon Douglas attempted to free him by bouncing a large rubber ball into Graham's hands. A hummingbird intermittently joined their game, darting in and out, advancing among them, then zipping off; holding, turning, coming back. Peggy lost points by swinging her stick at the tiny creature. It seemed drawn to the red school jacket worn by Gordon Douglas, as time and again it appeared out of nowhere, whipping towards him, then away again, leaving the boy giggling and clapping. "It likes you," Elsa told Gordon. She kissed one of his blushing cheeks. "But I like you more." Suddenly, Peggy checked her watch and announced that it was three o'clock.

"Oh Elsa," cried Graham David, "May we please watch our show now? Please may we, may we?"

"We have been so awfully good," Gordon Douglas said quietly.

"Yeah," added Peggy. "We played your stupid kraut game like you wanted."

Elsa narrowed her eyes at Peggy, focused again on the twins. "Okay, meine Kinder. You may."

They all hurrahed and went rushing inside. Elsa followed after them slowly, watching the hummingbird drop down one last time. It hovered outside the dark doorway, as if to peer in at the children.

"Gordon," Elsa sang out as she came into the house. "You have a friend here is wanting to see you."

The phone rang. Elsa caught it in the kitchen. In the next room she could hear Peggy telling the twins it was their fault: "You turned the TV on wrong and now it's broke! Good job, idiots!"

"Peggy!" Elsa called at them, as she picked up the phone. "Be nice! High-Low," she said into the receiver.

"Elsa, this is Gregory Martin. Has anything been disturbed?"

"High-Low, Mister Martin." One of the boys was bawling in the next room. Adult voices were pouring from the television. Someone was being wrestled to the carpet and someone was getting slapped.

"Elsa, get in here!" cried Peggy. "The idiots broke the TV!"

"Please repeat, Mister Martin."

"I asked—has anything been disturbed?"

"Elsa!" yelled Graham David. "Peggy slapped Gordon!"

"Gordon took his pants off!"

"Oh, Elsa, our TV show is not on. Please do come and fix the TV."

"I cannot understand you, Mister Martin."

"Don't you know?" asked Gregory Martin. "I mean, Lord! They're on McGregor Avenue, stoning the American consulate." Even from this distance, Elsa could smell the liquor on his breath. "It's absolute chaos out there." She envisioned him in his downtown executive suite with a glass of his usual drink (vodka sprinkled with ground black pepper) set before him, sighing wearily, his long, slim, nicotine-stained fingers pressed into his cheeks, un-successfully working to prop up his chin. "Haven't you been listening to the news?"

"Elsa!"

"Mister Martin, may I please place down the phone. I vill be back." She stalked into the next room. "VAT!?" she screamed at them. "The telephone is your fat'er. I am speaking to him."

"The idiots broke the TV," said Peggy once more, pointing at the set. It showed a gray-suited man sweating behind a desk as he read rapidly from a piece of paper.

"To repeat," the man said, "Our city today finds itself utterly without a police force. Apparently dissatisfied with the arbitration board's findings, the Policeman's Brother-hood has called an indefinite 'study session' in the Paul Sauvé Arena, saying they will stay for… for as long as it takes. And now we receive confirmation that indeed, our firemen have also announced a sympathy strike, effective immediately."

"Now we can't get our show."

"Peggy!" Elsa said. "It's not t'eir fault."

"Then how come this never happens when I turn on the TV? Hunh? Every time I turn on the TV—zip—our show comes on."

"It is t'e news," said Elsa.

"But whenever they turn on the TV, it won't turn on or nothing happens or it breaks, or all we get is damn news."

"Vat did you say?" Elsa asked. "Vat did you say?"

"You heard me! Kraut!"

The twins eyed them in fascination. "Now she's gon-na get it," Gordon Douglas whispered loudly.

Elsa moved to grab Peggy and slap her behind when Peggy suddenly blurted out, "Daddy's on the phone, Daddy's on the phone."

Elsa had forgotten. She returned to the kitchen. There was only a dial tone. She placed the receiver back in the cradle.

When she returned to the next room, the children were quietly watching the television.

"A car just blew up!" Graham David said excitedly.

"Aren't you going to spank Peggy?" Gordon Douglas reminded Elsa.

"Me?" Peggy asked innocently. "Why?"

"Because," Gordon told her quietly, "you said damn.*"*

"Ha ha!" laughed Peggy. "Now you said it, too. Now you're gonna have to spank Gordon, too! Ha ha!"

Gordon Douglas began to cry.

The man on television was describing how striking police were hijacking Quebec Provincial Police cruisers and using mobile police radios to block all frequencies of police communication.

The front door flew open and Kathryn Martin rushed in, laden with packages from Eaton's and Morgan's and Simpson's. "My children!" she screamed. "My lord, my children! Have they been hurt?!"

"Mama! Mama!"

Mrs. Martin went down on one knee and all three dashed into her open arms. "Yes, Graham, my sweet, are you okay?"

"Mama, Peggy said damn.*"*

"Yes, Graham."

"Mama, a car blew up!"

"Yes, Gordon."

"The idiots broke the TV, Mama."

"Yes, Peggy. Oh, yes, yes. Oh, my sweets, Mama loves you so much, you know that?"

Elsa stood a little way off. The family clenched together for such a suspended period of time, immobile, that Elsa felt she was watching a snapshot.

"Elsa?"

"Yes, Missus."

Kathryn Martin continued to speak without releasing the children. "Have we heard anything from Mister Martin?"

"Yes, Missus. He called. Ve spoke. The telephone... vas killed—"

"The line went dead, oh god. It's a war zone out there, my children. An absolute war zone!"

The twins let out a joyous holler: "Yeeeeeeeeaaaaaaah!"

"No, no, my sweets. No, no. This is it! It's the Quebec revolution come at last. Now nothing can stop them. Oh, god."

"Elsa—" began Peggy.

"Oh Elsa, my dear," Mrs. Martin cut in. "It is time you left now, my dear."

"Yes, Missus."

"Leave through the side door. Be extremely careful walking home. Do not speak to anyone. Lock your door. I'm sure you'll be fine."

"Yes, Missus. I vill see you tomorrow, t'en."

"Fat chance," said Peggy.

"Good-bye, meine Kinder," said Elsa, but the twins and Peggy, still held tightly to their mother's collar, did not respond. "Yes, good-bye," Elsa said again. She took up her bag of books and left through the side door, as Kathryn Martin always insisted.

Taking the turn onto Ste. Catherine Street, Elsa came upon a celebration of some kind: hundreds and hundreds of people deliriously clapping, dipping their arms in unison and kicking out their legs as they sang an up-tempo French song. Jugs of red wine were passed around. There were children in carnival costumes, gaily dressed as butterflies and angels and cowboys and pop musicians, hoisted in a swirling pageant of dusky color and handed over the shoulders of strangers while screaming with delirious happiness. There were lovers embracing in the center of the street, clinging together as if one of them had just returned from a long trip at sea; white rosebuds were being handed out to the crowd, and people were uncorking shaken-up bottles of champagne and blowing on noisemakers.

What a wonderful time the Martin twins would have here. She meandered in and out of the joyous crowd, content to be shoved and herded this way and that. The wind off the St. Lawrence discovered her, started her shivering. She found herself before a series of movie theaters. The marquees—their bouncing orange lights, their dark, neat lettering set against a panel of pale fluorescence—struck her eye with glee. It would be warm in there. Besides, it would be good for her English to see a movie. The Runaway Hit American Comedy! *read one marquee in small letters. This was what Brian would see, an American comedy. Elsa would be able to imagine him chortling until his sides ached, and this might make her feel better. And so she stepped to the box office, paid $1.25, and entered as* Take the Money and Run *was about to begin.*

In the middle of the movie, after Virgil Starkwell has been apprehended robbing a bank with a misspelled holdup note, and is sentenced to ten years in a maximum-security prison, the theater lights suddenly came on. People looked at each other in concern. "Ladies and Gentlemen!" bellowed an usher, stepping down the aisle, "Mesdames et Messieurs! There has been a telephone call... We have just been telephoned with... There has been a bomb threat and we must empty the theater immediately. Please, please do not panic. Please head for the marked exits as quickly as possible. Thank you."

Elsa joined the moviegoers, pressing their way up the aisle. The movie continued to play against the whited-out screen. Just before she entered the lobby, Elsa turned to look over her shoulder. Virgil had evidently made good his escape from prison. He was wrestling with the buttons on Louise's blouse.

The crowd swept her onto the street, where they lingered anxiously. They could hear, from the south towards Murray Hill, an animal-like howling drawing near. One of Elsa's hands instinctively went to her belly, as if she could hold the child in her, protect it from harm with one empty palm. Thousands of people crested the top of Murray Hill, smashing window after window and triggering a succession of store alarms. The moviegoers drew together, leaning against each other for support, shifting their balance towards the calm center of their huddle. The throng of window-smashers sprinted closer. "Québecois, dans les rues!" they were shouting. Although they appeared as one large body of wheeling limbs, a concentrated series of stamping boots and determined faces, distinct features became visible in their approach: a fringed leather jacket slipping to the ground, a shook-loose head of black hair. A chorus of shrill alarms climbed closer to Elsa. She had left her bag of schoolbooks in the movie theater.

The sounds of shouted slogans and breaking glass merged with the rising wail of alarms. "Québecois, dans les rues!" Elsa's hands were pressed over her ears. Oh Brian, please, just a sign, just a sign from you, just a sign will start the magic going. *And paralyzed in the huddling crowd, bracing for the mob's impact, Elsa felt once again the chill St. Lawrence breeze and started to shake uncontrollably.*

Suddenly someone placed a leather jacket about her shoulders from behind.

"Do not fear this," whispered a tender voice against her ear. "It's a wonderful thing, Mademoiselle Trop Jolie."

It was Gray Sweatshirt.

"Quelle coïncidence!" he yelled to the skies. "Terrible!" He fixed her with a grin. All around them were high-pitched sirens and clattering bells, people tripping and dodging and ducking and jabbing broomsticks into store windows. Elsa's fellow moviegoers had been scattered, their huddle broken open to dissolve into the general fluidity of the streets. Gray Sweatshirt motioned at one of the crowd. "Hey! Mon ami!" he called. "Lautey! Hey!"

Lautey, running low to the ground and growling like an attack dog, saw Gray Sweatshirt, suddenly let out a yelp of bliss, leapt into the air twirling like a ballerina and, landing, threw open his arms. "Hubert!"

"Lautey!"

"Hubert!"

"Lautey!"

"Hubert!"

Hubert motioned to Elsa, "This is..." He searched her face.

"Elsa!" she finished for him. They had to scream to be heard now. "Hello!" She offered her hand to Lautey in a gesture learned from the professor, the hand held stiffly away from the upper torso with the elbow bent and wrist limp.

Though she did not mean it as a joke, Lautey saw the ceremonious gesture and reared back with hysterical laughter. Then his laughter escalated to barking, as he stooped again close to the asphalt, limbs dangling comically. "Ruff," he said, sounding like a German shepherd. "Ruff. Ruff."

Hubert placed his hand on Elsa's back, simply a hand, placed there as if to steady her, and then he too—

though in a much more dignified manner—began to bark. "Ruff, ruff, ruff," he told Lautey with a great variety of doggy inflection—climbing from a lowly dachshund to a noble mastiff—and then turned to Elsa. "Ruff. Ruff ruff? Ruff! Ruff! Ruff-ruff-ruff-ruff?"

Elsa covered her mouth, giggling.

"Ruff ruff ruff!" sang out Lautey with operatic Golden Retriever earnestness.

Why not, thought Elsa. Conversation was clearly impossible in all this noise. "Ruffruffruffruffruff," she complained in snooty poodle-ish dialect. "Ruffruffruff-ruffruff."

Hubert motioned them over to the crashed window of Eaton's Department Store, where the alarms were especially shrill. "Ruff!" he barked, pointing at a mannequin dressed in a handsome thigh-length leather coat, tight leather pants, and leather motorcycle boots. "Ruff ruff ruff, ruff-ruff."

"He is saying that he absolutely must have that jacket," translated Lautey.

"Ruff, ruff!" acknowledged Hubert.

"Oh no!" Elsa protested. "Please! It is because Hubert has given me his." Elsa started to pull her arms out of the jacket. "Please do not do t'at. Take t'is one back!"

"C'est un fait accompli, Mademoiselle Trop Jolie!"

"But no! It is not right!"

Hubert was in the window, walking gingerly over broken glass, working to swivel the plastic torso and uproot the mannequin. He handed it down to Lautey, who so appreciated the feel of fine leather in his bare hands that he poured forth an ecstatic array of dog barks.

In the middle of Ste. Catherine Street, where normally nothing much took place, Hubert relaxed against the mannequin, struck a victorious match to a cigar. "Look, Elsa. Look!" Hubert beamed broadly. "Tell me we must replace the mannequin in the window."

It was true: all about them were looters; more than that, a sense of carnival, a tug of togetherness: costumed children photographed by newspapermen in flashes of light, groups of festive people having outsize puppet fights with storefront mannequins, dancers being helped up into cleared-out department-store windows and urged to stage a show while the crowd clapped along.

An airborne object flitted across her sight, and Elsa flinched. The thing spun, darted back, held itself aloft before her. It hovered at eye level. "Blaupunkt," Elsa said to Gordon Douglas's hummingbird.

"Do you know this little fellow?" asked Hubert.

Elsa nodded. "We are old friends."

Amid the clatter of alarms, the shouts and panic, Elsa felt a smile rising through her. A transparent blur of wings held the tiny bird before her, still as a miracle.

"What is it you have always wanted to do, Elsa?"

It was a familiar question. But now, for the first time in however long, she allowed herself to answer. What I have always wanted to do, she thought, is to walk somehow to the direct center of a country and settle there, among pastures and open highways.

Elsa slowly extended a finger to caress the apparently motionless bird. It danced away. She stepped towards it, again reached out; again, it danced away. It was leading her forward. She took another step, and another.

"Elsa!" yelled Hubert. "Don't move!"

She halted, looked about. She could no longer make out how she had gotten to where she presently stood. She was circled by broken glass, with mounds of jagged edges, piles of shards on all sides of her.

"Don't move!" he repeated. "I'll be there!"

If she stirred in any direction she would cut herself open. It was like the trick she had done with her brother, the conjurer, as a helpless girl in a box hedged with sword edges.

Elsa looked up querulously. The bird hovered just out of reach. Why, she wanted to ask. Why would you lead me to this dangerous place?

Elsa spotted a clear path to the bird and took another step, barely missed a jagged piece as her foot came down. The shard lightly touched her ankle, drawing a bead of blood. She took another step. The bird danced forward once more. It would lead her out. She could see that now. This bird would set her free.

"Elsa, please! You can't go any further! Stop! I'll be right there!"

But Elsa saw more from her vantage, saw that there was a passage through the broken glass, if she trod bravely, if she pursued the bird with care. The bird danced just beyond her grasp, always out of reach, as gingerly she stepped and stepped again.

Elsa now faced the smashed-open shop window bordering Eaton's. The little bird danced strangely in the display, its vibrating wings refracting out gleams and flashes as they caught the fluorescence.

Elsa crept closer.

"Wait!" shouted Hubert. Now he was at her side, urgently pointing out the shards still in her path. "You must be cautious!"

Elsa made no acknowledgment. Once more she reached to touch the feathers. The hummingbird seemed about to touch the topmost display shoes in the window. Seeing red, the bird was drawn to the shoes as though to blossoms.

The bird pulled completely away, out of the window and up. The moment seemed to snag. The entire street *seemed to be watching, pointing at the hummingbird as it lifted itself out of the chaos and disappeared into the night sky like an autumn leaf caught in an updraft.*

Elsa stared at the smashed-open display in disbelief, recognizing something within. Could it be...? she asked herself. Yes: somehow it was true.

Elsa knew these red shoes—had worn them before. She began to cry. Gordon Douglas's hummingbird had steered her back to the shoes, each sole a hand-crafted piece of cherrywood painted with a crescent moon and smelling heavily of Moroccan paprika, the leather glistening with gold sparkles, one size that fit both of them.

She extended one hand, her other hand in her jacket pocket for balance. Hubert stood directly behind her. To her right, Lautey paced in nervous circles. Someone nearby hollered, registering the purest sort of liberty. Elsa moved towards something even more elusive than the feel of a hummingbird in her palm. These were shoes, Brian had remarked, in which one could walk forever.

She was aware of her heart pounding in the tips of her fingers as she reached into the display.

Behind them a powerful flash exploded—the flash of a reporter's camera—or that of a distant explosion—or even a burst of light from a hummingbird's wings: Elsa could not be sure which.

Elsa felt herself released of everything, light-headed, gasping for breath through her tears, barely able as she sobbed to voice one word, inaudible to all but herself beneath the impossible cacophony of freedom: "Brian."

THE AUTHOR AND LIZ PHAIR MEET ATOP MT. EVEREST

THANKS

Nadia Comaneci
Dad (who chased off the cops after they ordered
us to turn down the amplifiers)
Mom (who urged me on)
Susan
Katherine
Steve
Mark L.
Megan
Janet
Mark D.

ABOUT THE AUTHOR

Camden Joy first attracted notice for the "manifestoes" on popular music and culture he pasted up all over New York City (later collected in *The Lost Manifestoes of Camden Joy*), and for his self-published "tracts," including *The Greatest Record Album Ever Told*. Since *The Last Rock Star Book*, he has published a second novel, *Boy Island*, and three novellas, as well as *Lost Joy*, a collection of his earlier writing.